FUN & GAMES

One of the customers, a man in a red-and-black-check mackinaw, had not been a customer but a spotter, one of Big Benny Laczko's stooges. The man had pulled a .44 Charter Arms Bulldog revolver from underneath his mackinaw and was swinging it up when Hilleli's big flat-topped bullet tore into the left side of his chest at a very steep angle and Kartz's hollow-pointed 9mm projectile popped him four inches below the hollow of the throat. Assassinated on its feet, Earl Scott's body jerked violently, first one way and then another, then crashed sideways onto a table filled with auto parts at the same time that Camellion kicked open the door and charged into the office. He was just in time to see two men getting to their feet, the large, broad-chested man with brown hair that resembled a rag mop reaching frantically for a weapon in his right rear pocket. Big Benny's fingers were tightening around the curved butt of a Ruger .357 Magnum as Camellion's 9mm bullet chopped into his right side, just above the belt. Laczko let out a strangled cry of pain and frustration and started to sag to the left. The Death Merchant's next projectile tore into his neck, just below the jawbone.

THE DEATH MERCHANT SERIES:

#54 in the incredible adventures of the

DEATH MERCHANT

APOCALYPSE U.S.A. !

by Joseph Rosenberger

PINNACLE BOOKS   (◎)   NEW YORK

DEATH MERCHANT #54: APOCALYPSE—U.S.A.!

An original Pinnacle Books edition, published for the first time anywhere.

First printing, March 1983

ISBN: 0-523-41998-8

Cover illustration by Dean Cate

Printed in the United States of America

PINNACLE BOOKS, INC.
1430 Broadway
New York, New York 10018

Immortality in this time continuum would be the most terrible curse of all, for it is this "life" that is unreal. Without realizing it, without knowing it, all that man does, from his art to his philosophies, from his building of cities to his exploration of space—it is all based on that which he tries to ignore: that his tomorrows are very limited, that his very being rests on the unstable foundation of his own mortality—that everything ends in Death.

—Richard J. Camellion
Warren, Texas

Special Adviser
Colonel George Ellis
of
Le Mercenaire

To the "Poet" and
"Wild Bill"—
L. V. C. has not
forgotten. . . .

Chapter 1

Twelve degrees below zero! If Richard Camellion could have made the choice, he would have preferred the cold to the tension eating at him and the other two men who were helping him gain access to the Farrell's Forty Flavors ice cream plant.

Down on one knee in the dirty snow, between Wally Chatters and Pini Hilleli, the Death Merchant glanced up at the sky. The darkness was so complete that it was impossible to tell where earth ended and sky began, where reality started and unreality drifted off into nothingness. One part of the reality was that he and the others were in Perth Amboy, New Jersey; moreover, it was four o'clock in the morning and he and the three other men were doing their best to prevent the possible deaths of from 12 to 25 million Americans. That was reality—*Plus a wind-chill factor of thirty below! I wish I were back in the Middle East!*[1]

"Can't you work any faster?" Pini Hilleli demanded of Wally Chatters, who wore a single-tube Cylops night-vision device over his eyes as his gloved fingers slowly turned the main calibration dial of the Celpit Circuit Clampotis mechanism,[2] which was known as a Clamper among specialists in the "dirty-tricks" trade.

"If you think you can do it better and faster, try it!" hissed Chatters calmly without looking up from the monitoring meter. Slowly, while peering through the Cylops night-vision device, he continued to turn the calibration dial—very slowly.

While the components of the Clamper were very complex, the device had only one function: to trick any intrusion alarm that

[1] We refer the reader to Death Merchant #53, *The Vatican Assignment*.
[2] A standing wave in which there is no horizontal motion of the crest. This results from the interference caused by the reflection of a wave train from a barrier that the wave train approaches with its crest parallel to the barrier.

depended on electricity for power, in this case the chain link fence three feet in front of the three men. The sensors of the Clamper revealed that the fence was pressure sensitized. Anyone cutting through it would instantly trigger a silent warning.

It was the job of the Clamper to make sure they could cut through the fence. It would do so by first breaking the circuit of the alarm system, then "clamping" the circuit together—"splicing" it, as it were—with its own power source, furnished by special nickel-cadmium cells, accomplishing all three operations in one four hundred thousandth of a second.

The Death Merchant adjusted the hood of his anorak, looked north through the chain link fence at the ice cream plant, and again wondered about the information that the Center in Langley had received. If that information was incorrect, all this would be for nothing. Two weeks of meticulous planning would dissolve in failure—*And we'll be back to square one!*

First, the time and the route of approach had to be considered—not an easy task because of all the variables, the main factor being escape if the operation fell apart. A strike during the daylight hours was not even feasible. The ice cream plant was on the northwest corner of Fairview Road and Pepperdine Avenue. During working hours, both heavily traveled streets would be clogged with traffic. An identical traffic situation would prevail on Lindsey, to the south, and on Wilson, to the east.

The surrounding blocks had to be very carefully reconnoitered. North, across Pepperdine, was an apartment house complex and its parking lot. No problem there, not during the wee hours of the morning. South, across Lindsey, was the Bayliss Shopping Center. Again, no problem.

That left only the block on which the ice cream plant was situated. South of the plant was what had been the Fairview Arms. At one time it had been a plush hotel, but it had been deserted for years. Now it was in the process of being torn down to make room for a parking lot. Half the ten stories had already been demolished. A crane, with a cable and iron-ball wrecker at the end of the cable, was parked to the north of the dying structure whose floors were open, their northern ends hanging precariously. However, there wasn't any danger. In complying with city regulations, the wrecking company had erected a high chain-link fence around the area, to keep out bums, curious teenagers, and others whose spirit of adventure might overpower their common sense. The wind had drifted snow around the

2

fence and over and around the rubble beyond the fence. Snow also clung to the exposed floors of the building, so that the wreckage resembled a bombed-out building of World War II.

An alley ran in the middle of the block, from south to north, from Lindsey to Pepperdine. East of the alley, starting on the northeast corner, was a health food store. Next to it was a pet shop, then a Yellow Front five-and-dime. On the southeast corner of the block was a Shell service station that closed at midnight.

"I have it—the current-density ratio!" Chatters announced triumphantly. "Pini,[3] get ready with the cutters. It will only take a second to make the splice."

"I'm ready," replied Hilleli. He stood up, stretched his arms within his Mountain parka, and unsnapped the two long handles of the large wire cutters he had in his gloved hands.

The Death Merchant whispered to Chatters, who was extending the three dish antennas of the Clamper, "Make sure the receiver on the detonator is turned on. If we can't retrieve the Clamper on our way back, we'll have to destroy it."

"The receiver is already on," Chatters said, "but it seems a shame to destroy it. It's like burning thousand-dollar bills—nine of them! That's what this instrument costs."

He turned the third six-inch dish toward the fence, flipped the power-surge switch, and the device began to hum. The circular-polarized-wave switch and the circuit-capacity switches were next. The "splice" had been made; the pressure-sensitive warning device on the fence had been rendered inoperable.

His breath condensing into a fog as he spoke, Chatters looked up at Pini Hilleli. "Go ahead and cut. The fence is no longer a threat."

As Hilleli approached the fence with the wire cutters, Chatters and the Death Merchant looked at the green-lighted volt "break" meter, almost holding their breath in tension as the Israeli snapped the first steel strand of the chain link fence. The needle remained at zero. The fence had been effectively neutralized.

While the Death Merchant had used devices similar to the Clamper, he was not familiar with the Celpit model; consequently, he said, "Listen, Wally. Are you certain we won't break the patched-in circuit when we move through the fence?"

"I'm positive," Chatters said without hesitation. "There's a latch-up actuator on the Clamper. We have a full sixty seconds to go in."

[3] Pronounced "Pie-Nee."

3

It took Pini Hilleli only four minutes to cut a five-foot-high three-foot-wide opening in the fence. No sooner had he used the cutter to snap through the last steel strand than Camellion lifted out the five-by-three-foot section and motioned to Chatters with his head, indicating he wanted the CIA "on-contract" agent to move through the opening.

Chatters, making sure of his footing in the snow piled on the side of the fence, pulled the hood of his Appalachian anorak over his head, hunched down, and moved through the opening.

"We're taking a terrible chance," Hilleli offered, his voice low and slightly unsteady. "It only takes one shot to bring the police."

Carefully the Death Merchant leaned the cut-out section against the fence. "The odds are on our side. If the police show up at the gas truck—should they stop and investigate, you and H. L. terminate them. It's that simple."

Camellion moved expertly through the hole in the fence, reared to his full height, stood beside Wally Chatters, and, pulling off his thick leather gloves, watched Hilleli, who had picked up the cut-out portion of the fence and was carefully placing it against the opening by firmly wedging the bottom into the snow.

Hilleli made a final check, glanced at the Death Merchant and Chatters, whispered, "Shalom," then turned and headed south toward the crane at the site of the half-demolished hotel.

Chatters had already removed his fur-lined gloves and had slipped on soft, electrically-heated deerskin gloves—the batteries secured to each wrist—and was holding a M923B 9mm Beretta autoloader in his right hand, a foot-long noise suppressor attached to the extra-long barrel. Almost forty, with a perfectly round head, a short, neatly-trimmed brown beard, and two cheeks full of freckles, Chatters kept watching each corner of the building, twenty feet in front of him, while the Death Merchant slipped on deerskin gloves, then pulled a silenced Beretta pistol from underneath his parka.

"All we need now is to bump into one of the guards," Chatters whispered as he and Camellion moved closer to the brick building, which had tall, narrow windows, the bottom of each window six feet above the ground.

"It's not very likely," Camellion said levelly. "The guards are depending on the fence to warn them of any intruders, and in this freezing weather they're not going to bother with outside patrols."

They walked carefully; yet their booted feet made crunching sounds in the snow. With the icy wind blowing finely powdered snow in their faces, they moved past the end of the lighted building where three dozen or more night-shift workers were busy making forty different flavors of ice cream.

The ice cream plant was a group of buildings that formed a square. On the south was the large L-shaped building—the bottom leg of the L situated from north to south—where the ice cream was actually made. The east end of the building contained the storage-refrigeration area. On the north side of the storage section was a corridor that moved into the two-story office building, which, connected to the storage section, was a north-south structure. A dock was on the north side of the L-shaped building, including the storage-refrigeration area. On the north side of the square was the long garage. In the northwest corner of the square was the plant security building, a one-story structure with the floor area of a small house.

The target was the office building.

Somewhere in that building—it had to be a secret room below the first floor—were nine men in the employ of one of the world's most dangerous madmen—Colonel Muammar Qaddafi[4] of Libya. No! Eight men. The ninth was a member of the East German *Staatssicherheitsdienst*—the SSD, the East German security service.

The Death Merchant and Wally Chatters would soon be creeping by the south end and then the east side of the office building; yet they would still have to continue along the east side, then move the full distance along the north side of the garage. There were four armed watchmen on the midnight shift, and those four had to be neutralized before Camellion and Chatters—the latter of whom some called the Widow Maker—dared enter the dark office building. The route would have been a lot shorter if they could have gone west and then have moved north along the west side—the front—of the L-building. They couldn't because of the wide double gate in the fence in front of the north end of the L-building and the south front of the security shack. Going all that distance, with the last fifty feet facing the front of the guard building, was too dangerous. Never did the Death Merchant violate his own special rules Never to taunt Fate was one of those rules.

---

[4] Qaddafi is the Westernized spelling. In the East it would be al-Qadhafi.

In spite of the darkness and the snow that had been blown into drifts and in places had formed lilliputian mountains with graceful ridges, Camellion and Chatters, making good time, quickly crept along the east side of the office building, hurried across the twenty-two-foot space between the end of the office and the east end of the garage, and soon were slinking west along the north side of the long garage, in which they could hear the sounds of men working on trucks. Engines were being turned over. There was some hammering and other noises.

Very rapidly, the Death Merchant and the Widow Maker approached the short north side of the guard shack, both men doing their best to ignore the bitter cold that in spite of their parkas, flannel trousers, twill wool shirts, and Ragg sweaters, penetrated to the very center of their bones. Little wonder. They had been out in the cold for almost an hour—and the humidity was almost 75 percent.

They paused at the northwest corner of the guard building and, covered by the darkness, looked out on Fairview Road. Even the streetlight seemed unfriendly, its white yellow glow apocalyptic. A Sender Bread Bakery truck went by, followed by a city salt truck, salt pouring evenly onto the icy pavement from hoppers on the rear end.

"The front door could be locked?" whispered Chatters, his tone indicating he was really asking, If it is, what then? He proceeded to remove the Cylops night-vision device from his face, after which he placed the bulky device into a black shoulder bag.

"I don't think it will be; the guards feel safe," Camellion said lazily. "But if it is, we'll open it—damn fast."

He reached underneath his parka and pulled a second weapon from a holster on a wide belt around his waist, this pistol a .44 stainless steel Backpacker .44 Auto Mag, a noise suppressor attached to the end of its 4½-inch barrel.

"You open the door," Camellion whispered. "I'll go in first."

"Let's get on with it," Chatters growled. "I feel like I have icicles on my pecker!"

They started along the west wall of the security building, hoping that if a car or truck passed on Fairview Road, the driver wouldn't notice them. However, the road was deserted, the glow of the streetlights falling only on ice and snow and loneliness.

Camellion pulled up short and looked around the southwest corner of the building. The door in the front of the building was only eight feet away, a small light burning above it. To the east, on the other side of the door in the center of the wall, was an eighteen-by-twenty-inch slanted one-way observation window. Forty feet to the south was the north end of the building, where the ice cream was actually made, its windows dark; however, the east-west section was lighted. The dock was deserted. To the east, the office building was dark, seemingly deserted. The sliding metal doors of the garage—seven in number—were down. Luminaire mercury lights mounted on the sides of the buildings made the square as bright as high noon.

"Okay. Let's do it," Camellion said. Without waiting for a reply from Wally Chatters, he turned the corner, hurried to the metal-covered door, stepped to one side, and waited as Chatters, coming up swiftly behind him, reached out, slowly turned the big brass knob, then jerked open the door.

Camellion moved into the building with such incredible speed that he surprised even Chatters. He startled the guards even more. Karl Haubold, his back to the Death Merchant, was pouring a cup of coffee. Ray Merkle, a heavyset dude with a head of thick, curly black hair, was leaning back in a swivel chair, his feet propped up on a desk parallel to the front and the back of the office. The third watchman, Arvine Chass, was seated at a table using spray-on leather from a Tannery can to soften a Sam Browne belt and strap and the rig's holster. His .38 Arminius revolver lay to his left on the glass-topped table.

Walt Cavander, the fourth guard, was in the room to the rear. He had just come out of the toilet and had reached the door between the two rooms when the Death Merchant stormed into the office.

The three guards in the front office were totally astonished, momentarily frozen in limbo at the sudden and unexpected appearance of Camellion and Chatters, during those few moments seeing only two parka-clad men with thick black stocking caps pulled down over their ears and kill weapons in their hands.

"What the hell—?" began Merkle, his lower jaw sagging.

It was Cavander who made the first fatal mistake. Only a portion of his right leg and a part of the front of his body was in the doorway between the rooms when he spotted Camellion and Chatters. Thinking that the two invaders hadn't seen him, Cavander jerked back and started tugging at the .38 Rossi revolver on his

7

hip. It was the last motion of his life. The Death Merchant, who could have seen a flea fly in a foggy field, hadn't missed Cavander.

I can't catch him, but I can sure blow him up! Camellion brought up the big stainless steel Auto Mag, instantly judged where Cavander would be in the next room, and pulled the trigger of the Backpacker AMP.

A *PHYYYT* sound came from the noise suppressor and the .44 flat-point bullet tore through the plywood wall, entering the wood a foot to the left of the doorway. Walt Cavander didn't even have the Rossi revolver out of its holster. The slug stabbed through the wall in the rear room and chopped him in the right side of the chest, the terrific impact lifting him up on his heels. The bullet, flattened out due to contact, tore through the top of Cavander's right lung and shot out his back, leaving a hole in which one could have stuffed a tennis ball.

Turned into an instant cadaver, Cavander made a helluva racket as he crashed to the floor, his body striking and turning over a clothes rack on which hung four mackinaws.

The hawk-eyed Camellion didn't hesitate. The big Beretta in his left hand lifted. A *PHYYYT* from the silencer! There was the zingggging sound of a sharp ricochet. The .38 Arminius revolver lying on the glass-topped table jumped a foot, along with a lot of glass, then fell back on the table, cracking more glass.

Arvine Chass jumped from fear and from three glass slivers striking him in the face, jerking back with such force that he almost toppled backward on the chair. Snorting through his nose, he managed to prevent himself from falling to the floor.

The front legs of the chair in which Ray Merkle was sitting came down with a loud sound as Merkle, almost falling sideways, took his feet off the desk and started to raise his arms.

Spilling hot coffee all over his gray uniform, Karl Haubold, having turned toward the Death Merchant, raised his arms, his eyes wide.

"There's no money h-here," Merkle said, a quiver to his voice. "This is only a g-guard office." Yet he knew by instinct that the two invaders were not ordinary heist men. Holdup men do not attempt to rob factory guard offices. Holdup men do not carry weapons to which silencers are attached. Merkle realized with a sickening dread that these two gunmen were seeking information about the mysterious men using the secret room off the basement of the office building. Merkle and the other watchmen on the night shift, as well as the guards on the day watch, didn't know who the men were or why they were there. They didn't want to know. All they knew and cared about was the extra $300 a week they were receiving to pretend the men in the basement didn't exist—and in cash, which meant the money was free and clear. No income tax! Why, a man could go into a store with fifty bucks and carry out all he had bought in two small sacks. After all, in these times, with a recession and all, didn't a man have a right to look out for himself and his family? Maybe the men hiding out in the basement were wanted criminals, or—? Forget it. Take the $300 a week and look the other way. Good jobs were not all that easy to get.

"Get over there by the wall with the other dummy," Camellion snapped to Merkle and Chass, motioning with the Auto Mag. "We want information, and if you have half the sense God gives half-wits in Holland, you'll cooperate."

Their faces ashen, Chass and Merkle—the face of the former bleeding from cuts—quickly complied and soon were standing next to Karl Haubold, who was almost hyperventilating from fear.

Camellion, glancing at Wally Chatters, who had taken a position to one side of the front door, which he had locked, pushed through the swinging gate of the wooden railing in front of the desks and walked closer to the three guards, amused at how they were staring at him.

"I want to know about the men hiding in the basement of the office," Camellion said in a pleasant tone of voice. "I want to know now."

Merkle, who was the boss of the night guards, took pride in being tough, on being a man among men. With more pride than common sense, he tried to sound firm and unafraid as he said, "We don't know what you're talking about, fella. Somebody's given you a bum steer. This is an ice crea—"

PHYYYT! The silencer on the 9mm Beretta in Camellion's left hand whispered. The weapon jumped, and a look of great surprise and shock flashed over Ray Merkle's face. A hole appeared in his gray uniform shirt, just to the left of his black tie. He blinked, his eyes closed, his legs turned to water, and he sank to the floor. In sixty-five seconds he would be a cold cut.

Arvine Chass and Karl Haubold drew back to the wall, horror shining in their eyes. Their mouths were as dry as dust, and they

9

found that it was only with effort that they could keep from trembling.

A smile broadened Camellion's mouth. "You boys may not like me, but Jesus loves you. Now, back to the men in the basement. Which one of you jokers wants to lie—then die?"

"They're there, those men, in the basement," Chass croaked in a weak voice.

"In a large secret room built off the north end of the basement, off the boiler room," Haubold added hastily. "Honestly, we don't know who they are or why they're there."

"It's the truth," Chass said in desperation. "We're being paid an extra three hundred bucks a week—and in cash—to forget them guys are down there. Honest to God, mister. That's all we know."

"Step it up," growled Wally Chatters. "We haven't got all night."

The Death Merchant stared at Chass and Haubold.

"Who pays you yo-yos the three bills a week?"

"Mr. Farrell's secretary," Chass answered quickly. "She comes around every Monday night and gives us the money in person. I don't know how the day guards are paid."

"Have you ever seen any of the men hiding out down there?"

Chass hesitated for a moment. "Only at a distance. Once, a few weeks ago, we saw two of them leaving by way of the main door of the office. We assumed they had a master key."

The Death Merchant nodded. "Are you saying that all the doors are controlled by a master key?"

"Yes. Four or five people—big shots—have a master key, and so do all the guards. It's the one hanging on our belts."

"I don't like people lying to me!"

Dread leaped across the faces of Chass and Haubold. "He's telling the truth!" Karl Haubold said in a panic. "We can't tell you anymore because that's all we know. We—"

PHYYYT! PHYYYT! Both the Beretta and the AMP made deadly sounds, and Haubold and Chass, their eyes wide for a moment, were shoved against the wall by the impact of the two projectiles. Chass folded and headed for the floor, a 9mm slug having cut a tunnel through the aortic arch above his heart. Killed instantly, Haubold went down like a heavy log, blood bubbling out of his chest from the large hole made by the .44 Magnum projectile. Pure death! Quick and painless . . .

Fascinated, Wally Chatters watched the Death Merchant amble

over to the dead Haubold, reach down, and unclip the master key and ring from the dying man's belt. Chatters had been a private contractor for years and had seen a lot of ruthlessness throughout the world. But Camellion was something else. He gave a new dimension to cruelty, killing as easily as most men breathe.

"Catch!" Camellion picked up a gray uniform cap from the desk and tossed it toward Chatters, who made a grab for it and missed. Camellion then took off his stocking cap and put on a billed uniform cap that had a red and silver badge with the words Farrell Security Department.

"I was under the impression you were going to render the guards harmless with the dart gun you carry," Chatters said. "I didn't know you were going to kill them."

Stuffing his stocking cap in a pocket of the parka, he put on the guard cap, then picked up the Beretta from the floor.

"I don't like people calling me 'fella,' " Camellion said. He put on the uniform cap—half a size too large—and cocked it to one side of his head. He then hurried toward Chatters, the gate behind him squeaking on its hinges as it swung back and forth.

"Now lay the real story on me." Chatters not only looked clever, he was clever. "And don't tell me we're going to walk right up to the main door of the office and go in."

The Death Merchant went over to the one-way glass observation window and looked out. "After killing the first guy, I had no choice but to smoke the other three. They could have IDed us. That would mean Murder One. They knew what they were getting into when they accepted the three hundred a week."

He studied the area outside through the window. The northside dock was empty. He could also see the door that opened to the storage area.

"We know that the storage room is connected to the south end of the office building," he said, turning from the window. "We'll use the storage room to gain access to the office. Under the circumstances, it's the best we can do."

"Dum de dum dum," hummed Chatters. Then—"And if we meet anyone coming out of the garage or bump into some of the inside workers? They're not likely to believe we're brand-new guards."

"We'll have to chance it." Camellion, having dropped the Beretta and the Auto Mag into the pockets of his anorak, opened the door and, with Chatters right behind him, stepped outside, the bitter cold stinging his face.

11

Chatters closed the door and together they hurried at an angle across the area to the steps at the east end of the dock. A few minutes more and they were facing the locked door to the storage room. Camellion soon opened the door with the master key and, very cautiously, he and Chatters stepped inside and pulled their weapons.

They found that they were in a grimy corridor lighted by several large bulbs in the ceiling. The air was thick with the smell of sour milk and the odor of vanilla and banana. From a distance they could hear the motor of the refrigeration system, its humming steady. In the south wall were several large refrigeration-type doors. Thirty feet to the east was a steel fire door, the door that separated the storage area from the south part of the office.

"I'm glad we brought grenades," whispered Chatters. "But I hope we don't have to use them."

"I hope we don't even have to fire a shot," quipped Camellion, "but I wouldn't count on it. Come on."

They moved to the fire door, Chatters walking backward in order to watch the outside door to the dock and another door that opened to the ice cream plant.

"Expect anything," warned Camellion, putting on his own Cylops night-vision device. "Even if we manage to get to the bums, they won't give up without a fight."

Chatters began putting on his own night-vision device. "This operation is ridiculous and we both know it," he snorted and buckled a strap behind his head. "We'll be lucky to get ourselves out and back to the van, much less capture one of the enemy."

"I know," agreed Camellion. "But this dump is the best lead we have. We have to follow it through."

He adjusted the light-gain control, then carefully turned the key in the lock in the fire door. He pulled out the key, dropped it into his pocket, took out the Backpacker AMP, pushed open the door, and, hunched, crept into the darkness. He paused and adjusted the integrated IR light source of the Cylops night-vision device as Chatters gently closed the door and began adjusting his own infrared night-vision instrument. Now the general office was bathed in twilight, the furniture standing out clearly.

It had taken several weeks for Redbird Group Alpha in Perth Amboy to obtain the complete floor plans of the office building. The Death Merchant and Chatters had memorized the diagram in

12

detail, until they knew the offices better than they did the lines in their own hands.

The general office was in the east end of the building, on the first floor. North of the general office was a hall, its west end opening to the main door. North of the hall was another corridor, this one moving north and south. East of the hall was a combination lunch room and recreation area for the office workers—Ping-Pong tables and what-have-you. West of the hall were the men's toilets, the janitors' supply room, and the office supply room. Against the north wall were the women's rest rooms. The steps to the basement were between the women's rest rooms and the office supply room, in the northwest section of the first floor. The stairs to the second floor, which contained Mr. Farrell's office and the offices of other executives, were in the center of the general offices.

Keeping low, Wally Chatters and the Death Merchant studied what lay before them. There were rows of steel desks and chairs, all looking lonely. Rows of mist green and desert sand filing cabinets, with a sprinkling of multidrawer storage cabinets and other equipment and machines one finds in the business office of a company—print-display calculators, Xerox copiers, data racks, etc.

On the east side of the room was a coin-operated coffee machine, next to it a sandwich machine. Next to the sandwich machine was a forms caddy and a large blackboard on a movable rack.

Three prefab offices—steel at the bottom, the upper part glass, no ceiling—were on the west side of the area. These were the offices of the head bookkeeper, the office manager, and the advertising manager.

A large divider—mist green—was between the general office and the stairs to the second floor.

"Personally, I'd rather be someplace else," muttered Chatters in a deep whisper. "This damned night work is getting me down."

"You'd die of boredom if you had to lead a normal life," growled Camellion, "or drink yourself to death."

Like two masked aliens from another world, they crept forward, moved east along the wall, then turned and hurried along the north wall, their destination the doors to the hall. In ten minutes they reached the double doors, pushed through them, moved into the hall, and in an instant absorbed their surroundings. The corridor was as empty as a tomb. All they could see were half a dozen folding chairs against one wall, a drinking fountain, and a decorator ash urn, cigarette and cigar butts sticking out of the sand in the round tray.

They crept to the door that opened to the next hallway, the one that ran north and south. Locked. After Camellion opened the door with the master key, he and Chatters moved into the second corridor and again were confronted with silence and emptiness, which, through the Cylops night-vision devices, was shrouded in medium twilight. However, halfway down the hall a small night-light burned from the ceiling. To their right was the door to the lunch-recreation room; to the left the three doors of the men's toilets, the janitors' supply room, and the office supply room.

Sixty feet to the north was another hall, this one between the women's rest rooms, the north side of the lunch-recreation room, and the north wall of the janitors' supply room. The steps to the basement—the most important steps in the building to Camellion and Chatters—were directly north of the janitors' supply room.

"What we need now is an extra dose of luck," Chatters whispered with conviction. "No telling who might have discovered the dead guards by now. One of the men in the garage or one of the workers in the plant could have gone into the guard shack for some reason. We don't have time to——"

"We're going to take the time," the Death Merchant snapped, deducing what was on Chatters's mind. "I don't like passing those rooms either without knowing what's inside, behind those doors. We'll investigate the lunchroom first."

What we really need is an Alpha One Unit,[5] the Death Merchant thought gloomily, moving toward the door of the lunch-room. *But we can't have miracles every day. . . .*

Tables and chairs, four Ping-Pong tables, several pinball machines, and a big empty silence in the lunch-recreation room.

"Let's get out of here," Camellion said. He had the urge to scratch his back but knew he would have to ignore the itch.

Wally Chatters, a Beretta in his right hand, was the first to reach the lunchroom door. He gently pushed it open, stuck out

[5] We refer the reader here to Death Merchant #48, *The Psionics War.* Much of the credit for the success of *The Psionics War* must go to Lieutenant Colonel John B. Alexander of Alexandria, Virginia, who supplied much of the research, for which we have our deep appreciation.

14

his head, and looked north. He couldn't believe what he was seeing. In the hallway to the north three men were walking west, no doubt toward the steps of the boiler room, the first room in the basement.

The totally unexpected appearance of the three men had been so sudden that for a moment Chatters had the idea that he was having a visual hallucination. Hallucination, hell! He could see the three clearly, there at the end of the north-south hall. Two of the slobs, in overcoats, had their arms filled with sacks, with what appeared to be groceries—two bags each. *Groceries!* At this hour of the morning!

It was the third man, Dieter Riggerman—wearing a leather jacket, over-the-shoe boots, and a brushed pigskin cap—who spotted Chatters outlined in the light of the overhead night-light and yelled a strangled kind of warning and started to reach underneath his jacket for a weapon.

Riggerman failed. Chatters raised the Beretta, body-pointed, squeezed the trigger, and put a 9mm hollow-pointed projectile through Riggerman's leather jacket and into his chest. The impact of the bullet caused Riggerman to stumble against Josef Vorst, another East German, who had dropped his two sacks and was attempting to reach the northeast corner of the janitors' supply room.

Hissein Dimouji had already dropped his two sacks of groceries and, as canned goods clanked and rolled around in confusion on the tiled floor, he ducked low and threw himself west, reaching the safety of the north wall as Wally Chatters fired again. *PHYYYT!* And a 9mm slug chopped into the right hip of Vorst, who yelled in fear and started to go down. He was halfway to the floor when Chatters popped him again, the bullet digging into the right side of the already mortally wounded man's rib cage. With a loud "*OHHHhhhhhhhhhhh!*" Vorst crashed to the floor, his chin hitting a can of tuna fish. His body jerked several times, then he lay still.

"Well, that shoves us in the sheep dip," sighed the Death Merchant, inwardly feeling disgust over what he knew was pure failure. "All we can do now is take the show off the road and get out of here."

He sighed again. All the work involved! All the trouble they had gone to! They had even bought a work van and had painted it green as part of the plan. After Perth Amboy Central Gas Corporation had been painted on both sides, the disguise was

15

complete. P.A.C.G.C. troubleshooter trucks were a common sight in Perth Amboy, the police never giving a second glance to one when they saw it parked. Besides, no cop in his right mind would be cruising around in a patrol car during those lonesome hours of the morning. Like uniformed cops everywhere, the Perth Amboy boys-in-blue did a vanishing act after midnight—to their favorite sleeping spot, more often than not with their favorite waitress.

"Maybe if we charged them—?" started Chatters, but the tone of his voice indicated he couldn't even halfway convince himself.

By then, Hissein Dimouji had reached the corner of the north wall and had pulled a 9mm Star PD .45 pistol. Muttering curses in Arabic, with a Libyan dialect, Dimouji leaned around the corner and triggered off two quick shots, the thunderous booms of the weapon shattering the stillness and bouncing back and forth off the walls with a dozen rolling echoes. But he had fired wildly and both slugs didn't come within three feet of Chatters, who instantly fired again. His bullet also missed, Dimouji quickly pulling back after he had fired.

"Does that answer your question?" Camellion said harshly. "Those shots were loud enough to wake the mayor and the chief of police, even if they live ten miles apart."

"You're right," conceded Chatters. "The sooner we get through the hole in the fence and to the van, the better I'll feel."

The Death Merchant took out the Beretta. "Listen! When I start firing, you run to the hall. Then you can cover me. Watch yourself. No telling who or what that shot has stirred up."

Camellion leaned around the edge of the doorway, the Beretta and silencer in his left hand ready, his eyes fastened on the corner of the janitors' supply room. "Get going," he said to Chatters, who got! He moved through the doorway, turned, then rushed south down the hall. He was almost to the first corridor when Hissein Dimouji tried to sneak a look around the corner. A third of his face and one eye was all the Death Merchant needed. In fact, the single eye of Dimouji would have been more than enough of a target for Camellion, who could shoot the balls off a bee at a hundred feet!

"Don't feel bad, stupid," muttered Camellion and brought up the Beretta at the same time that Dimouji's left hand and arm came around the corner. "A lot of people have no talent. And you've lived long enough."

16

PHYYYT! The Death Merchant's 9mm projectile struck Dimouji in the left cheek, sped across the roof of his mouth, and tore a bloody tunnel through the back of his upper neck. Blood pouring out his mouth, Dimouji dropped his PD Star and started the final fall of his life while the Death Merchant raced to the south hall and Theodore Benzil, Adolf Ducher, and four other men pounded up the basement steps, four of them armed with submachine guns.

Reaching the hall, the Death Merchant found Chatters waiting calmly by the double doors of the general office. Before Camellion could reach his partner-in-illegality, several SMGs roared to the north. The enemy was raking the corridor before charging down its length.

"Sub-guns!" Chatters said grimly when the Death Merchant reached him and began reloading the Backpacker Auto Mag and the big Beretta. "Damn it, don't they know the police will also want to question them! It doesn't make sense, their coming after us!"

"Oh yes it does." The Death Merchant shoved a full magazine into the butt of the Auto Mag. "They know they've been discovered. They don't have any more of a choice than we do. They have to escape too, and they have to get through us to do it. No doubt they have two or three escape vehicles parked close to here."

Chatters turned and looked toward the general office. "We have grenades; now is the time to use one or two."

The Death Merchant pulled back the slide of the Beretta, put the autopistol on the floor, next to the AMP, then reached into an inner pocket of the anorak and took out a K31 antipersonnel grenade. Colored red and the size of a baseball, the K31 had a main bursting charge of 12.6 ounces of TNT and was unconventional in that its perfectly rounded sides were composed of 17,000 slivers of metal glued together, each sliver a tiny needle that, after the grenade exploded, would fly through the air with the speed of a bullet.

He turned toward Chatters. "Wally, go to the southwest corner of the office and wait for me; I'm going to slow down our 'friends.' "

Chatters nodded and was gone, moving noiselessly among the desks and chairs.

Camellion couldn't be sure, but—*Do I hear footsteps in the other hall?* He didn't intend to hang around to find out whether

17

he was right or wrong. He pulled the pin of the K31 and rolled it northwest in such a way that it would come to a stop in front of the door to the north-south hall. Instantly, he picked up the AMP and the Beretta, pushed backward through the double doors, and stepped into the office just as the grenade exploded with a blast that shook the floor. He knew that the explosion probably hadn't harmed any of the enemy, but it would certainly slow them down and give him the time he needed.

He hurried south through the office, moving toward the southwest. In a short while he heard a loudly whispered "Over here!" from Chatters, who had taken a position at one end of a long metal stand on which rested a Heyer spirit duplicator, a desk-top addresser machine, and a punch-and-bind machine, a site from which he could watch the floor of the office and the door to the hall by the side of the storage area.

He looked at the Death Merchant through the Cylops night-vision device. Camellion seemed to be deep in thought. "What are we waiting for? That explosion won't stall them for long, old buddy."

"We're not going to leave the same way we came in," Camellion said. "That route's too long and we'd be exposed to Fairview Road."

Chatters was both curious and perplexed. "How then?"

"We'll ice as many as we can when they show up here, then open one of the windows on the southeast side with a grenade."

"A good plan," commented Chatters.

"It had better be or we're both dead. The only danger is that some of the cruds might creep around and come at us from either the west or the east on the south side of the building. We'll have to risk it." Camellion gave a long look at the double doors to the north. "I'm going to the southeast corner. We can catch them in a cross fire. If you toss a grenade, be damned careful."

"Just take care of yourself," growled Chatters, his professional pride wounded.

The Death Merchant crept between desks and chairs and other equipment and, soon reaching the southeast section of the office, got down by the corner of a steel L-unit work center. He was actually in front of the desks arranged in an L, with his back, fortunately, facing a row of filing cabinets. He was as surprised as Chatters when suddenly every fluorescent light hanging from the ceiling went on, turning the darkness into high noon with a skyful of sunshine.

Triple damn! But in the orchard of life some rotten apples must fall. . . .

Snuggled down, the Death Merchant and Chatters waited for the inevitable, waited for the terrorists to charge into the office, Camellion watching from the side of a desk, his right hand clamped around a grenade from which he had already pulled the pin.

He and Chatters didn't have long to wait. The lights hadn't been on a fourth of a minute when the double doors were pushed open and three men stormed into the office, their automatic weapons firing. Using a U.S. .45 M3 grease gun, Adolf Doucher darted to the left, Kahil Dindoudli, an HK 53 SMG in his hands, to the right. Heinrich Mann, triggering a 9mm Walther MP-K, charged down the center.

A hailstorm of swaged projectiles swept over the office, the .45, 9mm, and 5.56mm slugs wrecking everything they touched. Telephones exploded into junk. Electric typewriters and Dictaphones were instantly destroyed in the wave of metal. Crooked lines of holes appeared in the mist-green and desert-sand colored filing cabinets and in the steel sections of the prefab offices, whose windows dissolved as slugs broke the glass.

With loud ringing sounds, sub-gun slugs chopped into the coffee machine, the sounds immediately lost in the almost constant screaming of ricochets from high vel metal striking the steel edges of the desks and other pieces of equipment.

There wasn't any way that Camellion and the Widow Maker could fire at the three terrorists, not without rearing up and risking taking several slugs from the three vomiting submachine guns. They did the only thing they could do, the thing they were prepared to do, knowing exactly the strategy being employed by the three men—*Firing to keep us down, then pump us full of slugs when they find us!*

Camellion threw his K31 grenade first, an overhanded throw that carried the rounded red bomb to the center of the office, to his right, to the east. The grenade was still in the air when Chatters tossed his K31, throwing it on the west side of the floor, to his left.

Adolf Doucher saw the Death Merchant's grenade coming and did his best to duck, shouting, "*HANDGRANATE!*" to warn the other two men. He was dropping down, trying to reach the safety of the leg space under a desk to his right, when the grenade fell on a typewriter on another desk and exploded with a crashing

19

roar and a tenth of a second's flash of fire. Seventeen thousand slivers of steel flew outward and up like 17,000 rockets, thousands of the very tiny needles stabbing into desks and other objects. Thousands more shot upward and shattered thirty-one fluorescent tubes. At least 600 of the slivers pierced the right leg and the right hip of Doucher, who screamed in agony and fell to his left, the left side of the leg space underneath the desk, preventing him from falling completely to the floor. He might as well have been stabbed with 600 ice picks. Blood poured from his right leg, which looked as if it had been put into a giant pencil sharpener; more blood ran from his hip and, due to the proximity of the concussion, from his nose and ears.

BLAMMMMMMMMMMM! Wally Chatters's K31 exploded only twenty feet from Kahil Dindoudli and thirty-five feet from Heinrich Mann, both of whom were trying to drop to the floor between desks.

Dindoudli screamed like a woman, a high, shrill soprano that was chopped off in midair and turned into an animallike gurgle. The sneering gods couldn't blame the Libyan. Hundreds of steel slivers had performed instant surgery on his face. He fell, blinded and without a face, his face chopped liver, the fluid of his pierced eyes running down his shredded cheeks.

Heinrich Mann had been lucky. Although he had been only halfway to the office floor, not a single steel needle had struck his body. Only the concussion had dulled his senses, making his ears ring and a gong go off in the center of his brain.

Sprawling on the floor, still holding onto his Walther MP-K submachine gun, Mann scooted around on his knees and started crawling north. He had had enough. He'd crawl past the stairs and leave by way of the double doors.

He had crawled only ten feet when he was overcome by pure terror, his horror generated by a round red object that struck the floor—by the side of a desk—only four feet in front of him.

The Death Merchant had thrown another grenade.

Mann had only a single second to stare at the grenade and to realize that his life was over!

The explosion ripped off his head, tore off both arms, and tossed him eight feet into the air. Its clothes blown off, the corpse crashed back to the floor. Trailing streams of blood, it didn't resemble anything that had been human.

*   *   *

20

Camellion raised himself from the side of the desk and surveyed the office. Three-fourths of the lights had been put out, some by slivers, most by concussion. The office was a mess, equipment wrecked by machine gun slugs.

The Death Merchant chuckled. Edward Farrell had it coming to him. *I wonder how he'll explain it all to the police. And how are we going to explain our failure to Mr. G?*

He didn't waste any precious time. Blowing one of the windows would not be an easy task, not with a grenade. While all the tall office windows were covered on the outside with steel mesh, the mesh was not the problem. Making a grenade explode *against* the mesh was. Throw the pineapple too hard, and it would bounce off the mesh before it exploded. Throw it too lightly, and it would never reach the window.

I don't have any string either!

Holstering his two pistols, he turned sideways and glanced at Wally Chatters, who had raced across the room and was now beside him. "What are we waiting for?" demanded Chatters. "Let's get out of here. The police must be on their way by now. If they bottle us up in here, we'll have had it, and you know it."

"Watch both entrances," Camellion said coolly, "or else tell me how to control a grenade after it's thrown."

"Oh shit—just get on with it."

No string. No kind of cord. However, there were more than enough typewriter ribbons. Taking off his deerskin gloves, Camellion removed three ribbons from Royal office manuals and tied two ends together. He took the end of one ribbon and a third spool to a window in the center of the south wall, broke the bottom windowpane with a large Bostitch stapler, and, with some of the ribbon from the third spool, tied a K31 antipersonnel grenade securely to the steel mesh, fastening it in such a way that the pull-ring was facing north. Then he fastened the end of a ribbon to the ring and proceeded to play out the two tied-together ribbons, all the while moving to the north, Chatters duck-walking beside him, his head turning back and forth like an owl's. When Camellion reached the end of the ribbon, he tied it to the already cut ribbon of the third typewriter spool and played it out. When he came to the end of all three ribbons, he and Chatters were almost seventy feet north of the grenade.

They got down behind a desk and Camellion pulled steadily on the ribbon and freed the pin from the grenade. Five seconds later the grenade roared off, the big blast ripping off not only the steel mesh but most of the wooden molding.

Chatters commented as they ran to the window, "I guess you know that blast will be telling them what we're up to?"

"Do you have a better way?" Camellion paused in front of the window. "I'll go first." Beretta autoloader in hand, he started to crawl through the smoking opening. Once he had dropped the six feet to the ground and his feet were in the snow, he glanced in both directions while Chatters crawled through the window and dropped to the ground.

Chatters was standing up when Camellion saw the two men start to come around the southwest corner of the ice cream plant. Up came the Beretta; out went two 9mm hollow points through the silencer. A waste of ammo. The two men had seen him swing up the Beretta and had ducked back to the west side of the building.

Camellion and Chatters ran to the southeast corner of the office building and got down on the east side, Chatters instantly turning and watching the east side of the long structure and snarling, "This is the worst position possible. They can hit us from the west and the north—and here we are, out in the open. An SMG would be a luxury right now."

The Death Merchant, who had taken the remote control unit from his anorak, looked around the corner. "A luxury automatically becomes a necessity when you can charge it."

"Look, stupid! This is no time to be witty!" growled Chatters half in anger. "Let's use a grenade and blow a hole in the fence and get the hell away from here. Hear those sirens? They're not three blocks away."

"We're leaving in about one minute," Camellion said.

In the darkness, the two men who had tried to creep around the southwest corner of the plant could not see the Death Merchant, but since he was still wearing the Cylops night-vision device, he could see them clearly as they moved along the south side of the ice cream plant, SMGs in their hands.

"Well, damn it!" ground out Chatters. "What are we waiting for—the Fourth of July?"

"For a big boom!" Wondering how long it would take him to scrub the typewriter ribbon ink from his fingers, Camellion saw that the two men were practically opposite the Clamper on the south side of the fence. "A big boom—like now."

He pressed the red button in the remote control unit.

22

The explosion of the one-pound block of TNT in the Clamper shattered every window in the ice cream plant and the office building. The wall of pressure was what did the real damage. It not only killed the two men but picked them up and slammed them against the wall of the plant. They were still sliding into hell when Camellion pulled the pin of his last K31 grenade and tossed it west, along the fence. A big roar and the ping-ping-ping of steel slivers hitting the side of the building.

"Well, there went nine thousand bucks," sighed Chatters. "Halverson will love that."

The Death Merchant looked around the southeast corner and saw that, thirty-two feet away, a ragged six-foot hole had been blown in the fence.

"Now is the time to do it," he said. "Let's run like hell."

As if Satan himself were chasing them, they headed for the newly created hole in the fence.

The strike had been a total failure.

They still didn't know if the nerve gas had reached the United States!

Chapter 2

Orin & Bonnie Dunlip. Fine Antiques. Old English lettering—black on a white background, the wooden sign, supported by two wooden posts, to the left side of the long, twisting dirt road. Just off New Jersey State Highway 47, the dirt road led to a two-story white farmhouse that was 2.3 miles north of Keasbey. A little spit in the road, Keasbey was 3.9 miles northwest of Perth Amboy.

A pleasant couple in their late fifties, Orin and Bonnie Dunlip did sell antiques, all six rooms of the first floor of the farmhouse filled with reproductions of furniture from the American colonial period and various kinds of glassware. However, the work of the Dunlips involved far more than the selling of antiques.

On one side of the house was a two-car garage. Three hundred feet to the northeast of the house was a large barn. Built of concrete blocks and with a gambrel roof, the barn was painted Chinese red and was in very good condition. Although the color didn't matter—purple with pink dots would have done just as well!—the quality of the barn was vital. For one good reason. The entire second floor was listed in CIA files as CHERRY RED 6. In short, the second floor comprised a Company "Black Station."[1] At the moment, five hours after the Perth Amboy Central Gas Corporation van had fled the vicinity of the Farrell's Forty Flavors ice cream plant, Cherry Red 6 was a gloomy B-Station. No one liked failure, most of all the Death Merchant.

Camellion, who had changed into a tan heather turtleneck, redwood corduroy slacks, and Padmore chukka boots, leaned back in the Bentwood rocker and turned over in his mind H. L.'s suggestion to black-bag Eugene Dusenbury, one of the businessmen involved with the Qaddafi plot. Why not? They didn't have anything else going for them, not one single lead.

Duane Halverson, the only CIA career employee present and the case agent of Redbird Group Alpha, frowned at H. L. Kartz and continued to wipe the lens of his silver-framed glasses with a handkerchief.

"I think that after this morning's failure, Dusenbury and the other two American traitors will make themselves scarce, or at a minimum take extraordinary precautionary measures."

"I've taken that into account," Kartz retorted defensively. "I'm not exactly a newcomer in this business, or I wouldn't be here."

"That was not meant as a reflection on your ability," Halverson said stiffly.

Watching Halverson and Kartz, as well as Wally Chatters and Pini Hilleli, the Death Merchant considered the four a definite plus in the operation that was so vital that it didn't even have a cipher designation. *At least I have the trained help. . . .*

Hannibal Llewellyn Kartz—H. L was his nickname—was an expert in any number of fields vital to clandestine operations. Not quite thirty-five, he was tall, lean-hard like Camellion, and an authority on methods of assassination. An intense man who almost never smiled, Kartz had curly brown hair, a thick bush of a mustache, and eyes the color of freshly poured cement. Yet

---

[1] Technically not existing, a Black Station is always the base of operations for CIA dirty-tricks operators. In tradecraft lingo, such a station is referred to as a Home Drop. A Home Drop differs from a safe house in that only the members engaged in a specific mission use a Black Station.

Kartz had a serious flaw in his character. He was a nihilist and as such was an ardent admirer of—Adolf Hitler.[2] Conversely, a man such as Kartz, a man with such a preference for hero worship, was totally ruthless—exactly what the Death Merchant wanted and needed.

Wally Chatters had already proven his ability. With two college degrees, one in engineering, the other in electronics, he was a past master in bugging, although he preferred to refer to himself as a "specialist in nonconsensual electronic monitoring."

There was the Israeli. Only seven months in the United States, Pini Abel Hilleli hadn't made the grade with the Mossad—Israeli intelligence. He hadn't been able to join the Mossad because he had not had the right political connections, or, as one would say in Israel, *protektzia*.[3]

Sharp featured, with solemn dark eyes, long sideburns, and thick black hair, Hilleli, twenty-nine, was rather short and built like a baby tank—214 pounds of solid muscle. A karate and firearms expert, he was also an authority on ancient Egyptian poisons.

Duane Halverson? He doesn't count. . . .

While Halverson was officially the case officer of the group, in reality, he was only a figurehead without authority. It was Richard Camellion who made the decisions and was the true boss of Redbird Group Alpha. Halverson was only the liaison to Courtland Grojean, the director of the Company's clandestine service.[4]

The Death Merchant had to smile when he thought of the prissy Grojean, who was a master survivor. D.C.I.'s[5] and D.D.C.I's[6] might come and go—and did—but Grojean would remain until he felt like retiring. The Fox was too good at his job. There wasn't anyone around to replace him, except the

[2] Hitler will always appeal to the nihilists, for like Hitler, nihilists have no loyalties, no culture, no religious faith, and consider themselves a law unto themselves. They can only worship power and brute force. Hitler was the master nihilist, the master destroyer.

[3] The word really refers to an Israeli system in which patronage is a vital element in career advancement.

[4] This is the Deputy Director of Operations, or D.D.O.

[5] Director of Central Intelligence.

[6] Deputy Director of Central Intelligence.

Death Merchant himself. Impossible! Officially, Camellion was merely another tax-paying citizen.

Facing Camellion, with his back to the couch, H. L. Kartz leaned forward on the captain's chair, his gray eyes swinging to the Death Merchant. "Camellion, what's your analysis of the situation?" His voice was confident, his manner professional. "As I see it, we can either go after Dusenbury in New Haven, or one of the other two bastards taking Qaddafi's money and helping him."

The Death Merchant mentally thumbed through the files of his mind, seeing the histories of the three businessmen as a single picture.

Eugene Dusenbury owned and operated a large construction company in New Haven, Connecticut.

Verlin Dragg manufactured motor boat engines—outboards—in New Bedford, Massachusetts.

Keith Griesbeck was an engineer with his own consulting firm. He also owned a large junkyard. Griesbeck operated from Atlanta, Georgia.

"There's an old Italian saying," Camellion said thoughtfully. "If you want to be a good fishmonger, take off the tie."

"We're not selling fish." Kartz frowned in annoyance.

"No, we're not. But we are dealing with people," said Camellion. "Let's look at what we have. We know that the real owner of the ice cream plant is Dusenbury, with a seventy-four percent interest. Farrell was only a business front. According to the newscasts, he's in hiding. We can assume he's on the run."

Wally Chatters, his right leg dangling over an arm of the couch, laughed softly. "I feel sorry for the Perth Amboy police," he said. "They don't know what to make of all the cold cuts we left at the ice cream plant. They're convinced it wasn't a holdup—and why would 'terrorists' attack an ice cream plant? Farrell must be scared stiff. If the cops ever do find him, how's he going to explain all the cruds we terminated. How can he explain what they were doing there?"

"Where ever Farrell is, he can't be more worried than I was in the van," interjected Pini Hilleli, stirring his tea. "I almost had a stroke waiting for you and Camellion to show up and get in the van. As it was, we were only minutes ahead of the police. I felt even better when we ditched the van and H. L. picked us up."

If Kartz minded the interruption, his expression—always grim—

didn't show it. Still staring at the Death Merchant, he said in the same serious tone, "Farrell ran because, legally, the buck stops with him; he's responsible for what takes place at his plant. None of that means that Dusenbury will have to go into hiding. He's only the majority stockholder. He can deny any knowledge of the men and the secret room and be in the clear. Furthermore, there isn't any public connection between Dusenbury, Dragg, and Griesbeck."

"We can count on the FBI getting into the investigation," Halverson, sitting next to the Death Merchant, said matter-of-factly. "The Perth Amboy police are trying to make fingerprint identification of the men snuffed at the ice cream plant. It won't take long for the cops to start suspecting that the men were foreigners and ask the Feds for help. When that happens, Federal agents almost certainly will question Dusenbury once they learn he has the controlling interest in Forty Flavors." He looked from Kartz to Camellion. "That will open up a whole new ball game and won't make our job any easier."

The Death Merchant didn't comment. Kartz was not impressed. "All the more reason we should toss a net over Dusenbury, while the tossing is still one of our options—if he's the one we go after."

"If you ask me, the hit on the ice cream plant is going to make all the people working for Qaddafi have some second and third thoughts!" intoned Pini Hilleli. He put down the cup of tea and stared at Halverson and Camellion with a rather odd intentness. "Now the Libyans and the East Germans know that your Uncle Sam is aware of the plot. I have to agree with Duane. They will take any number of precautionary measures."

Wally Chatters said, "The three businessmen are the weakest links in the chain. We know it, and you can bet that the East Germans who are running the operation know it. For all we know, they might decide to silence not only Dusenbury, but also Dragg and Griesbeck. At least Dusenbury. If . . ."

The Death Merchant did give a lot of credit to Libyan strongman Muammar Qaddafi—*He has the acute cleverness of all dangerous madmen.*

A psychopath who planned ahead! There had never been any Libyan hit squads on the way to the United States to assassinate President Reagan. All of it had been a lie. A ruse! Just as the CIA had suspected. The defector who originally had reported

27

that he had heard crackpot Qaddafi order Reagan's murder had passed three different polygraph tests, indicating he was telling the truth. Also, his description of the hit squads' modus operandi exactly matched that of a 1979 Libyan assassination plot against then ambassador to Egypt Herman Eilts—a plot the supposed defector could not have known about in detail. Supposed defector? The man has since returned to North Africa.

Any trained agent knows how to fool a polygraph, mused Camellion.

It was now apparent that Qaddafi, helped by the East German intelligence service, had used the hit-men ploy for two reasons:

1. In order to draw attention to himself in the Arab world, where he had almost no political clout;

2. To steer the U.S. intelligence community from the real operation he was planning.

Qaddafi's real intention was mind-boggling—to the average person inconceivable! *Kaddafi intended to infect the entire eastern coast of the United States with VXB-2L6, the most deadly nerve gas in the world.* Colorless, odorless, and tasteless, the gas was so lethal that 1 part in 16 million would kill instantly if inhaled; within one minute if dropped on the bare skin.

Fifty pounds of VXB sprayed from the air, during a brisk wind, would kill every person in the New York City area, an estimated 13 million people.

Qaddafi was planning to use 640 pounds of VXB in liquid form.

Weeks earlier, Camellion had conferred with Courtland Grojean in an exclusive men's club in New York City. The Death Merchant had asked Grojean, "Are you certain there isn't a mistake?"

Not wanting to mash the sharp crease in his trousers, Grojean had carefully crossed his legs. "We're positive. Our information came from a very reliable source, one that in the past has been inerrable."

"An agent-in-place? At least someone close to Mr. Q?"

"I didn't say that."

"You didn't have to. What matters is that your information is accurate."

Grojean nodded. "We're certain that Qaddafi intends to spread VXB up and down the East Coast. We also know that American businessmen are helping him, working with the contingent who will handle the mission for Qaddafi—a dozen or more Libyans under the direction of Mischa Wolf's top agents.[7] We have the names of the three Americans. The poor fools think they're helping that damned sand crab obtain plans for a nuclear device. That alone is enough to earn them termination.''

"How much are they being paid?" asked Camellion.

"Each man is getting five hundred thousand American.''

A little smile ended on the left side of the Death Merchant's mouth. Grojean looked as if he had just stepped out of an exclusive men's shop. Normal for the chief of operations. He always looked that way.

"What went wrong?" Camellion inquired. "You're not paying me a hundred grand because we're friends. If the Company could handle it, you wouldn't need me.''

A pained expression blossomed on Grojean's face.

"Our major source didn't give us the details,'' he said, folding his slim hands. "At the time, while we were in contact with him, he didn't have them. By the time he got them—if he ever obtained them—it was too late. He couldn't make contact with our relay. We suspect that Qaddafi found out he was our man.''

"In which case Qaddafi knows that we know!"

"Maybe. Maybe not. From another source, one not privy to Qaddafi's plans, we learned that our man committed suicide. He put the muzzle of a gun against the roof of his mouth and pulled the trigger—a rather messy way to end one's existence. We assume he knew he had been uncovered. All Qaddafi can do is pray to Allah and wonder what we might know." Grojean had then paused and his voice had risen angrily, "I tell you, Camellion! That son of a bitch Qaddafi has got to be terminated with extreme prejudice. Sooner or later, we're going to use the most extreme sanction against that piece of camel shit.''

The Death Merchant's hand came from the sack in his left coat pocket and he put several carob-coated sunflower seeds into his mouth. He chewed for a time, then said, "Have you considered the possibility that Qaddafi might cancel the operation? Surely, he wouldn't want a finger pointed at him.''

"We can't afford to assume that he might cancel,'' Grojean snapped. "Let's face reality. That Arab maniac will try any-

---

[7] Marcus "Mischa" Wolf, the head of the SSD, the *Staatssicherheitsdienst*, the executive political police organ of the East German *Mfs—Ministerium für Staatssicherheit:* Ministry for State Security of the German Democratic Republic (DDR, East Germany).

thing. He's not all that crazy, but he does have a tendency to listen to his emotions in preference to common sense."

"What about the Soviets? Those old peasant pig farmers in Moscow would never give approval to such a monstrous plan. They're much too cautious."

Grojean went on, "The nerve gas was made in a laboratory close to Wau el Kabir. Wau el Kabir—it's in the armpit of Libya—is Qaddafi's main terrorist training center—but you already know that. Three scientists were involved in the making of the gas. One was a chemist from the United Kingdom. Another was from Czechland, the third from France. As for the Soviets— our evaluation indicates that the Soviets aren't aware of the plan. If they were, they would have taken steps to neutralize Qaddafi. Or they would warn us."

Camellion uttered a low laugh. "You mean that would be the commonsense thing to do on the part of the Soviets. But in this business, all sides have to play the waiting game. Everyone's afraid to make a decision. Why don't you say it how it is? The Russians wouldn't move against Qaddafi. In the first place, how could they, without making it look like an invasion. That's what it would be if they used force. Their status in the Arab world would drop fifty points below zero. And they wouldn't warn the U.S. It would be against their interests to do so." He looked directly into the eyes of a stone-faced Grojean. "For the same reason, we won't let the Soviet Union know what that nut in Libya is up to. It's against our interests. After all, what are millions of American lives in this little game of power?"

Not the least bit disturbed over the Death Merchant's brutal words, Grojean regarded Camellion calmly. "Please," he sighed, "let's not have any rhetorical nonsense." He continued with aloof graciousness. "We don't dare confide in the Russians. We can't because we have no direct evidence that the Soviets aren't aware of Qaddafi's scheme. Should his plan succeed—God forbid!—how do we know that the Soviets wouldn't use a preemptive strike against us? Naturally, that would be the end. We'd go down, but we'd take the Soviets with us. Should we go, the world goes. I can assure you of that. Very well. You have questions."

Camellion took a few more carob-coated sunflower seeds from his pocket. "Your man in Libya, the one who committed self-murder. Did he give you the information about the ice cream plant, or did you obtain the info from another source?"

Grojean's face cracked slightly—his version of a smile.

"Among other things, our source in Libya mentioned that Frank Farrell was only a business front for Eugene Dusenbury. At the same time, he also said that the first 'gas squad' was on its way to the U.S.—this was about six weeks ago—and that the men of that squad would hide out in the basement of some office. He didn't know the name of the building. Farrell's ice cream plant was the only thing visible. We took a long shot and guessed it might be his office building. We believe we're right."

"There are no other leads?"

"No. You'll have to start with the ice cream plant and hope for the best."

We did begin with the ice cream plant! A total failure!

". . . If Dragg and Griesbeck do a vanishing act," finished Chatters, "then what do we do?" He removed his leg dangling from the arm of the couch and gave the Death Merchant a hard look. "The sooner we grab one of them, the better chance we're going to have—or there'll be millions of corpses up and down the eastern United States. And we'll probably be among them!"

"It would upset the civilians at their breakfast!" Kartz said.

"We're going to black-bag one," Camellion said. "The question now, which one? Preliminary surveillance by Company street men indicates that Keith Griesbeck is very well guarded. As for Verlin Dragg—"

"But the odds are that Griesbeck, with his international connections, is our best bet," pointed out Kartz quickly.

"And it's a lot warmer in Atlanta," cracked Hilleli. Wanting to take a subtle dig at H. L. Kartz, whom he knew to be an admirer of Hitler, he added, "Or isn't Atlanta one of your favorite cities?"

The very perceptive Kartz instantly gleaned Hilleli's intention. He turned in his chair and glanced at the Israeli. "Since you believe so much in justice, and consider it justice that Americans have been deprived of their most fundamental civil right—the right of free association—why didn't you remain in Israel and try to do something about the racism that exists over there between Ashkenazic, and Sephardic Jews?"

Hilleli's face fell and anger flashed in his eyes.

"I didn't come to America because of any dislike of the Sephardic Jews," he said firmly. "There's a lot more to it. There's the annual Israeli inflation rate of one hundred percent, combined with ever-rising taxes. Worse is the damned bureau-

31

cracy. Why, it takes five or six years to get a telephone! Then there's the system of patronage, plus compulsory military service and the lengthy annual reserve duty—and the constant belt tightening."

"Belt tightening?" Kartz pretended innocence. "I don't know why there should be? Uncle Sam has given Israel untold billions since the creation of the Jewish state."[8]

Hilleli didn't have a chance to reply. The Death Merchant, aware that Kartz had once been young but would remain immature indefinitely, said easily but in a loud, firm voice, "Gentlemen, keep to the issue under discussion. The hell with social issues." His blue eyes jumped to Wally Chatters. "Wally, you always have an opinion. Whom do you suggest we grab—Dragg or Griesbeck?"

Chatters, now wearing a red flannel shirt, a bulky gray cardigan, and gray worsted flannel trousers, snapped shut his cigarette lighter and exhaled smoke.

"What happened to Eugene Dusenbury?" he asked.

"He's out of the running," Camellion said. "We don't know how soon the FBI will start investigating him. We don't want to cross swords with those Friggin' Bunch of Idiots. They would be too much of a stumbling block for us."

"In that case, my choice is Griesbeck," Chatters said promptly.

"He's well protected," intoned Duane Halverson. "In these times when businessmen are being kidnapped and held for ransom, Griesbeck has become paranoid. His place of business and his home are reported to have all kinds of electronic protective devices. There are guards at his home. But he's a millionaire and can afford it."

Chatters shrugged, his amused eyes on Halverson, whom he considered a red-tapist fool. "The bodyguards are not a problem. We kill 'em. We would have to proceed somewhat slower with the electronics. Understand, it would take a bit of time, perhaps as long as several weeks, depending on the overall plan we evolve regarding Griesbeck, mainly how we grab him and where. I suppose the 'how' will depend on the 'where.' "

"Pini, give me your opinion," Camellion said, still playing the devil's advocate.

"I agree with Wally," the Israeli replied. "We should grab Keith Griesbeck—for several reasons. First of all, whether we

---

[8] Roughly $24.26 billion.

net Dragg or Griesbeck, once we do, East German intelligence will know what we're up to. The one who is left—Dragg in this case—will have to go into hiding. So why go after Dragg when Griesbeck is apt to have more information about Qaddafi's plan—this based on his connections, which are international?"

Duane Halverson cleared his throat and watched Kartz get up and move the captain's chair to a position from which he could see Chatters and Hilleli, both of whom were on the couch.

"I have a suggestion I feel bears analysis," Halverson said. He glanced from Camellion to the other men. "Wally, you're an expert in bugging? Is that not so?"

"I'm one of the best in the business." Chatters folded his hands between his legs. "What are you driving at?"

"I'm thinking we might learn a lot after we grab Griesbeck," went on Halverson. "Then again, we might not. Think of the secrets we could learn if we could plant an infinity transmitter[9] in his vicinity, either in his office or in his home?"

Chatters smiled at Halverson. "Do you know what you're talking about? What do you really want—an interception approach or the wireless transmitter. With the former you have interception of phone conversations, interception of business' data communications to a computer service, or interception of conversations over direct-distance dialing networks between two or more people in different cities. It's the latter you want—and you can forget it. I'd have to have access to one of Griesbeck's phones for a harmonica bug. With a bug, access to the premises.

[9] Also called a harmonica bug. The switching device and mike amplifier must first be inserted in the target phone, after which the eavesdropper merely dials the target phone from his own phone. He then blows a harmonic note of a special frequency before the first ring, using a special device. It is imperative that he blow the note before the first ring of the target phone. This harmonic note activates the relay decoder circuit before the target phone has a chance to ring. This has the same effect as lifting the receiver of the target telephone. The harmonic tone establishes a connection by which the carbon mike acts as a room mike, with the amplifier boosting the signal level. The connection is broken when the eavesdropper hangs up his own phone. Distance is not a barrier. Phone from New York City and you can pick up a conversation in Los Angeles, provided you first had access to the target phone and "worked" it.

Why go to all that trouble—I mean, getting past the security devices—when we're going to grab him anyhow?"

"There should be some way, some method we can use," insisted Halverson.

"No go," said Chatters. "Terminal-box taps and all the rest of it are subject to detection devices, and we can be sure that Griesbeck has them. Whether we tap the phone or use a bug, a general purpose telephone analyzer could pick up any tap. A panoramic surveillance receiver could search the radio frequency spectrum and identify transmission emitted by any hidden receiver."

"Any kind of bugging would be too great a risk," Camellion joined in. "If Griesbeck's technical people discovered a tap or a bug before we were ready to move in, he'd fade, or increase personal security to the extent that we'd need a small army to get within ten feet of him."

"It was only a thought," Halverson said tentatively, shifting uncomfortably.

"Oh, don't feel bad," Camellion said cheerfully, feeling rather sorry for Halverson, who, like most CIA paper-pushers, had a limited perspective regarding violence. "That's why we're here: to consider all the possibilities."

Pini Hilleli looked at the other men, going from face to face. "Then it's settled? We go after Griesbeck?"

"Affirmative. We net Griesbeck," Camellion said. "We can leave either tonight or tomorrow morning for Atlanta. Griesbeck doesn't know what Qaddafi actually intends to do, but he will have to give us a positive lead we can develop to get to the people who do have the information we want."

"When and where the VXB is coming into the U.S.!" added Chatters gravely. "Or if the gas is already here, where is it?"

"All we need is a bushelful of miracles," growled H. L. Kartz.

"I have a suggestion." Hilleli sounded excited. "Since Griesbeck and Dragg aren't aware of Qaddafi's real plan, why couldn't we appeal to their humanity, to their sense of decency? After we grab Griesbeck, why not tell him the blunt truth? He doesn't want to see his family and relatives and friends murdered by nerve gas."

Chatters's large, round head turned to Hilleli, his freckled face mirroring surprise. "Damn it, of course we're going to

34

appeal to Griesbeck's sense of humanity—if he has any. What are you getting at? You also mentioned Verlin Dragg.''

''Appeal to Dragg, also, even though we're not going to black-bag him,'' Hilleli said quickly. ''It would be a simple matter for Company people to approach him. Why, they could walk right into his office.''

He looked from Chatters to the Death Merchant. ''What do you think, Camellion?''

Camellion shook his head. ''I doubt if Dragg would believe the truth. Even if he did, such a tactic would expose the entire show. We can't risk having any of this made public. The American people would demand harsh action against Qaddafi, and such action might not fit the plans of the idiots in Washington.''

H. L. Kartz made an obscene sound with his mouth and locked his fingers behind his head. ''Philosophically speaking, I wouldn't consider it such an earth-shaking tragedy if fifteen or twenty million people died from nerve gas. It's all relative. They'll die sooner or later anyhow. The way the world's going, probably sooner—in a nuclear conflict.''

Wally Chatters gave Kartz a long, hard look of disapproval. ''I've heard it said that nothing is so firmly believed as that which is least known. A good example would be that Jesus Christ came from Nazareth, even though Nazareth didn't exist historically until sometime during the eighth and ninth centuries. You're the second example, H. L. In some things you never act stupid. With you it's the real thing!''

Kartz regarded Hilleli with an air of disdain. Like all nihilists, Kartz considered himself superior to even the angels. He was not about to be insulted by a mere mortal!

''You're not being realistic, Pini,'' he said haughtily. ''People don't matter; they don't count. They never did and never will. They fight the wars and pay the taxes. Their leaders 'love' them and they die for their leaders. Right now the American people are being asked to pick up the expensive tab for a lot of crap they're told is vital to 'national security.' The irony of it is that at the very same time that Western bankers are struggling to arrange further loans to keep the Communist thugs afloat, to enable them to service and roll over their one-hundred-twenty-five-billion-dollar debt to Western banks and governments, American taxpayers are being told by those lying sneaks in Congress that they must 'sacrifice' their living standards to defend themselves against those same Commie thugs. It's you men who are the dreamers. The only two things that have ever really counted in a practical sense are money and power."

Kartz made a sweeping motion with one hand. "You'll be saying next that we personally are worried about the poor American people. Let's say it like it is. We're here because of the money, with the exception of Duane. He has to be here."

"You're full of it," Chatters said roughly, pulling at his short beard. "Sure, we know that money and power make the world spin. We don't dwell on it though or assign top priority to the moral wrongs of the world. There are a lot of things one accepts because one doesn't have a choice. Dwell on the ills of the world and you'll end up spending your days in a rubber-walled room."

During this short time, Camellion had vaguely been studying the reproduction of a Nantucket bench at the end of the room, to his right. Made of hand-planed pine, the bench—it was really a narrow table—had been hand-rubbed with golden linseed oil to allow for the patina of natural aging. On the top of the bench was a shiny brass London lamp, a reproduction of an oil lamp that had found its way to America in the early 1800s. Yet—if one let his mind wander, he might somehow get the feeling that the past was interwoven with the present, and ridiculously so. A Mura cordless telephone was on the solid oak table in front of the couch. Next to the phone was an IXO telecomputer, a portable data bank. A captain's chest was across the room; on it rested a large Sanyo Super Woofer boom box.

Weird. Sitting in this room, on the second story of a barn, discussing how millions of lives could be saved. Yet a proper setting for men who were equally as weird.

Especially Kartz. He's a genuine crackpot, but what he said is the truth. It is all relative in the long scheme of things.

Camellion suddenly thought of another irony, this one involving the mighty of the world. In reality, their power was zero! Cosmic forces were in motion, forces that would utterly transform world society within the next seventeen years, in the form of a catastrophe never before seen by modern man—*One that is impossible for the average man to even conceive. Men can never face up to what they think is total oblivion!*

There would be a literal shifting of the axis of the earth, and the planet would be tilted at a new angle so that the sun and the moon would appear to move in different orbits in the sky—*Unless*

Michel de Notredame is wrong! Well, he's been right on target for hundreds of years.[10]

The tilt of the earth would come during World War III—a nuclear holocaust—and usher in a new age, one of peace, one that would last for a thousand years, from A.D. 2000 to A.D. 3000, after which there would be a new horror, a new evil. Only this time man would not be fooled; he would be prepared, having developed a higher spiritual consciousness. At the end of the year A.D. 7000 there would be a universal conflagration in which earth would be destroyed. The planet would vanish in fire and smoke because its purpose will have been served, the material sphere no longer needed to support the physical body of man. By then, man will have left his material body and will have become pure spirit, as he was intended to be.

H. L. Kartz was saying in a voice that was one long sneer, "Strong-minded people don't end up on funny farms, even if they do know the world for what it really is. It's the daydreamers, the stupid liberals—"

"We have a job to do; let's get on with it and stop this gelastic bickering!" Camellion's sharp voice cut off Kartz in mid-sentence. The Death Merchant stood up, put his hands on his hips, and looked down, to his left, at Halverson. "It's settled. We're going after Keith Griesbeck in Atlanta. Duane, get on the radio and contact the Center. Use the nine-nine-nine five-digit code, with double scramble and black box. Tell Mr. G. that—"

[10] This is Nostradamus, the only truly accurate seer the world has ever known. Here is the actual quatrain in which he predicts the change of position of the sun and the moon. Only a tilting of the earth on its axis could effect such a change. The "twentieth year" is the year 2000.

The grand twentieth year ends, also the position
    of the moon.
It will hold a different monarchy in the sky for
    another 7,000 years.
Then the sun, too, will be tired of its place.
And at that time will my prophecies for the world be ended.

"I know how to use a shortwave and its security attachments," Halverson snapped. Giving Camellion an angry look, he got to his feet.

"Tell Grojean that we're going to Atlanta tonight. Tell him to get back to us at once with information about the Black Station we'll be using."

With a short nod, Halverson turned and walked from the room, taking long strides.

Wally Chatters got up from the couch. "I'll phone the airport and make sure the Cessna is ready for us."

He reached down for the Mura cordless phone on the coffee table but paused when Camellion said, "Hold on before you call. I want to tell the three of you about a new wrinkle in our operation."

"Don't tell me we're going to hitchhike from Perth Amboy to Atlanta?" joked Hilleli.

Chatters sat back down on the couch, his eyes narrowing.

"Let's have it, Camellion," Kartz said in that odd, vague manner of his.

The Death Merchant spoke with machine-gun rapidity. "Hilleli mentioned appealing to Verlin Dragg's sense of decency, to his concern for humanity as a whole. We know why we can't risk such a tactic. However, there isn't any reason why we can't grab both Dragg and Griesbeck."

"Oh, I can think of half a dozen good reasons," Hilleli said.

"Both of them! That would be some accomplishment," Kartz said heartily. "We net Griesbeck in Atlanta and Dragg in New Bedford—all at the same time. We're going to have to be twins and use teleportation to accomplish that bit of sheer impossibility."

Hilleli looked at Kartz as if he might be thinking of putting the Hitler lover's head into a meat grinder.

Chatters adjusted his dark glasses and lit another cigarette.

Before this is over, I'm going to zipper his mouth with my fist! Perfectly at ease in dealing with idiots and geniuses, Camellion said pleasantly, his eyes on Kartz, "The impossible is what nobody can do—until someone does it. We'll handle the grab in Atlanta and sync it with Company street men tossing a net over Dragg in New Bedford. All it requires is careful planning and constant communication."

"Hell yes! Why not go for broke?" Chatters said with a bitter little laugh. "After all, what do we have to lose?"

The Death Merchant's calm face didn't reveal what he was thinking—*Lose? Twenty million lives—and far more if Qaddafi succeeds. He would trigger World War III!*

Chapter 3

The same winter that had been unkind to New Jersey had also tortured the New York City area. The very same storm that had dumped millions of tons of snow on New Jersey had also paralyzed New York City. That first day, office workers had to remain overnight in their buildings. Cars were buried under mounds of white. Several days later, although the city was again functioning, snow was everywhere, along streets and sidewalks, shoveled into high mounds by several million hands and a million shovels and by hundreds of snowplows. On the lawns of houses and parks heavy wet snow lay three feet thick where the ground was level, with drifts often six to eight feet high—all of it covered with soot and other lung-cancer-causing debris so common in Murder City.

Staten Island had also been immobilized by the storm. Naturally this included West New Brighton, a little village on the north coast of the island. Snow had piled itself high around the two-story house on the edge of town, the storm of such intensity that Gunther Flegel and Manfred Halbritter had twice been forced to get out long aluminum extensions for the wide snow shovels and climb to the roof and push off snow to keep the roof from caving in from the weight. The roof had held.

From the large living room window, Gunther Flegel could look across the channel of Van Kull and see the haze above Elizabeth, New Jersey, to the northwest. Straight north was the haze and smog of Bayonne. A man with the kind of puppet face that didn't show its true age, the beefy Flegel didn't really mind the cold, being from Rostock, East Germany, where the winters are bitter cold, with icy winds constantly blowing from the Baltic Sea. Manfred Halbritter, Flegel's assistant, was also used to cold weather. He had been born and reared in Nuremberg.

The two other men in the living room might as well have been in Antarctica, as far as they were concerned. Having lived in Jamahiriya al-Arabia allibya[1] all of their lives, Abdullah al-Mansour and his aide, Suleiman Maghrabi, had been shivering for almost six weeks, ever since they had entered the United States. How they longed to be back in the land of sand and sunshine. First, these damned Americans, who were constantly helping the Israeli dogs, must be taught a lesson.

Flegel turned from the frosted window, walked back to the gold tubular framed armchair, sat down, crossed his legs, and smiled at al-Mansour and Maghrabi, both of whom were sitting on a round three-piece sofa-sleeper. Both men were wearing heavyweight flannel shirts, over which were woolen tweed zip-front jackets. The two Libyans were not taking any chances. Several days earlier, at the height of the blizzard, the electric heat had gone off, and the men had been forced to switch to the oil furnace in the cellar. Even though the oil furnace had kept the house at a comfortable seventy-eight degrees, the two Libyans felt more comfortable with electric heat. "It's warmer!" they insisted.

"We'll wait until the end of the week, then drive into New York and make contact with the courier from our legation in the United Nations," Flegel said. "The courier will give us final instructions as to how we will receive the drums of nerve gas."

"We already have most of the information," Halbritter said tersely in his thin, high voice. "The drums will be on board a ship. The vessel will have to be a freighter. It's the time of the year that bothers me. The Atlantic will be rough for months to come."

Half a head taller than Flegel, Halbritter had narrow shoulders and a head that seemed too large for his neck. Thirty-four years old, he had dark eyes under thickly browed overhanging banks of eye socket; his dark brown hair standing up a little like tufted grass. In spite of his bug-eyed appearance, Halbritter was one of the best agents in the East German SSD—a *Vertrauensmann* (a "very trusted person"). He was still a rank below Gunther Flegel, who was an *HV-Mann*, or *Hauptvertrauensmann*, that is, a leader.

"We still must have the name of the vessel," Flegel reminded Halbritter. "We must know its position in order to meet her.

[1] Arabic for the Libyan Arab Republic.

We must know how we are going to meet her and how we will make contact with the men who will take us."

"Men who will be obtained by one of the Americans working with us," Halbritter said dully. "I don't like it; I never did. *Mein Gott!* Look at the position we'll be putting ourselves in! We will have to trust the American swine."

Sitting in a tubular framed armchair, Halbritter took his feet from the ottoman and stood up, a look of deep concern on his face. "How can you trust men who are traitors to their own flag?"

"We can trust them because they're being so well paid," Flegel said smugly. "Naturally, there is some element of risk, but that's the nature of our business. We're in the United States, the most relaxed country in the world. These *Amerikaner* don't know the first thing about security. Why, we walked right into their country, right under their very noses."

Halbritter pulled at the bottom of his bulky-knit sweater-coat. "I'm going to the toilet. This American food doesn't agree with me. It's too bland."

He turned and walked slowly from the room.

Flegel, whose eyes seldom missed anything, saw apprehensive looks cross the faces of Suleiman Maghrabi and Abdullah al-Mansour. *Ach!* Those *unmenschliche Schweinehunde!*[2] Like all Arabs who are always out of their natural element while in Western nations, al-Mansour and Maghrabi were useless baggage, even though their presence was necessary. The two were Colonel Muammar al-Qaddafi's personal representatives. As such, they had come to the United States to observe everything that would be done, and later report in detail to the dictator of Libya.

Gunther Flegel had not been happy when he learned that al-Mansour and Maghrabi would accompany him and Halbritter to the United States.

He had protested to *Direktor*, Wolf whom he had known for years.

"*Mein Gott!* Why those Libyans are lower than the Russians. They're nothing more than *Leichenfresser!*[3] *Herr Direktor*. Isn't there some way we can push forward with the mission without the Libyans going with us to *Amerika*?"

[2] "Inhuman swine dogs."
[3] "Corpse eaters."

41

Nein, there wasn't. Oil-wealthy Qaddafi was giving the East German government $50 million in payment for the services of the *Staatssicherheitsdienst*. Qaddafi further insisted that his two representatives accompany the two top SSD agents. Other Libyans, who spoke English well and who had been educated in American universities, would go with other SSD men.

Flegel reflected that thus far PLAN Y was going as scheduled. One hundred and seventeen men in fourteen different groups, from six different vessels, had landed secretly on U.S. shores—on the coasts of Washington, Oregon, and northern California. Forty of the agents—thirty SSD and ten Libyans—had already made their way east across the United States and were in New York City. To a man, they spoke perfect idiomatic English and carried expertly forged identification—driver's licenses, social security cards, credit cards—that proved they were citizens from various towns and cities in the United States.

Acting as if they were strangers to each other, Flegel, Halbritter, and the two Libyans had been on the same Pan Am flight from Paris to New York. They had not had the least bit of difficulty at U.S. Customs after they had landed at John F. Kennedy International Airport. All their identification was forged, with one exception: their passports, which, while genuine, were of the "alias" kind.[4] Remembering how easy it had been to fool the U.S. Customs officials, Flegel felt good. A slight frown creased his brow. There had been a slight setback, but it had not been totally unexpected. The Libyans had suspected that Quamar Boutesi was a traitor and working for either the CIA or the KGB. Or could he be a double and working for both the Americans and the Russians? No one would ever know, except maybe the Americans and the Russians. Quamar Boutesi, the assistant chief

---

[4] The most serious type of passport fraud and the least detectable. Acquiring the passport hinges around obtaining a new birth certificate. The applicant searches the newspapers, the graveyards, and/or the local recorder's office until he finds a baby born at about the same time as himself, a child who died. He then proceeds to obtain the birth certificate—not an illegal act in most states. In most states, it can be handled via mail. Step number two is to acquire supplementary identification, such as a driver's license—the *sine qua non* of American IDs. The last step is to go to a U.S. Post Office and apply for the passport.

of the Libyan *Al Naqui-zam'i Mir-iza*,[5] had committed suicide before he could be questioned about his espionage activities. His wife could not be found; the couple's three children were also missing.

Director Wolf had suggested to Qaddafi's representative in Leipzig that Plan Y be canceled, his advice based on the premise that Boutesi might have given vital information to the enemy. Qaddafi had refused, pointing out that while Boutesi had given information, he could not possibly divulge what he didn't know—information, facts, data known only to Qaddafi, his three trusted aides, and half a dozen high-ranking East German intelligence officers.

Plan Y would be implemented. Colonel Qaddafi had spoken!

Gunther Flegel was pulled from his comfortable reverie by Suleiman Maghrabi, who, with Abdullah al-Mansour, was having morose thoughts about the loss of the men at Farrell's Forty Flavors ice cream factory and who proved that Flegel's optimism was not contagious by saying bluntly, "I fail to understand how we can drape a cloak of confidence over our shoulders in view of the disaster at the American ice cream factory nine days ago."

Right behind him added Abdullah al-Mansour, who also did not speak with the least trace of an accent, "It is evident that the son-of-whore Boutesi somehow obtained the names of the American capitalists who have betrayed their own country and gave those names to the Central Intelligence Agency. That is how the CIA knew about Mr. Farrell and his place of business. What assurance do we have that, right now, the Americans aren't preparing to swoop down and arrest all three businessmen?"

"We have been all through that," Flegel said, underlining each word carefully and looking through narrowed lids at the two Libyans, both of whom carried passports identifying them as Italian-Americans. Suleiman Maghrabi was Vito Romiro of Brooklyn, New York. Abdullah al-Mansour had the name Salvatore Manganni. He "lived" in Queens. Both men spoke fluent English.

"Before we even left Europe, we thoroughly discussed Quamar Boutesi and the type of information he could have passed to the Americans," Flegel said, getting to his feet. He had tried to sound patient and pleasant and hoped that none of his dislike of the two Libyans was showing. "The conclusion then was that

[5] The Libyan intelligence service. Actual translation is "Protective Bureau of the Sacred Nation."

there wasn't any way that Boutesi could have obtained the name of the three Americans. Even Hassan Khatib Jasiiji, the chief of Libyan intelligence, knew the names." He leaned over slightly and peered accusingly at al-Mansour and Maghrabi. "Or, are you intimating that one of Qaddafi's chief assistants is an agent for the American government?"

A tall man, with a head of thick black hair and lazy eyes whose upper lids never rose very far and were decorated with heavy lashes, Suleiman Maghrabi refused to be tricked by Flegel's attempt to make him feel guilty. Al-Mansour didn't fall for the trick either.

Maghrabi said steadily, "We are saying that if Boutesi didn't inform the CIA about Farrell's ice cream plant, then how did American intelligence obtain the information?"

Abdullah al-Mansour said, "The fact still confronts us that only Idris Ghradeh and one of your own agents, Heinrich Reinner, escaped from the ice cream plant. The rest of the squad was killed." He paused, his eyes carefully probing Flegel. He then continued with a kind of smoldering resentment that was definitely disquieting. "Another fact that might indicate a severe weakness in our security is that the American, Frank Farrell, isn't even one of the three traitors working with us. Can you deny those truths, Herr Flegel?"

Gunther Flegel couldn't and didn't try to. Not a man to hedge, an individual who didn't believe in retreat, he promptly admitted, as he walked to the cabinet bar across the room, that East German intelligence didn't know how the CIA had learned about the ice cream plant. "We can be sure of one thing," he reassured the Libyans, pouring Scotch into a glass, "there isn't any possibility of the CIA's knowing about Keith Griesback and Verlin Dragg. Since Quamar Boutesi wasn't aware of their existence, he couldn't have given their names to anyone; and Dragg and Griesbeck have never had any dealings with each other. Both of them are strangers to Eugene Dusenbury. By the way, Dusenbury no longer matters. It is possible that he will be questioned by American authorities because of Frank Farrell. Fortunately, he doesn't know anything of importance. It's Dragg who has arranged for the aircraft and Griesbeck who will make arrangements for us to meet the vessel. All Dusenbury can confess to is that he arranged nine different hiding places, safe houses, and that he was involved in a plot to steal plans for the neutron bomb."

44

Flegel turned, took a sip of Scotch without looking at the Libyans, hurried across the room, and returned to his chair, pretending not to notice, or be disturbed by, the questioning stares of Maghrabi or al-Mansour, the latter of whom said at length in a low, severe voice, "Yet the Americans know that our leader, His Excellency Colonel Muammar al-Qaddhafi, is responsible for the scheme, supposedly to steal the plans of the neutron bomb. I ask you: suppose Quamar Boutesi managed to reveal our leader's true plan to American intelligence? By Allah! What is to prevent American naval and air forces from attacking our country?" His voice rose in volume. "With a determined strike, they could crush us overnight. We are a small nation!"

You're a nation of dumb swine! thought Flegel, who leaned back and said aloofly, "It was Colonel Qaddafi's decision to proceed with the operation. The risks were pointed out to him. Even so, the Americans can't strike against your nation. If they did, they would have to tell the world why. They can't do that without letting the world know how vulnerable their defenses are."

Manfred Halbritter, coming back from the john and entering the living room, had heard Flegel's words and now he said as he sat down, "Let's assume the Central Intelligence Agency does know about the VXB nerve gas. What can they do about it? They don't know that Dragg and Griesbeck exist; they don't know that we and our men exist."

"But they could know that the nerve gas is to be distributed over the East Coast of the United States," Abdullah al-Mansour said with exasperating calmness. "If so, our job will be more difficult."

For a long moment, Flegel looked at al-Mansour, who was about forty, had high cheekbones, and was a big man who looked as if he had loose skin. His upper lip was decorated with a long, thin mustache and he was half bald.

"Not at all," Gunther Flegel replied with equal calmness, swishing the Scotch around in the thick, tall glass. "We'll only have to be more cautious, and since we're going to be extremely guarded to begin with, it doesn't make any difference." He looked up from the glass and grinned, showing big but even teeth. "While the gas is being spread, we'll be nowhere in the general areas. We'll have taken flights to the American West Coast several days earlier."

"It's our four Libyan pilots who will be taking the risks,"

45

Suleiman Maghrabi said sullenly. "It is they who will be flying the aircraft."

"That is how your colonel wanted it," retorted Halbritter, tilting back his head. "In fact, he insisted."

"The pilots will not be in any real danger, when they spread the nerve gas," Gunther Flegel said blandly. "The gas will be behind the airplanes and, being heavier than air, will sink to the ground immediately. The pilots will simply keep on going until they are out of range; one hundred sixty kilometers is only a short distance in an aircraft."

"It is still a great risk," said Maghrabi. He slowly rubbed the end of his chin with the thumb and forefinger of his right hand. "Frankly, we feel that you are underestimating the ability of the Americans. While they are known for their naiveté in international matters, they are not stupid."

"Have you two considered the length of the East Coast of this nation?" Flegel said in a loud voice. "When you add up all the twisted shorelines of coves and bays, you get a length of almost thirty-two hundred kilometers, or two thousand English miles. There isn't any way the Americans can watch that much coastline."

"This is a very rich nation," Halbritter said happily, reinforcing Flegel's optimism. "There are thousands and thousands of private boats and airplanes and literally millions of automobiles. How can the CIA keep track of them all?"

Al-Mansour and Maghrabi, naturally pessimistic because of their desert background, gazed solemnly at the two East German agents as if they were mentally rehearsing what they were about to say—a habit that irritated the two German intelligence officers, who considered the two Libyans on a par with bedbugs and just plain weird. Maghrabi and al-Mansour could sit for hours without (seemingly) moving, without changing or shifting positions.

At length, Suleiman Maghrabi spoke in a sly tone. "A lot of your views and contentions are built only around pure hypotheses; and there are some inconsistencies we must consider."

Flegel looked up sharply. "It's better to work on the basis of a hypothesis based on known fact than to have no hypothesis at all."

"What inconsistencies?" demanded Halbritter, grasping the arms of his chair.

"Idris Ghradeh and Heinrich Reinner reported that only two men were in the ice cream factory," Suleiman Maghrabi said coldly. "Doesn't that strike you as inconsistent? Only two men!

Ghradeh and Reinner also reported that those two also seemed anxious to avoid contact with the American civilian police. The proof that this is so is that the two men were nowhere around when the American civilian police arrived. Our intelligence service may not be as sophisticated as yours, but we find it ludicrous that the Central Intelligence Agency—in its very own country—would send only two men to investigate a stronghold of an enemy!''

Gunther Flegel burst into laughter.

Manfred Halbritter smiled and reached for his cigarettes.

"There isn't any inconsistency," Flegel said expansively. "It's only normal, that is, for the Americans. Your trouble is that you don't understand the various interlocking layers of authority in the United States. For example, in the Soviet Union the militia is under the firm control of the KGB. In our nation, the *Volkspolizei*,[6] or VOPO, is subservient to our SSD. A much different police complex exists in this foolish nation, which believes that citizens have rights."

"Due to all the American 'freedoms,' " sneered Halbritter.

"The CIA does not control the other American police agencies," explained Flegel in a condescending tone. "The CIA cannot give orders to the local police of each city—except in national emergencies—and, believe it or not, the CIA must uphold all local and state laws, laws that are imposed on the rest of the population. The two CIA men at the ice cream factory fled because they did not want to be arrested by the Perth Amboy city police. How could they have explained what they were doing there?"

Maghrabi and al-Mansour glanced at each other in amazement, as if a great revelation had been disclosed to them.

"There's the state police and the Federal Bureau of Investigation—the famous FBI we were warned about," said Flegel, chuckling. "And *state* in this case does not mean 'national.' It means that each American state has its own police that patrol the state's highways. The FBI is national and connected to the Justice Department of the federal American government."

Appended Manfred Halbritter, "Those agencies cooperate with each other, yet function independently. As you can see, it's a system that works to our benefit."

"Or to our disadvantage," spoke up Suleiman Maghrabi.

[6] People's Police.

47

"Working in close cooperation, those various police agencies could pose a serious problem for us."

"*Nein*—NO!" Flegel was vehement. "The CIA wouldn't dare risk letting the civilian police know the truth. There would be too much danger that the American people would learn the facts. There isn't a controlled press in the United States, as odd as that might seem to us. The police are always getting money from reporters in payment for tips."

"We shall see," Maghrabi said soberly. He neither sounded nor looked convinced.

Neither did Abdullah al-Mansour. Like Maghrabi, al-Mansour had a reason, and that reason was the disaster that had occurred at the ice cream plant. Only two CIA agents had attacked.

But they had killed the American guards and eight men of the group of Libyans and East Germans.

Only two men!

Maghrabi and al-Mansour were worried and uncomfortable, feelings they kept carefully hidden from the two East German infidels. This cold United States was alien to them—a frozen hell whose defenders fought like devils.

Chapter 4

More snow and chilling cold. Yet Atlanta, Georgia—the home of Coca-Cola, the second highest large city in the United States and the business headquarters of the entire southeastern United States[1]—was warmer than the New York and the New Jersey area. Nor had there been a recent snowstorm.

That morning at 1029 hours, when the Death Merchant and his tiny group expertly hijacked the tractor and trailer, the temperature was twenty-nine degrees above zero and the sky, with long streaks of cirrus clouds, was bright with sun. There was less than six inches of snow on the ground and none on the roads and highways.

BARDOLOW INDUSTRIES—in large black block letters on

[1] Atlanta is at an altitude of 1,175 feet. Denver, 5,280 (one mile). More than four thousand national business and industrial firms have district and branch offices in Atlanta.

the white sides of the trailer, and in smaller black letters on both doors of the cab. In smaller letters in red—Manufacturers of Gas Stoves, Refrigerators & Related Kitchen Products. Rome, Georgia.

Rome was less than sixty miles northwest of Atlanta.

Dressed in heavy-duty coveralls, a quilt-lined zippered work coat, and billed work cap, Camellion drove carefully, handling the big rig with an easy dexterity, his eyes on the ribbon of road.

Next to him, Wally Chatters, similarly dressed, glanced at the mileage on the speedometer, then carefully checked the map in his lap. Finally, he announced, "We're less than seven miles from eighty-five. You're sure you know how to get onto twenty-nine?"

The Death Merchant should have been annoyed with Chatters. It was the fourth time he had asked the question since they had taken over the rig just south of Marietta. Camellion should have been irked, but he wasn't. Maybe it was because Chatters had a naturally friendly voice, a ready smile, and was always willing to listen to the other fellow's point of view—the exact opposite of H. L. Kartz, whose mouth had been going full steam since they had left the Black Station on Dresden Road in North Atlanta, a suburb northeast of Atlanta.

Kartz might have been a modern Don Quixote tilting at windmills of various wrongs, but much of what he said was the truth. Camellion and Chatters had to agree when he said that Billy Graham was either "the most naive man in the world" or a hypocrite.

"Graham goes to the Soviet Union and the Russians make him look like a dummy,"[2] Kartz said. "Graham gives a sermon over there and tells the Soviet people that they should obey the authorities and that he thinks Christians and atheists can work together. He didn't say a single word about the Soviet invasion of Afghanistan, or how the Soviet Union ignores human rights and supports world terrorism. It's morons like Graham who make it easy for the Communists."

The federal government came in for its share of criticism, Kartz raging that millions of tax dollars were being wasted by "grants given by idiots to idiots. The biggest dumbbells of all are those bureaucrats in the U.S. Department of Health and Human Services. Those morons gave over eighteen thousand dollars to some weird outfit in Maryland to study the '*coming out*

---

[2] During May of 1982.

49

process of coping strategies of gay women.' Imagine! Eighteen grand so a group of half-witted eggheads can figure out why queer broads like to eat pussy!''

Kartz said that the same ''crackpot group''—the Department of Health and Human Services[3]—also gave a grant of $167,724 to a center attached to California State University in San Francisco. ''This grant was for a study—get this!—a study of 'civil liberties and sexual orientation!' ''

Kartz had a name for people who protested the arms race—leftwing trash. ''Isn't it strange,'' raged Kartz, ''how these protesters didn't say one single word about how the Soviet Union is putting the finishing touches on the greatest arms buildup in history, an arms buildup that was provoked by no perceptible act of aggression from the West.

''The Soviet Union is also the nation that has designed its thousands of warheads on land-based missiles to destroy two legs of our strategic triad with one stroke.

''But the left-wing 'save-humanity-from-the-bomb' scum didn't mention this. They also ignored the fact that the Russians ignore treaty commitments and even now are using chemical and biological warfare against rag-tag tribesmen in Southeast and Southwest Asia in contravention of the 1925 Geneva protocol on gas warfare and the 1972 biological convention. But Uncle Sam should make himself defenseless!''

''That's the trouble with a democracy,'' Chatters had commented. ''Anyone can have his say, no matter how silly his platform is. Maybe that's why a democracy never lasts long. It soon wastes, exhausts, and murders itself. In all of world history there was never a democracy that didn't commit suicide.''

''The way we're doing now with the Soviet Union,'' Kartz had said, ''For a time, I thought President Reagan might stand up to world Communism. But he's proved that he's only all talk.''

---

[3] All this is true, and only the tip of the iceberg of fiscal hemorrhage. Under the now abandoned Comprehensive Employment and Training Program, $41,000 went to a feminist outfit to produce the all-nude *Leaping Lesbian Follies.* Another $640,000 funded nearly half of the staff of the Gay and Lesbian Community Service Center in Los Angeles; the grant was intended to provide ''education about gay lifestyles and gay people's problems''!

"Yeah—but he's an expert at making the poor poorer and the rich richer."

Richard Camellion, forever a realist of the first order, couldn't have cared less about the pinheads in the federal government. He had always placed politicians on a level below child molesters and rapists.

All that mattered was the success of the mission.

It was possible that their luck had changed. The Cessna had taken off only hours ahead of another ice and snow storm that had dumped another foot of frozen wet stuff on the eastern United States of America.

Once Camellion and the other four men had reached the Black Station on Dresden Road, he had been surprised to find a very efficient network, a fifteen-person team with a leader and a deputy, the various sections using Hebrew names taken from the days of the week.

Yom Rishon ("Sunday") consisted of two shooters specializing in silent assassination, using handguns and other weapons.

Yom Shani ("Monday") was two men who acted as guards and drivers.

Yom Shlishi ("Tuesday") was two people, a man and a woman, to rent apartments, cars, and to furnish logistic support.

Yom Rvii ("Wednesday") consisted of six to eight people who would track the target, learn his habits, all his movements, and determine the time and place of the hit, or the grab, and to provide the escape corridor for the *Yom Rishon* and *Yom Shani* people.

Yom Chamishi was two men for communications, with one man at a secret post near the operation, the other at the Black Station for a direct link to CIA Central in Langley. Only Barry Newheart, the leader, and Virgil Lindsey, the deputy, were CIA career "government employees." The remainder of Blue 15 network was composed of "private contractors" who had undergone training in weapons, karate, memory enhancement, infiltration, shadowing, and techniques of being unnoticed and unobtrusive.

Camellion had first let Newheart and Lindsey know who was running the show—politely but firmly. That first meeting had taken place eight days earlier. The next day, he had met with four members of the *Yom Rvii* group, whose leader had brought a thick Subject-Data File on Keith Reeves Griesbeck.

Thirty-nine years old, Griesbeck was married, had two children, and lived in Avondale Estates, east of Atlanta. His father was German, his mother English, this latter explaining the *Keith* and the *Reeves* in his name. Very successful as a consulting engineer in hydraulics, Griesbeck had a number-one rating in Dun & Bradstreet.

"If you wanted to terminate him, it would be easy," Edith Caines, the leader of the *Yom Rvii* group, told the Death Merchant. "You want to kidnap him. We can't grab him at his home in Avondale Estates. It would be next to impossible."

A stout woman in her late thirties, with short brown hair and a pair of shrewd deep gray eyes, she explained that Avondale Estates even had its own private police force. "And they're good. The police patrol regularly, day and night. That suburb is better protected than Beverly Hills. In addition, many of those swells have their own private guards. Griesbeck has three. They live over the garage."

Which left Keith Griesbeck's place of business, his suite of offices in the Fludgion Building on Forrest Avenue, in downtown Atlanta. On the eleventh floor!

Caines and Maurice Ehlers, the latter of whom was another member of the *Yom Rvii* group, promptly and enthusiastically suggested that Griesbeck be taken in his office. They had worked out a plan, right down to the last detail. Four of the group would enter the office as clients and put everyone to sleep with dart guns, including Griesbeck. The members of *Yom Rishon* and *Yom Shani* would then show up and, disguised as ambulance attendants, carry the unconscious Griesbeck out on a stretcher to a waiting ambulance. As for the people rubbernecking, they would learn that Griesbeck had suffered a heart attack.

After studying the operation proposed by the two, the Death Merchant vetoed it for one good reason. It was too risky. There were too many variables, too many "holes-in-the-blanket," too much that could go wrong.

More discussion, more close scrutinizing of the Subject-Data File. Griesbeck was basically a workaholic. He didn't have any hobbies. He didn't belong to any clubs. He was faithful to his wife and never looked at another woman. He and his family were members of the Third Baptist Church in Avondale Hills. He did have one great, overriding fear: that he or some member of his family might be kidnapped. He was also a creature of habit and was very predictable as to where he would be at any given time of the day, give or take fifteen minutes. What intrigued the Death Merchant was that Griesbeck went to Big Benny's Salvage Yard every Thursday, arriving promptly at noon. He and Big Benny, the part owner and operator of the yard, would then have lunch together. Griesbeck would then leave about two in the afternoon.

The salvage yard was off Georgia 29, two and a half miles southwest of the William B. Hartsfield Atlanta International Airport.

"Big Benny" was Bernard Laczko, a big brute of a man who owned 46 percent of the salvage yard. Keith Griesbeck owned the remaining 54 percent. Old and fast friends, Griesbeck and Laczko had grown up together and had known each other since their days in Public School No. 4.

"You're sure that Griesbeck goes to the salvage yard every Thursday at noon?" Camellion asked Edith Caines and Maurice Ehlers.

They were positive. "We've been watching his every movement for three weeks," stated Caines. "We have ascertained that Laczko and Griesbeck have lunch together because they're old friends. They never associate socially because they occupy different social positions."

Could Griesbeck be grabbed at the restaurant where he bought the lunches? No way. Big Benny ordered the lunches from a roadside cafe a mile from the salvage yard.

"Every Thursday? You're positive!"

"We're certain of our information. Griesbeck's been going to the salvage yard every Thursday for four years, ever since he and Laczko went into business together."

Did they happen to have a sketch plan of the salvage yard?

Yes, they did.

The Death Merchant studied the diagram for a long time, then analyzed a road map of the surrounding area. On the basis of his analysis, he decided that they would throw a net over Keith Griesbeck at Big Benny's Salvage Yard.

Edith Caines and Maurice Ehlers were not in agreement. The expressions of the two other members of the *Yom Rvii* group present showed that they too were skeptical. Lindsey and Newheart, two well groomed men a few years from forty, were not enthusiastic over what Newheart said was a "next-to-impossible venture." He said, "Camellion, it would seem to me that going after him at the junkyard would be just as dangerous as making the try at his office."

With one foot on the seat of a chair, Newheart tapped the large state map on the table. "The moment a shot is fired and the police find out there's trouble, they'll block all the highways. Why, we wouldn't get five miles before we ran into the state police. Then what?"

"You're right," Camellion agreed. "But suppose a helicopter lands right in the junkyard and picks us up." He tapped the map and looked slyly at the surprised Newheart. "Right here, only a hop, skip, and double jump northwest of Atlanta is Dobbins Air Force Base. All we have to do is radio Grojean and . . ."

One hand firmly on the big steering wheel, Camellion used his other hand to push the dark glasses higher up on his nose. The sun glistening off the snow on the sides of the highway was bright, and driving a large tractor and trailer was not an easy job.

"Are you deaf?" asked Chatters. "I asked you if you knew how to get onto number twenty-nine?"

"As I told you before—yes," Camellion said easily. "We turn right on the underpass at Red Oak. We then turn right again when we reach twenty-nine. We go east. The salvage yard will be to our right. We can't miss it. Ask me again a few minutes from now!"

Chatters faked a little laugh. "Okay, okay! I admit this operation has got me uptight. It's just that so much can go wrong. Suppose the signal isn't picked up at the air base. Or say something goes wrong after the helicopter lands near Bill Arp?"

"If you want to walk the route of the complete pessimist, include the possibility that we might drop dead," Camellion said with a slight smile. "Or a drunk driver might slam into us!"

"He's saying that you have to accentuate the positive and try to ignore the negative," said H. L. Kartz, who was sitting next to Chatters, by the right side door of the tractor. "The early Christians were experts at thinking positively. They were also good at ignoring translations when those translations didn't suit the propaganda they were putting out. The word *Elohim* is a good example."

Chatters turned to the Death Merchant, who, glancing in the big side mirror, saw that Pini Hilleli and Arlon Chalker, in the Toyota Starlet, were right behind him. "Camellion, what in hell is he talking about—and come to think of it, what does religion have to do with our grabbing Keith Griesbeck?"

The Death Merchant knew that if he didn't explain to Chatters, Kartz would—and that explanation would be a long-winded lecture!

"Does *Elohim* mean 'God?' That's the question," Camellion said. "You see, in Hebrew, *Elohim* is the plural form of *Eloah*. *Eloah*, in the singular, appears forty times in the Book of Job. *Elohim* is therefore not 'God' but 'gods.' In the West, most Bibles see *Elohim* as a 'plural of majesty' and translate it as 'God' throughout the text. Bibles of the Russian Orthodox Church, however, translate it sometimes as 'God'—notably in Genesis—and sometimes as 'the angels'—notably in Psalm Eight."

"That's just the information I needed this morning," muttered Chatters. "We're about to get shot out—maybe—and you birds rattle about biblical translations!"

"The point is, dear boy," said Kartz, "when you read Genesis within the proper context, it becomes a consistent story of colonization of earth by astronauts from another planet—spacemen who 'came from the sky' and became 'angels' in human memory."

"OHHHH boy!" sighed Chatters. "The people I get involved with!"

Shot at! A distinct possibility—and not by the state police either! thought the Death Merchant.

Edith Caines had explained that Big Benny Laczko had served five years in the Georgia State Penitentiary for assault with a deadly weapon and that he had solid connections with the Atlanta underworld. His (and Griesbeck's) salvage yard was the largest in Georgia, with more than sixty people working in the complex, most of them tough ex-convicts.

"We can assume some of them will be armed," Caines had said.

There was far more—all a big minus as far as the operation was concerned. The Georgia police and the FBI were convinced that Laczko was running a chop shop at the salvage yard—dismantling stolen cars and selling the parts. They couldn't prove it; they couldn't catch him.

In response to Camellion's pointing out that it didn't make sense for Griesbeck to be a part of a chop-shop operation—the man was already wealthy—Caines said that the way the CIA had it figured, Griesbeck wasn't aware of how his old friend Laczko was making "spare change" on the side.

"More likely," said Caines, "he suspects what Big Benny is doing and, because of their friendship, is looking the other way. The danger is that the FBI might have men stationed watching the yard—or even placed among the workers."

Possibly. If so—it was a danger that would have to be risked.

The people of Blue 15 had worked frantically. The Death Merchant couldn't drive into the salvage yard, go right into the main building, and grab Griesbeck in Laczko's office—too chancy. He and the men with him would have to appear legit; they would have to have a reason for being there.

They needed a large truck of scrap iron, the truck of some company that regularly did business with the salvage yard. A lot of messages later to the Center solved the problem. In two days, Bardolow Industries, of Rome, Georgia, would be sending twenty-three tons of scrap metal to Big Benny's Salvage Yard. A tractor-trailer deal that would be leaving in the morning.

Perfect! All the Death Merchant had to do was hijack the rig.

How do you hijack a large tractor and trailer on a multilane highway? First, you have to make the driver stop—and not just any place either. He has to pull over and stop at the right place.

A lot had to be guesswork. More had to be assumption based on the logic that the driver would pull off at the first convenient spot, depending on how the rig was disabled. Camellion and his people found that "right place" on Highway 41, a few miles south of Marietta, close to the Marietta National Cemetery. Should the driver have a flat at the top of a certain grade, the nearest area where he could pull off the road was 150 miles ahead. Close by, where the driver would park, was a long billboard advertising ROLAIDS—the perfect place to hide a vehicle.

There were two problems. The first was the timing, the second the state police. Suppose a state police car stopped after the driver of the rig pulled over to the side of the road? The first could be worked out. Three cars would wait until the tractor and trailer came roaring down the road from Rome. They would follow the rig, one car pulling around and go ahead so that the driver would not become suspicious and think he was being trailed. The second problem was not really a problem, as there was only one answer. If the state police stopped, the operation would be canceled.

The first part of the project went off as planned, with Camellion, Kartz, Chatters, and Emos Figg following the tractor and trailer—it looked as large as a moving van—in a Datsun Sentra four-door wagon. When no other vehicles were passing or coming from the opposite direction in the other lanes, the Death Merchant shot out one of the right rear tires of the trailer with a silenced 9mm Omni Llama autopistol.

As he and the others had assumed, the driver of the huge vehicle pulled off the road onto the area 150 feet ahead, the closest available spot. The Datsun Sentra also pulled off. Seeing that there were three men in the cab, Camellion and his companions inquired if they could be of some assistance, an offer that was declined with smiles. After all, changing a wheel on a trailer filled with scrap iron wasn't the same as changing a wheel on a car.

As the driver and the other two men pulled out a large jack from a compartment on the side of the tractor, he glanced at the Death Merchant and the two men with Camellion. "What are you guys waiting for? I said we don't need no help."

"We've never seen a wheel removed from one of these big babies," Camellion replied. "You don't mind if we watch, do you?"

The driver gave Camellion a pathetic look. "Hell no, if you ain't got nothin' better to do."

It took the truckers only fifteen minutes to place boards for the foundation of the huge jack and change the flat tire. Once the driver and the other two men had left the rear corner of the trailer and were by the tractor, where they couldn't be seen from the road, Camellion shot all three with a B14-M needle gun. The 200 milligrams of phencyclethylamine in each needle took effect instantly and the three men dropped unconscious to the snow.

Merwin Boradus, who had driven a resold United Parcel Service van,[4] painted dark green, behind the ROLAIDS billboard, now drove the van close to the right side of the tractor-trailer. Quickly, Camellion and the others carried the three unconscious truckers into the van and handcuffed their hands behind their backs—a precautionary measure that wasn't necessary. The three men would sleep for several hours. After the operation was completed, the three truckers would be turned loose on the outskirts of Atlanta.

Merwin Boradus—he looked like he should be in high school—got into the UPS van and drove off.

[4] UPS vans are not resold by the company until they are ready to fall apart. Most people buy them for the body, not the engine. They repaint the body, mount it on another frame with engine, and use the vehicle, as a rule, for a camper.

By then, Pini Hilleli and Arlon Chalker—the latter of the *Yom Shani* squad—had driven up in the Toyota Starlet. Chalker got into the Datsun Sentra and headed south. He would park close to the salvage yard and, pretending to have engine trouble, act as Communication One and a lookout. Not only would he radio reports back to the Black Station on a closed band H-D16 transceiver, he would also warn the Death Merchant if—should things go wrong—the state police came charging down the highway.

The Death Merchant, H. L. Kartz, and Wally Chatters had transferred their own hand-held Ferris H-D16 transceiver and two MAC Ingram 9mm submachine guns to the tractor, and now they climbed in. Camellion shifted gears, fed oil to the diesel, and pulled the big rig onto the highway and started driving south.

Smelling oil and feeling a twinge in his gut—*The muscle didn't heal properly from the gunshot wound![5]*—he saw the green and white sign coming up on the right side of the highway—RED OAK. 1 MI.

Before Wally Chatters could open his mouth, Camellion said, "I know. I turn right at the underpass just south of Red Oaks. You don't have to remind me."

Chatters turned his big freckled face toward Camellion. A man who could appreciate a joke on himself, he grinned. "It's your show, Camellion," he said with a small laugh. "If you miss the turn and we wind up in Augusta, I'll be the first to let you know it."

Camellion didn't miss the turn twelve minutes later. In a short while, he turned right onto Georgia 29, a two-lane blacktop. They soon passed The Home of the Confederacy, the roadside diner where Benny Laczko bought the lunches that he and Keith Griesbeck ate.

The salvage yard was only one mile away.

"Do me a favor," H. L. Kartz said to Chatters. "Spell your last name backward—now, without thinking."

"*S-R-E-T-T-A-H-C!*" Chatters promptly spelled, giving a surprised Kartz a smug look. "I learned that trick years ago. It's a standard Company test question to see how fast you can think on

[5] See *Death Merchant #50*, *The Hellbomb Theft*.

58

your feet, and it's as dumb as believing that Lee Harvey Oswald knocked off John Kennedy!''

Kartz pretended ignorance. "Oh? I thought he did!''

"We all know damn good and well that he didn't,'' growled Chatters. "He was only the perfect patsy—''

"Get with it, you two,'' Camellion said gruffly. "We're practically there.'' He glanced at his wristwatch—1150 hours, or ten minutes to twelve noon. We're right on schedule!

"Wally, get on the H-D16 and tell Newheart and Lindsey that we're about to move into the salvage yard.''

They passed Arlon Chalker. The Toyota Starlet was parked to the right, on the shoulder. Chalker had the hood up and was pretending to be checking the carburetor. Finally—there it was— the entrance to Big Benny's Salvage Yard.

Big Benny's Salvage Yard was as weird looking as it was huge—a unique "city" composed of piles and piles of rusted metal—wrecked automobiles, old motorcycles, and other kinds of vehicles, plus old stoves, refrigerators, metal tables, and ten thousand other different metal items that had outlived their usefulness.

Beyond the parking lot for customers going to the auto parts shop was a wide wooden walk that led to the auto parts building 150 feet to the southwest. The parts shop was a 120-foot-long shed, with the first 20-foot section, to the north, being Big Benny's operations office.

In front of this building there was an acre or more of stacked tires. Automobile tires, farm tractor tires, tires for trucks of all sizes—row upon row of old rubber, waiting to be processed and sold.

There were two entrances, side by side, for trucks. The first one was for pickups and other small trucks, for private individuals who might have some junk from around the house and/or yard to sell, say a wrought iron patio table that had rusted or whatever.

The second road was for large trucks from companies that had tons of scrap to be unloaded. A crane, with a large flat magnet at the end of a steel cable, handled the scrap from the large trucks. The crane was in the scrapyard into which the two roads opened.

North of the two roads were the long stripping sheds where automobiles were ripped apart. Seats, engines, and windows were removed—all rubber, all plastic, all wood, all fabric until there was only the naked metal body, which was then hauled out

59

to the crusher, not far from the crane. The crane would pick up the steel body with the magnet and deposit it in the "grave" of the crusher, a twenty-two-by-nine-by-eight-foot receptacle. A worker would seal the lid and a hydraulic ram would then reduce, by squeezing, the body of the car into a block of metal twenty inches square.

"Here goes nothing," Camellion said, and started to turn the steering wheel to the right.

"Yeah," mumbled Chatters, "and if all is going well up north, Company boys should be walking into Verlin Dragg's office in New Bedford."

Kartz snorted and puckered his lips with disdain. "I think it's a damned nutty technique they're using, pretending to be FBI agents."

"Rather clever, if you ask me," Chatters said. "I still don't see why we couldn't have used that gimmick with Griesbeck."

"You know why," Camellion said in a dry monotone. "Griesbeck's the kind of guy who wouldn't buy it. If trouble started and we didn't have a chopper, it would be goodbye-charlie!"

"I don't see Griesbeck's Olds," Chatters said cautiously. "Wouldn't it be a joke if he didn't show today for some reason. Hold it! I think I see his car. Anyhow, it's the same kind of car he drives, a silver gray Cutlass Ciera."

"That's Pini's job; all he has to do is get the license number," said the Death Merchant and headed the tractor for the road marked To S-Yard. Large Trucks Only.

He glanced in the big rearview mirror to his left, mounted on the outside, and saw that Pini Hilleli was driving the Toyota between the two tall posts of the entrance.

"On your guard, boys," Camellion said easily. "We're coming to the scale. Wally, be sure you keep the lid of the box closed until you have to use the H-D16."

He guided the tractor and trailer onto the long scale, a man who worked in the salvage yard motioning him forward with both hands. Camellion moved the rig very slowly, finally stopping when the man raised his hands and pushed outward, indicating that the entire rig was on the weighing scale. The Death Merchant shut off the engine, glanced around the cab, then opened the door on his side and started to climb out. Kartz and Chatters started to get out on the other side while Jake Jergabowski, the man who had waved Camellion ahead, hurried toward the

60

rig. He was joined by Jackson Eaton, another yard employee. Both men wore leather coats and caps with earflaps.

Wally Chatters didn't have any earflaps on his cap, but he did have an earplug in his right ear, of the type worn by people who are hard of hearing. The small pickup mike was pinned to his right breast—and it was a blind. The wire actually ran to a small Varda 730L-4 walkie-talkie fastened to his belt. On low volume, the transceiver was on.

Stepping on the rung beneath the door, Camellion glanced at his watch—12:14 P.M. *On the mark!* By now, Emos Figg, a member of the *Yom Shlishi* squad, would have turned around in the Ford Ranger pickup he was driving and would be watching Highway 285 for Georgia State Police cars. Should the operation get fouled up and the state cops be alerted and come charging down the highway, Figg would contact Chatters on the Varda. In turn, Wally would warn Camellion and Kartz.

The Law of Knowledge is in effect! thought the Death Merchant, stepping onto the wet ground thawed by the hot sun. The more data input an organism has about various phenomena either inside or outside the organism, the greater the possibility the organism has of solving problems and thus surviving—*And getting a specific job done. Knowledge IS power!*

The sublaw was the Law of Knowledge of Self. Constant review and analysis of the contents of one's own mind and body lead to more effective survival. *This is "Know Thyself." Brush aside the moral conditioning of society and the religious claptrap and know who you really are!*

The Death Merchant and the men with him did know who they were, knew what they could do and what they couldn't do.

If we can't do the job, if we can't grab Griesbeck—who can?

Jergabowski and Eaton reached the rig and looked at Camellion and Kartz and Chatters with cold, unfriendly eyes, Jergabowski appearing puzzled as he scratched a red-veined cheek with several days' whisker growth on it.

"You're from Bardolow, huh?" he grunted. "You guys are new. What happened to Whimpy and Freddie?"

"Yeah, this is the first time we've made this run," Camellion said roughly. "We dunno about the other guys. We heard they had a couple of gals along the route they was shacking up with. The boss didn't go for the lost time. That's what we heard."

"You still going to look for that radiator?" Kartz asked Camellion.

"So whatcha got this trip? The usual, I guess?" Jergabowski said, then loudly blew his nose, using a gloved thumb and forefinger.

"Twenty-three tons of scrap," Camellion said, then laughed. " 'Course, we don't expect you to take our word for it."

"We ain't," sneered Jergabowski. He jerked his hand and threw a long string of snot from one finger. "We don't take nobody's word about nothing around here. Man, you can't believe nobody these days."

"You guys move off the scale," Jack Eaton said to Chatters and Kartz in a heavy, raspy voice. "I'll weigh the rig and scrap. Then you can drive over to the crane and get unloaded. You drive back on the scale and weigh in again. The difference is what you get paid for—got it?"

"It's your yard," Chatters shrugged.

"You'd better believe it, fella," Eaton said and started for the scale house a very short distance away.

Wally Chatters and H. L. Kartz moved off the metal floor of the scale and joined Camellion and Jergabowski, who were standing to one side.

"I asked if you was gonna look for that radiator?" Kartz again said to Camellion. "Maybe they got it in their small-parts shop."

"Say, you got radiators up there?" Camellion looked at Jergabowski and jerked his head toward the southwest. In the distance he saw that Pini Hilleli was halfway to the small-parts shop—*Which means he's passed all the cars in the parking lot. Either it's Griesbeck's Cutlass or it isn't. If it is, we go to work. If it isn't—we go home.*

"Shit, man! We got damn near anything you'd want for a car," Jergabowski said. "Hell, go up there and look. See that boardwalk? It'll take you right up to the parts shop."

Nodding his thanks, his hands snuggled in the side pockets of his work coat, Camellion turned to Wally Chatters. "Frankie, you stay here. You can drive. Me and Les, we'll mosey on up there and see if we can find that damned radiator."

"Sure thing, go ahead," "Frankie" said and spit on the group. He locked eyes with the Death Merchant for a brief moment. "Get what you gotta get," he said, the subtlety of his tone carrying the real meaning. "But remember that we ain't got all day to hang around here."

"Yeah, we know," the Death Merchant said. He turned with Kartz, who also had his hands in the side pockets of his work

62

jacket, his right hand folded around the butt of a Raven 25 ACP autopistol; in shoulder holsters he carried two Smith & Wesson Model 39 9mm autoloaders, each weapon holding fourteen cartridges. Eight spare magazines were scattered throughout his pockets.

Kartz and the Death Merchant, taking long strides, hurried toward the wooden walk that led to the small-parts shed, their eyes momentarily swinging to the crane and the awesome crusher, both of which were in operation. There was a loud, ringing sound as the flat, five-foot-in-diameter electromagnet at the end of the cable stretching down from the boom of the crane made contact with the body of a 1979 VW Rabbit. The crane operator began winding in the cable and the VW Rabbit, dirty snow falling from it, was jerked free from the stacked pile of automobile bodies. The crane operator raised the Rabbit twenty feet in the air, swung the boom of the crane to his right, then began lowering the steel body of the VW until it was six feet above the "grave" of the crusher.

"He really knows how to work those controls," muttered Camellion.

The crane operator switched off the magnet and the body of the Rabbit crashed into the steel-sided "grave," after which a worker—twenty feet away in the crusher's control house, pulled back on a lever that controlled the lid. The lid swung over the top, clanged into place, and locked itself. The man now pressed a button.

There was a short, loud whoosh, then a loud grinding and crushing sound, with the rammer molding the body of the Rabbit as easily as one shapes a handful of putty. Another sound, the hissing of escaping air, as the ram cylinder was drawn back into striking position and the lid over the "grave" slowly folded back.

The crane operator's job was still not finished. He carefully lowered the magnet into the steel-sided cavity of the crusher and lifted the block of metal so that it hung only five feet below the end of the boom. He then swung the crane completely around and gently deposited the block on a stack already fifteen feet square. Again the boom swung and the operator began lowering the magnet toward another car body.

"Think of having to make a living like that poor slob in the crane," Kartz said. "Sitting up there all day, making little ones out of big ones."

"Maybe so, but his job is safer than ours," replied Camellion. "Anyhow, it's all relative and similar to what you said about the loss being of no consequence if millions got gassed on the East Coast."

They stopped at the entrance of the small-parts shop, which was at the southwest corner of the shed, and turned and looked toward the scale. Chatters was driving the tractor and the flat-bedded trailer toward the crane. Both Camellion and Kartz knew that so far Lady Luck had been with them. So very much could have gone wrong but hadn't. So much had been on pure supposition. The Death Merchant had shot out the outer right rear tire of the eighteen-wheeler. Suppose the driver had decided not to stop. The other wheels and tires would have supported the weight. Yet the weight could have shifted with one tire gone; and so Camellion had assumed that the driver would stop, and he had. Other things could have fallen apart. It is not an easy task to change a wheel of an eighteen-wheeler. The driver and the two men with him had used heavy planks as a foundation for the large hydraulic jack. But suppose the ground had been too soft?

There were only a dozen customers in the long building with the low ceiling. Due to hot-air blowers in the four corners, there was ample heat, although the giant shed was constructed of corrugated iron on the outside and plywood siding on the inside.

A low chuckle came from Camellion and his mouth twisted into a small grin.

"You find this amusing?" growled Kartz.

"I was thinking of a slob I know in Southern California, Rance Galloway. That yellow-backed freak is so full of hot air he could warm up all of Atlanta during the middle of an ice age!"

Everywhere were auto parts, piled on long tables, on racks on the walls—seat covers, floor mats, AM/FM stereo radios (some with cassette players), hoods, fenders, bumpers, hubcaps for ten different makes, beam headlamps, replacement vinyl convertible tops, rooftop carriers, hitch accessories, steel tow bars, springs, shock absorbers, blocks, cylinders, connecting rods, rod bearings, main bearings, timing gears, crankshafts, rings, pistons, oil pumps, gaskets, etc.

Camellion and Kartz sauntered past several men inspecting Cyclone exhaust headers and saw that Pini Hilleli was toward the north end of the shed, pretending to be looking at battery chargers. They also spotted the door to Bernard Laczko's office. It was an ordinary wooden door with a black porcelain knob and a brass Yale lock set in the wood. Two rough-looking men sat on folding chairs six feet to the left of the door. They were doing more than guarding the door to the office. It was also their job to keep an eye on the customers and prevent shoplifting.

Nonchalantly, the Death Merchant and H. L. Kartz ambled to a position that put them to the left of Pini Hilleli, with Camellion next to the Israeli, who ignored him and Kartz. All three were only twenty-three feet south of Jules Schultz and Roy Cubbage, the two guards.

Subtly, Hilleli turned his back to the guards and whispered, his lips barely moving, "The Cutlass belongs to Griesbeck all right. It has his license number. He has to be in the office."

He doesn't have to be in the office, but more likely than not he is! Camellion unzipped his work jacket, then moved around Hilleli toward the end of the table, his eyes playing over power inverters and ammeter and vacuum gauges as he studied Cubbage and Schultz with his peripheral vision—*big, slow, and half stupid.*

Kartz followed him.

In theory, Keith Griesbeck, the target, was only thirty to thirty-five feet to the north. *But we must be sure he's there before we send the signal to Dobbins AFB.*

Camellion walked around to the end of the table and, with Kartz following, turned his back to Schultz and Cubbage.

"Go with me," he whispered to Kartz. "You ride shotgun and cover me."

"Do it!" Kartz muttered.

Camellion turned and walked leisurely toward Schultz and Cubbage, the dour-faced Kartz several paces behind him and to his right.

Glancing up, Cubbage and Schultz were about to ask Camellion what he wanted when suddenly the two men found themselves staring into the black muzzle of a Llama Omni autopistol and Kartz's Raven 25 autoloader.

His nostrils flaring, Cubbage started to get up.

"Don't!" Camellion warned the fierce-eyed slob, "not unless you want a slug in the center of your pea-sized brain. The key to the office door. Which one of you has it? Or is it unlocked?"

Schultz's plum-sized Adam's apple bobbed up and down like a cork in water. "The door's locked from the inside," he said, his voice steady. "It's never used. We ain't got the key."

"Uh huh, and I think you're a lying piece of trash!" snarled the Death Merchant. "What you need is a bullet in the kneecap to make your tongue flap in the right direction."

It was then that Roy Cubbage did the most stupid thing of his thirty-four years: rearing up, he made a desperate grab for Kartz's .25 automatic.

Kartz didn't move half an inch. He simply squeezed the trigger of the Raven, the explosion sounding like the crack of a whip. The cabbage-faced Cubbage didn't hear the shot. His eyes as round as saucers, his mouth open in a long and narrow **O**, he sat down heavily on the folding chair, a small blue black hole in his lower forehead, just above the nose.

Well! That blows the icing off the cake! Knowing that Kartz's shot might as well have been a siren going off on the roof, the Death Merchant calmly put a 9mm projectile into Schultz's wide chest, the shot sounding three times as loud as the little blast from Kartz's Raven. The echo was just getting off to a good start when Camellion's second round smashed through the Yale lock on the door, and there were two more shots, one from a Smith & Wesson M-38 9mm autopistol that Kartz had jerked out, the other—a veritable BERROOMMMM!—from Pini Hilleli's Smith & Wesson Model 29 .44 Magnum revolver.

One of the customers, a man in a red-and-black-check mackinaw, had not been a customer but a spotter, one of Big Benny Laczko's stooges. The man had pulled a .44 Charter Arms Bulldog revolver from underneath his mackinaw and was swinging it up when Hilleli's big flat-topped bullet tore into the left side of his chest at a very steep angle and Kartz's hollow-point 9mm projectile popped him four inches below the hollow of the throat. Assassinated on its feet, Earl Scott's body jerked violently, first one way and then another, then crashed sideways onto a table filled with auto parts at the same time that Camellion kicked open the door and charged into the office. He was just in time to see two men getting to their feet, the large, broad-chested man with brown hair that resembled a rag mop reaching frantically for a weapon in his right rear pocket. Big Benny's fingers were tightening around the curved butt of a Ruger .357 Magnum as Camellion's 9mm bullet chopped into his right side, just above the belt. Laczko let out a strangled cry of pain and frustration and started to sag to the left. The Death

Merchant's next projectile tore into his neck, just below the jawbone.

The second man—*He's dressed in Sunday-go-to-meetin' clothes!* —stood as if paralyzed, in front of a folding table on which was a plate of fried chicken and all the trimmings.

Keith Griesbeck had been found!

Chapter 5

Just as love without deep concern is pure lust, so things and conditions around Big Benny's Salvage Yard were not necessarily as they seemed to be. For instance, the old two-story Klavin house, 517 feet southeast of the yard, across Georgia 29. The clapboard structure badly needed several coats of paint, and the two old cars in the front yard, both blocked up on their axles (the 1969 Ford sedan was without an engine), didn't add to the decor.

Over the years, as the area around the airport had started to grow, more than one real estate developer had tried to buy the house and the ten acres around it. Janeese Klavin and his wife Josephine always refused to sell, their rejection a lucky break for the local FBI in Atlanta. For four months the FBI had been watching the salvage yard from a second-story room on the northwest corner of the house.

The Feds had not had to use too much persuasion to get the Klavins to give permission to use the house as a surveillance station. "Bud" and Josephine Klavin hated Big Benny and the men who worked at the salvage yard. During the summer months, there was always loud music coming from the yard, that filthy rock music that always praised drugs and licentious sex. And all year the workers—always drinking on their way home—threw empty beer cans in the front yard as they roared by in their cars.

FBI technicians had replaced the ordinary glass of one window with a special two-way glass and then agents had settled down to watch the yard, day and night, around the clock.

Special Agents Mark T. J. Blair and Steven D. Gogas had been on duty in the second-floor bedroom since 6:00 A.M. that morning, taking turns watching the entrance to the yard through powerful binoculars and now and then putting fresh film into the 35mm motion picture camera that, mounted on a tripod, was pointed at the entrance of the salvage yard and was constantly photographing anyone who entered or left Big Benny's. Blair and Gogas also took turns listening on a P-2000 EMP parabolic microphone that was pointed at the yard. The EMP had an effective recording range up to three-quarters of a mile.

Well trained and observant, Gogas and Blair first became suspicious of Arlon Chalker, who had parked the Toyota Starlet nine hundred feet north of the yard's entrance on the west side of the highway. At first, the two Feds had figured Chalker was just another unlucky motorist with car trouble. They became suspicious when, after fifteen minutes, Chalker didn't walk to the salvage yard and seek help or phone for a wrecker to tow him to a garage. He acted suspiciously in other ways too. At times he seemed to be more interested in Big Benny's than getting his car started. Decidedly unusual!

Good little *F*riggin' *B*unch of *I*diots that they were, Blair and Gogas got out a sixty-power telescope, read the license number of the Toyota, and wrote it down on their report pad.

"He could be with the GBI,"[1] suggested Blair.

Gogas stroked his mustache. "I don't think so. We'll find out after the boys downtown check the license number."

Gogas had on the headphones and was listening through the parabolic mike during the time that H. L. Kartz terminated Roy Cubbage with a single bullet from the .25 Raven autopistol.

"I could swear I just heard what seemed like a shot," exclaimed Gogas. "I can't be sure."

"Well, keep listening," suggested Blair, "but I seriously doubt if you heard a shot. Who'd be fool enough to fool around with those hoods, and with that slicker Griesbeck there having lunch. Man, I'd like to see that son of a bitch hit with a ten-year rap."

Gogas almost jumped when the parabolic mike picked up the sound of the Death Merchant's killing Jules Schultz and shattering the lock in the door; and, seconds later, of H. L. Kartz and Pini Hilleli's blowing away the boob with the Charter Arms Bulldog.

The roar of Hilleli's .44 Mag was particularly distinct. Even Blair heard the shot faintly through the closed window of the house.

Steven Gogas jerked off the headphones and stared at an

---

[1] Georgia Bureau of Investigation.

astonished Mark Blair. "By God! There's a shoot-out going on over there!" Gogas was almost breathless with excitement. "What do you think we should do, call the state police?"

"Are you crazy?" Blair was horrified. "If we phone the state boys they'll get the credit. Where will that leave the Bureau? We'll end up transferred to some place like Phoenix, or Nome! We'll wait a bit and see what goes down."

"We can't sit here and do nothing," insisted Gogas. "Any idiot will know that we could hear the shots from up here." He wrinkled his nose and sniffed the air. "Do you smell that? What is it?"

"Oh hell, it's Old Lady Klavin making home-made chili again," Blair said. "I think chili is all they live on—and corn bread!"

Chapter 6

The well-dressed Keith Griesbeck looked so confused that the Death Merchant assumed it would have taken him two hours to watch "60 Minutes." Tall, Griesbeck was built like a slender boy, although his hips were wide and he had an oddly shaped head, his wide, lower jaw making his forehead seem more narrow than it actually was. Always conscious of his appearance, he wore a herringbone Haddington wool tweed jacket, a bright red doeskin vest with brass buttons, and worsted navy flannel trousers. Camellion, who had no trouble detecting custom-made clothes, wondered why the shoulders of the tweed jacket looked knobbed like the padded shoulders of football players.

"There isn't anything of value here," Griesbeck said. He had automatically raised his hands above his head, and his low voice was calm; yet Camellion and Kartz—the latter pulling a Varda walkie-talkie clipped to his belt—detected small notes of fear in his tone. "If you men have any sense, you'll—"

"Shut up and consider yourself kidnapped. Turn around and put your hands behind your back." The Death Merchant glanced briefly at the corpse of Big Benny sprawled out on its back, eyes closed, the lower left leg bent inward; Camellion then turned his attention to Griesbeck. While he used his left hand to snap the steel bracelets around Griesbeck's wrists, Kartz spoke into the walkie-talkie. "We have the package. Send the signal."

"You—You'll never get a-away with this," Griesbeck suddenly burst out. "It's—it's insane." He looked first at the Death Merchant, who had pulled his second Llama Omni and was keeping an eye on a door on the southwest side of the room; then Griesbeck turned to H. L. Kartz, who had raced across the office and had taken a position by the door that opened to the outside. With a Smith & Wesson M-38 9mm autopistol in each hand, he was watching the door with the shot-out Yale lock, as well as the two windows toward the front of the office in the opposite wall.

The Death Merchant motioned toward the door in the rear corner, waving the Llama Omni close to Griesbeck.

"Where does that door lead to?" he asked the man, his voice a deadly warning.

H. L. Kartz interjected, "I know there's a room that sits back from this office and is connected to it. I can see the front of it and one corner through the windows."

"The door—back there is the lockers and showers for the men," Griesbeck replied. "That's why you'll never pull this off. There must be several dozen in there eating lunch."

"You had better hope we do," Camellion said coldly. "When we die, you die, my friend. Count on it!"

"But you don't—"

"Shut up!"—*And those men are experienced! That's why they haven't tried to storm in here. They're playing it cautious, and that makes them dangerous!*

Kartz fired two rounds so unexpectedly with his right pistol—and without a word of warning—that both Griesbeck and Camellion flinched. The loud roars were followed by the sound of broken glass falling from one window.

Reacting instantly, Camellion spun and fired both Llama Omnis, sending two HP 9mm projectiles popping through the wooden door in the corner of the office. Concurrent with his firing, there were two shots far away, toward the outside entrance of the long small parts shed.

Pini Hilleli was either in serious trouble—or dead.

"Two men," explained Kartz, now down on one knee. "They were trying to come around the front corner of the locker room. I didn't hit them."

The Death Merchant quickly shoved Keith Griesbeck to the wall on the window side of the room, pushing him to a position several feet to the right of the door in the corner of the office. "Yell and tell them not to fire," ordered Camellion, "nor to interfere with us in any way when we leave. Tell them that if we go down, you'll go with us."

Deep fear in his brown eyes, Griesbeck did as he was told, shouting out the message in a loud voice. The response was not expected—three shots from the other side of the door, from the locker-shower room. Two of the slugs, coming straight through the wood, struck the opposite wall. The third, fired at a sharp angle, knocked over a brass antelope ornament on the dead Big Benny's desk and then buried itself in the wall to the left of the door that opened to the parts shed.

"I've been trying to tell you, they don't give a damn about me!" a panicky Griesbeck almost shouted to Camellion, who now had to conclude that he had made a serious miscalculation. Equally as bad, he and Kurtz were in a very dangerous position, with two windows and three doors through which the enemy could fire—*Double damn!*

"You were Benny's partner in this operation!" Camellion said to Griesbeck, who was flush against the wall, streams of perspiration flowing down his cheeks. "And yet they would just as soon see you dead?"

Each word Griesbeck spoke was draped with sadness. "His *silent* partner," he said. "None of the men here at the junkyard knew my hands were in this pie. To them, I'm just the dandy businessman from downtown Atlanta! Since I called out to them and not Ben, they must assume he's dead, which he is. They were loyal to Ben. They'll gladly see me dead if they can revenge him by knocking off you two birds. You guys have trapped all three of us, don't you see that?"

Camellion saw! He sensed that Griesbeck was telling the truth, the shots through the door being ample proof. It all added up to one hideous fact: *We can't set foot out of this building without Big Benny's boys blowing us away!*

Another grim absolute: It would take the helicopter only fourteen minutes to take off, fly to the salvage yard, and land in the customer parking lot—*Only we won't be in the center of the parking lot! Not at the rate we're going!*

"This is a bust!" called out Kartz. "Our waiting is more ridiculous than a hope chest in a whorehouse. Let's kill him and make a run for it."

Before Camellion could tell Kartz that he didn't have any

faults, that he was simply hopeless, Pini Hilleli called from the other side of the door between the office and the small-parts shed, "It's me! Don't fire! I'm coming in!"

"Come in on your hands and knees!" yelled Camellion, thinking fast.

The door swung open and Hilleli, a .44 Magnum revolver in his right hand, started to crawl into the office. He was almost through the opening at the same time five shots rang out from the locker-shower room. The thugs had heard Hilleli call out and were shooting through the other door at a very steep angle in an effort to hit him. Three of the projectiles struck the wall to the left of the door. Two more went through the doorway. Both would have struck Hilleli, had he not been crawling on his hands and knees. He didn't panic. He kicked the door shut with his right foot, crawled quickly to the left side of the desk, and stood up, saying, "Now I know why you had me get down. Two men were waiting on the outside; they fired at me. They must have heard the first shots we fired." He looked around the office. "It seems we're not going anywhere from in here either!"

"Watch him," Camellion said, indicating Griesbeck. He reached underneath his coat, pulled the Varda 730L-4 walkie-talkie from his belt, and switched it on. He knew that when he contacted Arlon Chalker, Wally Chatters would also receive the message.

The Death Merchant soon had Chalker on the walkie-talkie. Quickly explaining the situation, he told Chalker what he wanted him to do, finishing with, "Do you think you can do it? If you can't, we're as good as dead—over."

"I'll give it a try." Chalker's voice, coming back through the walkie-talkie, did not seem happy. "I'll smash right through the wooden fence and try to swing to the front door of the office. Anything else? Over."

"That's it. Good luck and out." The Death Merchant then said, "Wally, did you get all that? If you're not in a position to answer verbally, buzz me on the set. And did you send the signal to the air base? Two buzzes for yes to both questions. One for no.

Buzzzzzzzz—buzzzzzzzz.

"I want you to use one of the SMGs and open fire on the corner of showers and locker room. It's the room attached to the office. Keep the men in there pinned down. The only other way out for them is through the door in back. By the time they sneak all the way around the shed and come at us from the inside, Arlon should be here. Two buzzes if you have it all straight."

Buzzzzzz—buzzzzzz.

"Okay—out," Camellion said. He switched off the walkie-talkie and shoved it back on his belt. "Pini, you watch the door to the shed. "I'll keep an eye on the door to the locker room—and you"—he shoved a Llama pistol against Griesbeck's chin—"be good. But then, you don't have much of a choice, do you?"

Camellion had moved to the wall and Hilleli was down by the desk when, far to the front of the office, a MAC Ingram SMG chattered a three-round burst, then another three-round burst. A few seconds later, a much longer burst.

"What the devil is he doing?" Kartz said, staring out the window he had shot out. "He's not firing at the corner of the locker room."

"Oh boy!" muttered Camellion. "I'd like to know what my horoscope said for today."

Chapter 7

The diesel engine of the crane was making a lot of noise, and there was more racket when the magnet dropped the sheets of scrap iron packed on wooden pallets it was lifting from the open trailer of the Bardolow Industries rig. Wally Chatters, after driving the rig into a position from which it could be reached by the crane, stood with Jackson Eaton and Jake Jergabowski watching the operation, each second seeming like an hour to the Widow Maker.

It was the sharp report from the Death Merchant's Llama and the big BEROOOMMMM from Pini Hilleli's Smith & Wesson Magnum that put an end to the waiting and wondering. Even through the CHUG-CHUG-CHUG of the diesel, Gillie Hawkins, the operator, heard the two shots and the shots that followed. Hawkins shut off the crane's diesel, leaned out the window, and yelled down, "You guys hear that?"

Eaton and Jergabowski certainly had. Both had swung around, intense concern on their faces.

"Yeah, we heard them shots," Jake Jergabowski shouted

back to Hawkins. "Sounded like it came from Big Benny's office. Something ain't right up there."

"We should get up there," Eaton suggested to Jergabowski, "and see what the hell is going on. That dressed-up dude Griesbeck's up there having dinner with Benny and—you don't think they had an argument, do you?"

"Don't be stupid!" sneered Jergabowski, staring toward the office in the distance. "Shit, they go way back. They was even in grade school together—an we ain't goin' up there. Who knows what we might be gettin' into. We'll wait here and see what—" He grabbed the left arm of Wally Chatters, who had started toward the tractor and trailer. "Hey, where you goin', sport?"

Chatters roughly jerked his arm away. "Back in the cab," he said. "I'm goin' where it's safe. I didn't drive from Rome to get my butt shot. Hell, for all I know, my two buddies who went up to the parts shop might be dead. What kind of a massacre factory you guys runnin' here?"

"Hell, they're safe," laughed Eaton. "It's just some of the guys who maybe got carried away in an argument." He glanced at Hawkins, who was climbing out of the crane. "We'll finish unloading you when we find out what the hell's goin' on."

Chatters hurried to the big tractor, climbed in, and, hunched far down in the seat, pulled one of the two pistols he carried in shoulder holsters, a SIG-Sauer 9mm job, which he placed on the seat. Then, looking through the windshield and seeing that Eaton, Jergabowski, and Hawkins had gone to the front of the crane, he pulled the two Ingrams and the spare magazines in the canvas bag from underneath the seat. H. L. Kartz's voice was coming through the earplug of the Varda walkie-talkie, telling him that "We have the package—send the signal" as Chatters was leaning around with his hand in the sleeping compartment, tugging at the cardboard box that contained the Ferris H-D16 transceiver. It wasn't necessary to operate the H-D16 in the regular manner. The set had been precoded to a single VLR channel and would emit one long signal when the set was turned on and the TALK button pressed.

Chatters removed the box from the sleeping compartment, placed it on the floor in front of the seat, and took another quick look at Eaton, Jergabowski, and Hawkins. The three men were still squatting down in front of the crane and weren't looking at the tractor. Chatters tilted the H-D16 transceiver and started extending the telescoping antenna, his mouth becoming a tight, bitter line when he heard two shots from the small-parts shed. Right behind them, the sharp crack of two more rounds! A split second later there were several more shots, these sounding as if they were from the outside, at the opposite end of the building, close to the entrance of the parts shed.

A cold, vicious anger churning in his stomach, Chatters put a foot of the antenna out of the right side window, after which he turned on the transceiver and pressed the TALK button, holding it down to the count of twelve and watching the red light blink close to the TALK button. Good. The signal had been sent and would be picked up by the special receiver at Dobbins Air Force Base.

Three rapid shots from the office end of the building! Feeling helpless, Chatters began returning the antenna to the well in the transceiver. At length, he closed the lid of the cardboard box and checked the two 9mm Ingram submachine guns. Each weapon had an extra-length fifty-round magazine—100 rounds, actually, since two magazines were taped together reverse style. What he hated the most was his awareness that all he could do was wait—and wait—while knowing that Camellion, Chatters, and Hilleli were in serious trouble.

He lifted his head and looked through the front windshield. The front of the crane was sixty feet to the northwest of the cab, the boom extending over the trailer. Eaton, Jergabowski, and Hawkins were still in front of the crane. Only something new had been added. Eaton was holding a .357 Lawman Mag revolver. A Heckler & Koch .380 PP pistol was in the left hand of the burly Jergabowski.

Very suddenly—five rapid shots from the office end of the small-parts shed. Only "quiet" noise through the walkie-talkie's earplug. Half lying on his left side, Chatters toyed with the idea of contacting Camellion. Better not. Don't bother him. Wait. Yeah—sit here like a bump on a log and wait . . .

Unexpectedly, words were coming over the walkie-talkie through the earplug: Camellion was asking Arlon Chalker to drive the Toyota Starlet into the salvage yard and try to whack out the gunmen close to the far entrance of the small-parts shed; then Chalker's replying that he would try to pull up in front of the office.

"Wally, did you get all of that?" The Death Merchant also wanted to know if he had sent the vital signal to the air force

75

base—two buzzes for Yes, if he was not in a position to answer verbally, meaning if he were talking to some of the workers and could not take the walkie-talkie from underneath his coat. Chatters, lying as he was on his left side, used the more expedient method of buzzing a reply with the ON/OFF button.

Camellion had orders for him: *Open fire on the corner of the locker-shower room. Got it?''*

Chatters had it—two more buzzes.

He didn't waste time. He picked up one of the Ingrams, picked up the SIG/Sauer, shoved it back in the shoulder holster, and looked up through the windshield. The three men were still there in front of the crane. "Time to get a lesson from the Gospel of Saint Die!" muttered Chatters.

Listening to Chalker roar up the entrance of the salvage yard, Chatters opened the door on the right side with his left hand, keeping the Ingram SMG in his right hand down. Quickly then, still using his left hand, he rolled down the window of the door.

Eaton, Jergabowski, and Hawkins had also heard the racing engine of the Toyota Starlet and had turned to the south, toward the driveway. The three were staring to the left of the rig as Chatters pushed open the right side door, shoved the Ingram through the open window, and opened fire, very very sure of what he was doing and how he was doing it. The first three-round burst hit Jackson Eaton squarely in the chest, killing him before he even suspected what had happened to him. The second three-round blast blew up Jake Jergabowski and turned the front of his jacket into tattered leather that soon became soggy with thick blood; he fell like a balloon that had suddenly lost all its air.

Gillie Hawkins, leaning over the end of one of the tracks of the crane, was the third man on the end. He tried to save himself by falling to the north side of the crane, but he was a few seconds too slow. Six hollow-pointed projectiles caught him in the left thigh and the left hip and helped him finish his fall. With a loud scream, he hit the ground, rolled over on his back, and lay still. Eaton and Jergabowski were equally as still.

With a loud, smashing sound, the Toyota crashed through the three-foot-high fence at the west end of the parking lot, Chalker hunched low over the wheel and thinking that $1,000 tax-free bucks a day was poor compensation for the risk he was taking.

Between the end of the parking lot and the front of the small-parts shed there was the wide wooden walk (seven feet wide); there were also piles of junk composed of every conceivable item ever manufactured in the world of modern man. Junk lay scattered right up to the left (or south) side of the boardwalk. In contrast, there was a five-foot space on the right (or north) side of the boardwalk. This was more than enough room for the Toyota Starlet; in fact, the right side was the only "route" possible for Arlon Chalker, who was hunched over the steering wheel—provided he didn't mind being tilted to the right, since the left side wheels of the Toyota would be on the boardwalk seven inches off the ground. Even so, with the vehicle bouncing, Chalker headed it straight toward the small-parts building, his speed at better than forty miles per hour, a fully loaded 9mm Hi-Power Browning on the seat beside him. Chalker was unaware that Wally Chatters was about to lend a hand.

Chatters didn't waste time. As soon as Hawkins crashed to the ground, Chatters jumped from the cab, switched the Ingram to full auto, and, resting the SMG on the hood of the cab, aimed at the north side of the locker-shower room. The little weapon chattered, slugs jumping from the short barrel as Chatters raked the north side of the building.

Three men had been on the north side of the building; however, on hearing the first three bursts from Chatters's SMG, the three had wisely fled to the rear door of the shower room and warned the other eleven men. They were fleeing to the west side of the small-parts shed when more than two dozen 9mm projectiles ripped through the corrugated iron sheets that composed the outer wall. Due to their angle of entry, many of the projectiles had spent most of their force and power; they thudded against the inside of the inner plywood wall. Twelve, however, zipped all the way through the plywood. One stung Perry Burddoff in the right side. Almost all of its power spent, it lodged against a rib. Burddoff howled and stumbled sideways, fully conscious and not seriously wounded. He managed to stagger out the rear door, groaning and thinking he would never see the sunset.

Another Ingram projectile caught Clyde Minndler in the right side of the neck, just below his ear. The bullet was weak, but still powerful enough to bore all the way through the flesh and lodge itself in the fleshy part of his tongue. Minndler did his best to scream. He couldn't. His mouth was full of blood, dribbling over his lips and down his chin, then splat-splat-splatting on the floor. In a crucifixion of agony, he wobbled from side to side, trying to call after the other men to help him. They kept on going, leaving him in the dark capital of the Twilight Zone. The other men were just in time in their hasty exit. Chatters pulled the empty magazine from the Ingrams, reversed it, along with the fully loaded magazine taped to it, thrust the top end of the loaded magazine into the weapon's loading slot, felt the first cartridge engage, cocked the weapon, aimed, and cut loose. This time he directed the stream of slugs at the east wall of the locker room, crisscrossing the iron sheets (really, a thick tin) at about five feet from the ground. Another fifty 9mm projectiles cut into the building—all wasted, save two. Bleeding to death and fainting from pain, Minndler was going down, his legs more limber than wet spaghetti, as the two slugs banged him in the back of the head and lodged in the skull bone.

The loud shrieking sound of tires digging into the ground, of rubber being burned and tortured. Frantically, Chalker turned the steering wheel to the right, the Toyota rocking back and forth on its shocks. For a micromoment, Chalker almost lost control of the car and its left side came dangerously close to the front of the shed, the metal of the car coming within an inch of the metal of the shed.

Sixty feet more to the outside door of Big Benny's office!

His hands gripping the steering wheel, Chalker shot the Toyota Starlet to the north, turning the wheel first to the left, then to the right, doing his best to dodge single items of junk ahead. He managed to swing past half a dozen stacked wheels, avoid a rusted gear set that was minus its housing (of a rear axle), and barely missed a wooden box filled with armatures, solenoids, and half a dozen overrunning clutches.

Ah—there was the door of the office—there, to the left. Breathing heavily from tension, Chalker slowed slightly and prepared to swing the car around so that its rear end would be facing the east side of the office. However, he was going too fast and misjudged the distance. The car jumped east like some runaway mechanical monster. The trouble was that all of the rear of the vehicle didn't clear the shed. The left rear side of the Toyota slammed into the door of the office with a loud, crashing sound, the terrific impact sending enormous splinters of wood flying inward and tearing the rest of the door off its hinges.

Muttering under his breath, Chalker slammed on the brakes, the tires screaming on the gravel.

*   *   *

FBI agents Steven D. Gogas and Mark T. J. Blair were having their Big Excitement of the day. Only a very short time ago, while watching Arlon Chalker through the sixty-power telescope, they had seen him suddenly straighten up from underneath the raised hood and stand as if petrified, as if his joints had suddenly been locked. Even with the telescope, the two Feds could not see the thin wire running from the earplug to the Varda walkie-talkie snuggled in an inner pocket of his work jacket.

"What the hell do you think is wrong with him, T. J.?" asked Gogas, puzzled. "He's standing there like someone's stuck a rod up his ass!"

"It looks to me as if he's listening to something or for something," Blair said, very slowly turning the focus knob of the telescope.

Gogas blinked rapidly. "Listening? To what? Cars passing on the road!"

"Hey! Look!" hissed Blair.

Chalker became alive with activity. He got into the car, turned on the ignition, and started to drive toward the entrance of the salvage yard.

"By God!" Blair became so excited he almost knocked over the telescope. "That proves he was stalling and waiting around for something. Whatever's going on in Big Benny's place, that bird is part of it." He looked at Gogas. "Steve, we've no choice. We've got to call the state police."

"Yeah, you're right," agreed Gogas, starting to wipe his face with a handkerchief. "We'll call the locals, then phone the Bureau in Atlanta. That's—"

The Toyota was turning into the salvage yard when Blair and Gogas heard the chattering of a submachine gun in the distance!

Chapter 8

Flat on the floor, not far from the north wall, the Death Merchant heard the Toyota Starlet and felt that the vehicle was moving too fast for safety. Accordingly, he yelled at Kartz, "H. L., get away from the door."

The shouted warning was wasted. The words were jumping out of Camellion's mouth when Kartz, against the wall to the right of the outside door, darted to the southeast corner of the office.

Pini Hilleli remained by the end of the desk. Next to him, on both knees, was an ashen-faced Keith Griesbeck, a suspended-in-space-and-time expression on his face—reminding Camellion of a yodeler who had forgotten the lyrics!

Joked Hilleli, "Did Arlie say he was going to park by the office or crash into it. From the sound of that engine, he—"

The crash cut him off. The left rear end of the Toyota Starlet smashed into the door of the office, the impact—along with a microsecond's sound of wood being ripped and torn apart—sounding almost like an explosion.

Pieces and chunks of wood of various sizes and lengths flew inward, one three-foot length stabbing across the room and spearing itself over Pini Hilleli's head, missing him by only four inches. It sailed across the desk and landed on the floor on the other side. Another chunk hit the desk, smashing the face of a clock. Several more lengths, resembling mammoth splinters, landed on Camellion's back and right thigh. They only weighed a pound each and the Death Merchant wasn't injured.

"I think that Chalker's arrived," Kartz said dryly.

As if Chalker had heard him, the horn of the Toyota began a furious honking.

Not in any mood to appreciate Kartz's ill-timed humor, the Death Merchant jumped to his feet, looked at the door to the long shed, and said to Hilleli, "You watch the package. If he gets cute, shoot off one of his earlobes."

"Let's move it!" Kartz said impatiently. With a quick glance at Camellion and at Hilleli, who was jerking Griesbeck to his feet, he moved to the right side of the shattered doorway. "In another five minutes the chopper will be here and no doubt the police."

Hilleli shoved a scared-stiff Griesbeck toward the door. "What about the men in the locker room?" he said to the Death Merchant, who was walking backward and still watching the door to the small-parts shed. "Wally's slugs might have winged or even neutralized a few, but the rest of the *baizeh chei-eh*[1] must be waiting for us by now at the southeast corner; and if Wally's line of sight doesn't take in that corner, some could have

---

[1] Yiddish. Means a "vicious animal," usually refers to an "inhuman person."

slipped inside through the regular entrance and be coming at us right now"

"Keep an eye on the inner door," Camellion said. "I want to size up the situation."

"Size up—hell!" spit out Kartz, glaring at the Death Merchant. "That chopper will be here in less than five minutes."

Camellion's left arm brushed against the cracked casing on the left side, which was bulging outward. He saw that the rear end of the Toyota was twelve to fifteen feet from the shattered door and that the vehicle was parked catercornered so that the front faced the southeast. As for Arlon Chalker, he had stopped honking the horn, had opened the left front door, and, having turned around, was leaning out and starting to shout for them to make a run for it. Only the *run* managed to get out of his mouth. There were loud reports from four handguns to the south, three loud clanggggsss, and a short cry of pain from Chalker, who pitched sideways, tumbled from the car to the ground, and lay still. A single .357 Magnum projectile had shot through the open right window and—since he had turned around in the seat—had hit him in the left side of the head, an inch above the ear. He was dead by the time he was halfway to the ground.

More slugs came from the southeast corner of the shed. *BANG!* The right front tire went flat. *BANG!* The right rear tire went down. *Thud-thud-thud!* Two bullet holes appeared in the right side door. A third bullet hole was in the body of the Toyota, a foot to the left of the door.

A Smith & Wesson M-38 autopistol in each hand, Kartz cursed in frustration. It was agony to stand there with handfuls of iron and not be able to return the fire—unless he wanted to expose himself and get blown up!

"Damn those shitheads to hell!" he raged. "They're making sure we'll never get to that damned car!"

"Time to put a stop to it!" Camellion snapped. "It's intermission time and if we don't hurry, we won't get any boxes of popcorn!"

Before either Kartz or Hilleli could ask him how, Camellion turned and raced back to the door between the office and the small-parts shed. He shoved one of the Llama Omnis into his belt, gently opened the door, pulled the Llama from his waist, and darted into the shed, going in low to the left—and a good thing he didn't go to the right!

While the other hoods waited by the south end of the shed,

Simon Moulder and Ferd Vetch had slipped into the long shed, entering through the southeast door, intending to move north into the office and engage in a bit of back-shooting.

Forty feet from the Death Merchant, both men were in the middle aisle when Camellion came through the door. Vetch, very fast for a fat man, brought up his Thomas DA .38 autopistol and snapped off two quick rounds in the direction of Camellion, who ducked to the left a very thin slice of a second before Vetch's thick finger pulled the trigger. The first .45 300-grain flat-nosed slug burned the air within an inch of Camellion's right shoulder, buzzed on by, and broke into the office wall. The second big projectile missed forty times farther to the right, since Camellion was moving left, away from the slug, moving and throwing himself to the floor as he fired both Llama pistols.

"AAAAUWWWWWKKKKKKK!" Vetch's high scream sounded like the crazed cry of a wounded catamount.[2] One hollow-pointed 9mm Llama bullet tore into Vetch's blubber gut; the metal tore through the rectus sheath, stabbed through the ascending colon, and tunneled out through his back. The second 9mm projectile struck him in the fundus portion of the stomach and, going upward, lodged against a rib. Shock to the nervous system started the blackness squeezing Vetch's consciousness. The impact between slugs and flesh had started him going backward, and he felt himself going down, the floor coming up to meet him, and, a stranger to himself, he was helpless in preventing it.

Although a quick thinker and no stranger to violence, Si Moulder wasn't sharp enough in the brain department to save his own life. A wise man, thinking ahead, would have instantly dropped to the floor, as the Death Merchant was doing. Moulder, afraid Camellion would gun him if he tried that tactic, counted on speed, forgetting that it takes natural-born talent and a lot of practice to react instantly, aim by instinct, and whack out a moving target.

In a crouch, Moulder snapped off a shot with his Dan Wesson M-14-2 revolver, the result a waste of a .38 cartridge that burned the air a foot over Camellion's back.

The roar of the Dan Wesson still loud in his ears, Moulder hesitated as he debated whether or not he had hit Camellion or whether the Death Merchant was headed to the floor on his own. That half a second made the difference between life and death

---

[2] Mountain lion, cougar, panther, puma.

for Moulder. By the time he decided to drop down and fire underneath the long counter, which was actually a long table, it was far too late.

The Death Merchant had decided on the same tactic!

Moulder was dropping to his right knee when Camellion, flat on his belly, fired both Llama Omnis. The 9mm hollow point stabbed into Moulder's left ankle, hitting the bone in front. The second projectile banged him a few inches below the right knee. The bullet would have smacked him in the right ankle if he hadn't been in the process of getting down on his right knee, a movement he didn't complete. With a loud yell of pain and surprise, Moulder started to fall back, feeling as if he had been hit in both legs with sledgehammers. His head was only a microsecond away from striking a leg of the opposite table when Camellion fired both Llamas again. Both slugs, zipping in at an angle, hit Moulder in the midsection, one cutting through his liver, the second smashing through the spleen. Camellion fired the Llama in his left hand and put a third bullet into Moulder. This slug went underneath Moulder's chin, cut through his tongue and the roof of his mouth, and skidded to a halt toward the top of his now useless brain, thirty-eight millimeters from the top skull bone.

The Death Merchant was too experienced in the ways of quick and violent death to jump to his feet. Other gunmen could have entered during that one-half a minute shoot-out. Almost positive he could hear the faint *thub-thub-thub-thub* of a helicopter rotor in the distance, he waited. He couldn't be sure about the helicopter. There was too much noise. Big Benny's men were still firing from the southeast corner of the shed, only now, Kartz was somehow managing to return the firing. Kartz may have been an opinionated racist and fascinated by Hitler, but he was a number-one "iron man" when all the chips were down.

Camellion scooted under the table and crawled forward between the legs of the counter another six feet. He was still trying to make up his mind about whether he was actually hearing a *flub-thub-thub-thub* when another sound jumped to his ears, the furious chattering of an Ingram SMG. There was no mistaking the rapid *duddle-duddle-duddle-duddle*.

Chatters! He's tangling with the jokers in the two wrecking sheds! I have to narrow the odds in our favor, and I've only a minute or so to do it!

He reared up and looked at the entrance to the southeast. The door was closed. Apparently the two gunsels he had whacked out had been the only two to sneak back inside the shed. His eyes jumped to the south wall, on which hung scores of mufflers. The trick was to put slugs between the mufflers into the wall. No problem. Camellion could have shot the butt off a bee at a hundred feet. Wishing he had his Auto Mags, he raised the two Llama Omnis, sighted in, and began to pull the triggers. The two pistols began to crack, the Hornady high-velocity projectiles stabbing into the plywood at between four and five feet from the floor, Camellion spacing out the slugs in a line ten feet long.

The magazines were soon empty. Camellion dropped to the floor, snuggled underneath the counter to his right, quickly reloaded the two well-worked autopistols, got to his feet, had another look at the southeast door, then turned and sprinted toward the door between the shed and the office. Wally Chatters's SMG was still firing short bursts; the hoods in the two wrecking sheds were still throwing slugs at him. To make matters worse, the hoods by the southeast corner of the long shed were still tossing lead at the office door and the Toyota. The real spit in the face of success was the fact that the chopper was definitely only a short distance from the salvage yard. He could hear the thub-thub-thub-thub of its rotor plainly over the racket of gunfire.

Once Camellion was inside the office and back at the wrecked doorway, he saw that H. L. Kartz was firing around the right side of the doorway. He'd lean out, snap off a shot, and pull back—all too fast to hit any of the target, too fast to even toss a slug by instinct.

"We'll never be able to use the car," Pini Hilleli said in a lofty, objective tone. "Hear the chopper? We're going to have to put wheels on our feet!"

"We're going to have to run for it," growled Kartz, shoving a fresh magazine into one of his Smith & Wesson M-38 autopistols. "We can't get to the chopper and, unless I'm having an auditory hallucination, I also hear sirens!" His eyes became curious as he watched Camellion reach underneath his coat and pull out a Varda 730L-4 walkie-talkie. "You're going to contact the eggbeater?"

The Death Merchant nodded. "Always plan on prime rib, but be prepared for lunch meat," Camellion said bluntly. "I ordered the bird to show up with a couple of .50 cals, just in case. It's a good thing I did."

Hilleli went "Tch, tch, tch," then said, "Newheart and Lindsey will have a triple hemorrhage when they learn that the Company people in the bird had to get their hands wet. They were only supposed to sit down and pick us up."

"Who gives a damn what those two bureaucrats think," Kartz said vehemently. "Get on with it, Camellion."

Camellion got! He made contact with the chopper, which was only 4,000 feet to the northwest and flying at 1,700 feet. In response to Camellion's call, Maurice Ehlers's anxious voice came through the speaker of the transceiver in Camellion's hand. The Death Merchant promptly told him that the chopper's twin .50 Brownings would have to take out the hoods by the southeast corner of the long shed, then rake the two sheds and any police cars that might enter the salvage yard.

"We were only supposed to land and lift you out," Ehlers said reproachfully.

"You monolithic moron!" Camellion snarled into the walkie-talkie. "Do as I tell you, or you can explain why you didn't to the Q boys.[3] You have a diagram of the layout of the yard and know where everything is. Do what I have ordered—right now. Over and an immediate confirm."

"Confirmed."

Fifty to sixty percent of any black-crash operation is the planning, which more often than not involves—for reasons of security—members of the various branches of the armed services fooling each other. The paradox is that they aren't aware they are "closing the street"[4] on each other!

A case in point was the UH-1B helicopter that, with pilot, copilot, and Maurice Ehlers, had lifted off from Dobbins Air Force Base, with the two Company men dressed in U.S. Air Force fatigues. The CIA had pulled a lot of wire with Pentagon brass to get the chopper routed. The Pentagon had issued orders not only to the commanding officer at Dobbins AFB, but also to top officials at Fort Campbell Military Reservation in Kentucky, and the top people at the Crane Naval Ammunition Depot near Burns City, Indiana.

Ostensibly, the UH-1B, with extra-large fuel tanks, that had lifted off from Dobbins was going to the military reservation in Kentucky. A UH-1B would arrive at Fort Campbell Military

---

[3] CIA assassination experts.
[4] Intelligence slang for officially pulling the paperwork wool over this or that branch of the service.

Reservation, only it would be an eggbeater that had taken off from Crane Naval Ammunition Depot in Indiana. Earlier, the chopper had been flown from Chanute Air Force Base in Illinois. Conveniently, the records of that particular helicopter would be lost in the files at Chanute AFB, and it would no longer exist.

There had also been the special problem in repainting the UH-1B Huey while it had still been at Dobbins—a task accomplished within a certain hangar during the small hours of the morning, with the six airmen who had participated being sworn to secrecy, under the U.S. Secrecy Act. Breathing one single word of the triple repaint job could mean either a $10,000 fine or ten years in prison—or both. Unofficially, Maurice Ehlers told the airmen that if they ever confided in anyone, they would have a strange but fatal accident.

The UH-1B Huey had lifted off looking like any other air force chopper, with UNITED STATES AIR FORCE and its ID number all proper and in the right places. Roy Wohlwend, the pilot, had flown at only 860 feet until he was within six miles of Big Benny's Salvage Yard. Wohlwend had then taken the chopper up to 2,500 feet, where the icy winds had dissolved the first coating of paint, the UNITED STATES AIR FORCE and the identification numbers; the cold then ate away, flake by flake, the blue and white, leaving only the coating of jet black that the airmen had painted over the UNITED STATES AIR FORCE, the ID, and the blue and white coloring of the craft.

The roaring of the chopper's rotor was thunderous as Wohlwend revved down the Lycoming T53 free-turbine turboshaft and Ehlers, sitting beside him in the cockpit, a diagram of the yard on a clipboard on his lap, directed him to the south side of the small-parts shed.

In the main section of the bird, Ferris "Blubberlips" Bensinn, wearing a direct-boom-mike headset, had buckled on safety straps. He pulled back the port side door and swung the .50 caliber heavy Browning into position on its mount.

In a very short time, Ehlers spoke into the mike of his own headset and, as Wohlwend swung the bird toward the shed at only 100 feet, gave Bensinn his instructions.

Blubberlips opened fire twenty seconds later, for a moment seeing only uplifted faces, startled and frightened faces, before scores of large .50 caliber projectiles rained down on them. Almost instantly, six men were ripped apart, torn into bloody shreds by the scores of Spitzer flat-based slugs that butchered them. A seventh man began to run to the west, but Bensinn didn't bother with him. One man was not a threat.

Immediately the chopper swung east. Blubberlips heard Wohlwend's voice in the headset. "We're going to hover over the parking lot. You rake those two long sheds that face the east and chop apart any police vehicles that might come into the yard."

"As good as done," Blubberlips said coldly. He was used to killing people, having become very good at it in Vietnam. He had snuffed many of those little gook mothers during rabbit shoots. Yes sir, those had been the days.

Extermination in the Delta had been rather decentralized, with decision being made by FACs[5] who had flown around looking for signs of guerrilla activity! And man, the weapons they had used! Like napalm that rolled and splattered over a wide area and burned everything in sight it touched, suffocating those slant-eyed bastards who tried to escape by hiding in tunnels.

"Daisy Cutters," bombs that exploded in the water, had been another great weapon, a favorite that was used against peasants—Cong sympathizers—hiding in rice paddies. But CBUs[6] were the best. They contained tiny bomblets that could be expelled over a wide area. Hell, with a CBU a pilot could lawnmower for considerable distances, killing or maiming the little treacherous mothers on a path several hundred feet wide and scores of yards long. Why, with one type of CBU, a plane could shred an area a quarter of a mile wide and a mile long with more than 2 million steel fragments. Hot damn!

Roy Wohlwend had the helicopter in position, its nose pointed to the south so that Blubberlips could fire from the port side. The bird was only 80 feet above the center of the parking lot.

The Death Merchant and the other three had heard the .50 caliber projectiles striking the south end of the shed. For only five or six seconds they had heard the sharp loud clangs of the slugs boring through the corrugated iron and the plywood, and then striking the mufflers and other items on the south wall of the shed.

By looking around the edge of the office doorway, they could see that the savage firing had accomplished its purpose. One of

[5] Forward air controllers.
[6] Cluster Bomb Units.

the enemy was sprawled out, his head and shoulders lying just beyond the southwest corner of the shed.

Keith Griesbeck suddenly burst out in a hoarse croak, "Y-you're barbarians! He—he machine-gunned all of them!"

"Yeah—they fell faster than pigs on a freeway," Camellion remarked, "but the term *barbarian* is relative. But you should be an authority on barbarism since you're working for that kook Qaddafi!"

It was then that the Bell Huey chopper opened fire on the two long sheds where automobiles were stripped, hundreds of .50 cal projectiles stabbing through the tin roofs. The racket was enormous, for each .50 caliber projectile also struck a part of an automobile, and most of those parts were made of metal. Eleven men were by the inside west wall of one side, another nine by the west wall of the second building. Seven were ripped into bloody bits by Blubberlips's first blast. Four lost their heads and rushed out a door in the southwest corner of the building. All four were promptly shot down by Wally Chatters, who was firing from one side of the rig's tractor and almost out of ammo. Blubberlips again raked the sheds, up and down and back and forth. Eight more men were terminated.

The Death Merchant, Kartz, Hilleli, and Griesbeck left the office and ran toward the parking lot in that kind of zigzag permitted by the terrain, Kartz in the rear, then Hilleli and Griesbeck, the latter moving as best he could with his hands cuffed behind his back, Camellion acting as forward guard. But no shots greeted them on their way to the parking lot as they raced to one side of the boardwalk.

They reached the parking lot and, feeling the strong downdraft generated by the chopper's twin-bladed rotor, got down by the side of a Datsun wagon in time to see the first two patrol cars of the Georgia Highway Patrol turn into the entrance of the salvage yard, sirens screaming. A short distance behind them, still on the highway, were four more state police cars. None had a chance against the heavy Browning machine gun. The first two vehicles seemed to fall apart. Dozens of projectiles, cutting into the engines, first stopped the vehicles. A moment later, the inside of the two police cars resembled a battlefield. Scores of projectiles stabbed through the windshields and roofs, killing almost instantly the four men inside each car. Ripped seats became soggy with blood that flowed over torn pieces of leather coats and bits of flesh and chips of bone. Pieces of glass lay thick on the bloody corpses and a cool wind began spreading the sweet odor of death.

Roy Wohlwend began to bring the helicopter down, and as he did so, Ferris "Blubberlips" Bensinn opened fire on the other Georgia State Police cars that had stopped because the way was blocked by the first two wrecked vehicles.

To Bensinn it was Vietnam all over again, and, as he exploded one police car, then riddled the fourth one with a hail of .50 caliber slugs, he recalled how a FAC could employ either "Recon by smoke" or "Recon by fire." In the first case the pilot drops a smoke grenade and if anyone runs from the explosion he is presumed guilty and napalmed (if he runs into his house), or machine-gunned (if he darts into the rice paddies). "Recon by fire" is based on the same principle except that CBUs are used instead of smoke grenades, so that if the victims do not run they will be killed anyway.

The really effective method, recalled Blubberlips, was the "carpet" raid that could explode fifty square miles of jungle into flame. In such an area, fire bombs killed everything, friend and foe and animals. Such a raid could be almost as effective as defoliation, which could "kill" 300 acres in four minutes.

The last state police car exploded in a ball of rolling bright fire and dark smoke as slugs ruptured the gas tank, parts and pieces of the vehicle flying all over the highway. Traffic on the two-lane highway had stopped, both to the north and the south, and lines of cars were forming. Hot damn! Blubberlips again thought of Vietnam and of the motto he and his unit had had regarding defoliation—*Only You can Prevent a Forest!*

The skids of the Bell UH-1B touched the gravel of the parking lot, Maurice Ehlers frantically motioning from the starboard side of the cockpit to Camellion and the other men, gesturing for them to hurry up and get aboard. The tiny group, including Wally Chatters, who had run over to the Datsun wagon, quickly got aboard the roaring chopper, and Roy Wohlwend lifted off and swung the bird to the northwest. At 750 feet, Ehlers slid open a port of the cockpit glass to his left and shoved out a package of 900 red handbills. The strong wind quickly began to scatter them, and they started to float downward like giant bloody snowflakes.

In the salvage yard below there was only death and destruction, a carnage that would be reported in the world's press as the worst terrorist attack ever experienced by the people of the United States.

Having closed the starboard side door and securely latched it, the Death Merchant turned and grinned at his three "partners-in-crime."

"This is as much fun as you can have with your pants up! Everyone agree?"

"It got damned lonesome in that rig," growled Chatters, "and I was down to the last magazine. That's a hell of a way to run an operation."

"You should complain!" chided Hilleli. "I was stuck with looking out after this *chazzer!*"[7]

Kartz's cement-colored eyes fixed themselves on the Death Merchant and he fingered his thick mustache. "We're still not secure," he said in his funereal voice. "We can congratulate each other when we're thirty miles from Bill Arp and headed toward Atlanta."

Keith Griesbeck, who considered all of them card-carrying kamikazes, stared at the Death Merchant with the fear and fascination of one face to face with a shark. Camellion, smiling back at him, sensed the man's utter panic and felt that *All we'll have to do is point a weapon at him and say, "Talk!" and he'll spill all he knows.* Camellion knew that Griesbeck wasn't the conventional Rance Galloway; he wasn't a coward. He was a realist while still brainwashed by the peculiar brand of American morality—*Which is why he considers us barbarians! He's a victim of the Great American Dilemma. All of us—we're half Puritan, half vulgarian, and half-liars—the sons and daughters of Cotton Mather and Jonathan Edwards. Part of us hustles the Big Buck while the other part mews nonsense homilies about money not being able to buy happiness or love or health or what have you. We're a nation of pretenders, of hypocrites—and we resent those "ruthless" people we are not. And as a nation—we kill better than most people. The average American will learn this the hard way during World War III, when our own streets run red with blood!*

Roy Wohlwend's voice, coming over the speaker, jerked Camellion from his philosophical reflections:

"We're only fourteen minutes from Bill Arp."

[7] "Pig," a "piggish person."

Chapter 9

"That's about the dumbest suggestion I've heard since we took off from Atlanta International!" H. L. Kartz said scornfully, looking angrily at Virgil Lindsey, who was in the seat across the aisle from him, and who had just suggested the possibility that maybe they could obtain the help of the Cosa Nostra once they were in New York City. As Lindsey had pointed out, the Company had very good contacts within the Mafia. "I wouldn't trust one of those garlic snappers if I could hold his soul in a matchbox," finished Kartz. "Hell, I'd just as soon trust a U.S. senator!"

"What's that supposed to mean?" asked Lindsey, who was a medium-sized man with narrow features and a receding hairline. For six years he had been a "street man." He was a career employee. "What do senators have to do with the mob?"

Kartz snickered. "I'm speaking of in-depth political protection that goes all the way to D.C. Don't you know that the Mafia is bigger than U.S. Steel?[1] That means money, and money means power. It's that power that helps to elect politicians."[2]

Lindsey stared for a moment at Kartz, sensing that trying to carry on a conversation with him was similar to trying to stop an elephant with a flyswatter.

Lindsey sighed and reached for the lever underneath the arm of the seat. "I'm going to get some sleep; it's almost fifteen hundred hours." He tilted back the seat and snuggled down with his back half turned to Kartz.

In one of the last seats in the six-passenger Cessna Crusader, Pini Hilleli leaned far out and whispered to Camellion across the

[1] Bigger than U.S. Steel since the Cosa Nostra takes in some $30 billion a year, of which $10 billion is net profit.
[2] Experts estimate that the Mafia exercises varying degrees of control over some twenty-five congressmen as well as thousands of lesser political figures. President Kennedy gave a presidential pardon to Jake (the Barber) Factor after the hoodlum contributed $10,000 to the Democratic party. In 1968, Factor was revealed to be the largest financial contributor to the Democratic party's presidential campaign. Money—mob money—talks, even with U.S. presidents.

aisle, "Is it true? Is organized crime that firmly entrenched in your country?"

"Our country," corrected the Death Merchant, who had been looking out the small window at the stars. "The Company is obtaining citizenship for you. And it's true. The Mafia in the United States has assumed a position of supremacy that is total and absolute, with every Mafioso believing it is his inalienable right to rob and steal, plunder and murder, to deal in drugs, prostitution, and what-have-you. But it's violent street crime that the average American has to worry about. It exists because of half-witted do-gooders who still haven't learned—after thirty years of rising crime—what any good cop could tell them: that there isn't any such thing as 'rehabilitation.' "

"Isn't that a presumptive statement?" asked Hilleli.

"Negative. A lot of let's-coddle-the-criminal comes from the U.S. Supreme Court itself. For example, in 1972 Justice Thurgood Marshall wrote that 'punishment for the sake of retribution is not permissible under the Eighth Amendment.' That's first-rate stupdity! The element of retribution—call it vengeance if you want—does not make punishment cruel and unusual—*it makes punishment intelligible and distinguishes punishment from therapy.*" His blue eyes flickered over Hilleli. "Rehabilitation may be an ancillary result of punishment, but we punish to serve justice. We punish criminals by giving them what they deserve. Anyhow, that's how it should be. It isn't. Because it isn't, crime is rising."

Hilleli thought for a moment. At length he said, "What I find ridiculous is how your—our—government pampers certain classes and groups. I find it a paradox that certain study programs are permitted to teach minority racism in high schools and colleges where majority racism is forbidden. To me that's nonsense, dangerous nonsense. It will wreck the education system in time."

"It already has," Camellion said. "Intellectually, we're already a third-rate nation. The pygmies are at the controls, and savages have taken over the classrooms. The animal trainers are sleeping . . ."

Camellion turned and resumed looking out the window, watching space and the quiet stars.

Feeling that the Death Merchant wanted to be alone with his own thoughts, Hilleli leaned back on the seat and closed his eyes, trying to convince himself that he didn't miss the sights and sounds and smells of Yisroel.[3] He supposed that thousands of other Israeli immigrants in the United States were equally as lonely, pretending to be happy while missing the homeland they loved.

Ironic, thought Hilleli, that Jews from Israel had become a source of manpower for the United States. While Jews the world over end their prayers with *Leshana Haba'a BiYrushalayim* ("Next Year in Jerusalem"), one out of every ten Israelis was still contemplating *Leshana Haba'aBeNew York*, or Miami, or Los Angeles, or Chicago, or—? All would have the same reason for wanting to leave the Promised Land:[4] they had become tired of the constant pressure, of living in an armed camp, and of the unparalleled sacrifices being constantly demanded of them.

They didn't like the compulsory military service and extended annual reserve duty. They didn't like the severe housing shortage—a working couple with a joint income of $1,000 a month found it impossible to raise the $100,000 that a two-bedroom apartment in Tel Aviv or Jerusalem would cost. They didn't like the all-powerful bureaucracy—it often took five or six years to get a telephone. They didn't like the annual inflation rate of 100 percent, combined with very high taxes.

Added to this was the growing gap between Sephardic Jews and Ashkenazic Jews.

Telling himself that life was already much better in the United States, Hilleli drifted off to sleep.

The Death Merchant's mind was not focused on Israel. Methodically, Camellion reviewed the events of the previous day. The Bell Huey had landed as scheduled in the woods six miles north of Bill Arp, a small town of less than five hundred people on the Chattahoochee River (really a creek), southwest of Atlanta. The transfer to the two cars and the U-Haul moving van with its big snow tires had gone smoothly. The two vehicles were six miles away and on a main road that led to Atlanta by the time the six pounds of C-4 exploded and scattered the eggbeater all over the snowy clearing in the woods. (That evening the *Atlanta Journal* reported that the helicopter "possibly used by the terrorists" had crashed in the woods.)

[3] Hebrew: Israel
[4] People, Israel's most precious commodity, have become a major export. Fifteen percent of the 3.9 million population have chosen to live elsewhere. This would be the equivalent of 34 million Americans leaving the United States.

Terrorists? The red leaflets dropped by Maurice Ehlers were supposedly from the *Movimiento de Acción Revolucionaria*, or MAR, one of the major terrorist groups operating in Mexico—and Marxist to the core. The "demands" of MAR were outrageous and totally impractical (which Camellion had done deliberately—a return of the Southwest to Mexico, a return of former Mexican territory "stolen by American imperialists in their greed to acquire land."

"We will free our Latino brothers in the United States!"

"Death to Capitalist Imperialists who step on the throats of the people!"

Grojean won't like that, I'm sure.

There hadn't been any difficulty in the transfer from the vehicles, which had driven to a large garage on Simpson Street in Atlanta. By 1730 hours, the group, with the target, were in the Black Station on Dresden Road in North Atlanta.

The home of Professor Sanford Wittenjohn, who taught political science at Oglethorpe College, only seven blocks away, the Victorian house was the perfect cover for a Black Station. It had a large wooden front porch with railings, sunny bay windows, fish-scale shingles, and turn-of-the-century "carpenter's lace." The house also had what the other Victorian houses in the area didn't have—a small, soundproofed room built off the full basement.

It was to this small room that Camellion & Co. took the very uncomfortable Keith Griesbeck.

No sooner was the door to the secret room closed than H. L. Kartz snapped, "Electric shock should turn this son of a bitch into a long-playing record."

However, intensive interrogation was not necessary with the subject. As Camellion had earlier surmised, all they had to do was look at Griesbeck and tell him to start talking—after Camellion had told him that they were well informed about his working for Colonel Muammar Qaddafi, one of the most dangerous men in the world—". . . which makes you an unregistered foreign agent," Camellion said. "That in itself is good for twenty years in a federal penitentiary."[5]

"You were duped, dummy!" Wally Chatters said with a laugh. "Qaddafi's made a sap out of you. He's tricked you into

[5] The actual penalty is five years in prison or a $10,000 fine, or both.

thinking he wants the secret of the neutron bomb, and you believed him, sucker!''

The Death Merchant put a foot on a wooden box, leaned down on the leg with his forearm, and glared down at Griesbeck. ''The East Germans are also in on the act! You didn't know that, did you, stupid? The East Germans and Qaddafi aren't after the 'secret' of the neutron bomb. There isn't any 'secret' involved with the neutron bomb. Any nation with the technical resources can make such a weapon.''

Camellion then told the wide-eyed man that Qaddafi's real plan was to spread nerve gas over the East Coast of the United States—''VXB-2L6 gas. It's the most deadly nerve gas in the world, so powerful that should Qaddafi's plan succeed, there will be from fifteen to twenty-five million corpses. Your wife and children, all your friends and relatives that you have on the East Coast—they'll all die. Think about it! Think of how you will be largely responsible for twenty million murders!''

Duane Halverson leaned down close to Griesbeck, who sat dejectedly on a plain wooden chair, staring up at the circle of accusing faces.

''Tell me, Griesbeck. What do you call a man who helps murder his own family?'' he asked harshly. ''What can you call such a piece of scum?''

''B-But I didn't k-know Qaddafi's real plan!'' protested Griesbeck in a loud, almost hysterical voice. He started to stand. Wally Chatters, behind him, grabbed his collar and jerked him down.

''And now you do know!'' Camellion said, a note of threat in his low voice. ''Tell us everything you know or we'll make you wish you were dead a hundred times over and then some.''

Motioning a lot with his hands as he talked, Griesbeck confessed that he had dealt with only one man of the other side, an Algerian, Akram Ndrangheta, who was an undersecretary with the Algerian Delegation to the United Nations. And how had Griesbeck met Ndrangheta? Surely not in Atlanta over black-eyed peas and corn pone!

Griesbeck explained that he had met Ndrangheta in New York City while he was on a business trip concerning a project his consulting firm was handling for the Algerian government. ''It had to do with irrigation of the desert around Ghardaïa in northern Algeria. We were to supply the valves for the automatic flow and shutoff of the water and supply data in regard to absorption of water into the soil at specific times of the day, depending on factors that—''

"We're concerned only with Qaddafi!" cut in the Death Merchant. "Get to the point."

Griesbeck explained that he and Akram Ndrangheta had become quite friendly as the months had gone by and the two of them had gotten together for any number of meetings, in New York, in Atlanta, and twice in Atlantic City. It was on the fifth meeting that Ndrangheta had slyly asked Griesbeck if he would like to make some tax-free money for himself by working for him—$500,000.00! How? Ndrangheta wanted the secret of the neutron bomb. Would Griesbeck be willing to help him get it?

"Just like that, huh?" sneered Barry Newheart, his voice full of skepticism. "You're expecting us to believe that this Ndrangheta came right out and offered you half a million dollars to help him grab the supposed 'secret' of the N-bomb! Next you'll be asking us to believe that General Custer loved Indians!"

"Even more strange is that Ndrangheta should come right out and mention Qaddafi," said H. L. Kartz, his cruel eyes ice-picking Griesbeck.

"He didn't mention Qaddafi," Griesbeck quickly corrected him. "He never did. I . . ."

It was during a meeting with Ndrangheta and another Algerian in New York City that Griesbeck, having drunk too much, had lain down in a bedroom in a suite of rooms that Ndrangheta had rented. Getting up several hours later, he had heard Ndrangheta and the other man talking in the next room and—"I listened at the door and heard Qaddafi's name mentioned three or four times. It was then I deduced, from the way they were talking, that Qaddafi was behind the scheme."

Asked Pini Hilleli, "What was the name of the other Algerian?"

"Salech, Salich—something like that," said Griesbeck. "That was his first name. I don't recall his last name. It was—was—I want to say 'Bokker.' I really don't r-remember."

H. L. Kartz blew cigarette smoke at Griesbeck. "My thinking is similar to Mr. Newheart's. It seems peculiar to me that Ndrangheta should come right out and ask if you wanted to help him acquire information about the neutron bomb."

Kartz didn't anticipate Camellion's answering for Griesbeck.

"It's no great mystery," the Death Merchant said, looking at Kartz. "Any of us in this room can size up a man and know if he has larceny jumping around in him waiting to get out. A trained intelligence agency can do this ten times faster. I hardly think that Ndrangheta is an amateur.'' His steady gaze moved to Griesbeck. ''I'm more curious why Ndrangheta should have tried to recruit him at all. Suppose you tell us, Griesbeck.''

''H-He said it was because I know people in Washington.'' Griesbeck seemed to swallow with difficulty. ''A few physicists my company has worked with on certain projects. Of course, I f-found it all difficult to believe, but—but—''

''But the money made up your mind!'' Camellion said.

A guilty expression bloomed on Griesbeck's face. ''The first payment was two hundred and fifty thousand in cash. I was to receive the remainder after we had the vital information about the bomb.''

The Death Merchant asked the vital question. ''You did receive orders. Ndrangheta had something for you to do. What was it?''

''I didn't have anything to do. The last time I met Ndrangheta— it was several weeks ago in Jacksonville, Florida. We decided to meet in Florida because—''

''Get to the point!'' barked the Death Merchant.

''Ndrangheta said that within a month I would have to make arrangements for some men to meet a ship that would be arriving in the United States,'' confessed Griesbeck. ''When I''—in spite of the extremely valuable information that Griesbeck had just revealed, none of the men revealed their wild elation over the possibility that the VXB-2L6 gas was being smuggled into the United States by an oceangoing vessel—''asked Ndrangheta when the ship would be coming in and where it would be docking, he said he'd tell me at the proper time.''

''Did he say how many men?'' inquired Virgil Lindsey, who was a tall, bony individual with a quick manner, a receding hairline, and a red face, although he drank only moderately.

''All he said was what I've told you. I did gather that the ship would be outside the harbor, wherever the port might be. I mean—quite a distance out.''

The Death Merchant removed his right foot from the wooden box filled with handguns that were ''cold'' pieces.[6] ''Did Ndrangheta give any further indication of when you would make these arrangements? Think! Anything at all pertaining to the time?''

---

[6] Weapons that can't be traced—usually used for ''wet'' affairs— assassinations.

Griesbeck shook his head. "No. There wasn't anything except that it would be within a month."

The Death Merchant's eyes flicked with a weird, preternatural fire.

And that meeting was two weeks ago. Within a month. That leaves us very little time!

"I'd like to know something," said Pini Hilleli, who was new to the intelligence game. "Didn't Akram Ndrangheta take a big risk in asking Griesbeck to work against the U.S.? Suppose Griesbeck had reported his offer to the FBI?"

"That wasn't really that big a problem," Camellion replied, accenting his Texas drawl for the hell of it (and to keep the men around him confused). "If Griesbeck had reported the offer to the FBI, the Feds would have begun watching Ndrangheta and used a cross-triple tail. Sooner or later they would have wired Griesbeck to get the plot down on tape. Then they would have moved in and arrested the sand crab. Being a diplomat, he couldn't have been prosecuted. He would have been deported and that would have been the end of it."

Hilleli didn't seem convinced.

Looking directly at Camellion, H. L. Kartz was all business. "Well, you're in charge. When do we leave for New York?"

A long report by shortwave had been sent to Grojean at Langley Center—black box and triple-reverse scramble, in the ultrasecret code used only by the Fox and the Death Merchant.[7]

Camellion's recommendation: Blue 15 network should proceed to New York with all possible speed and make arrangements to black-bag Akram Ndrangheta. In the meanwhile, what information did the Company have on Ndrangheta and a man whose name could be Salech or Salich Bokker. (Note: Spelling is phonetic).

The reply from Langley Center: *Will send requested information in three hours. Make arrangements to take network to New York. Your plan approved. J. Brent.*[8]

He didn't say a single word about the Movimiento de Acción

---

[7] The code is composed of words from the Mohican Indian language. Phonetic since the Mohicans did not have an alphabet. Each word is reversed; two letters of each reversed word are used to indicate a certain letter of the English alphabet. The message is then keyed out.

[8] One of Grojean's many code names.

Revolucionaria! reflected Camellion. *He must be slipping or very worried. No doubt very worried. He's too crafty to slip.*

Camellion leaned slightly forward as the Cessna Crusader dipped into an air pocket. The two TSIO-520 Continental engines purring smoothly, the airplane was at 19,000 feet and cruising at 198 knots.

The Company did have information on Akram Ndrangheta. The oily Algerian had been posted for twenty-six months at the United Nations. As a matter of security, the CIA routinely snooped on members of the various foreign delegations. Ndrangheta first attracted Company attention when it was noticed that he seldom attended UN meetings, even though he was an undersecretary. What then did Ndrangheta do? For seven months the Company had shadowed the man. Ndrangheta went to a lot of UN parties, as well as gala get-togethers by Americans. He even had a few friends in New York's exclusive Racquet Club. But he never did anything suspicious. He never associated with people—foreign or American—who were on the Company's active list. Married and the father of three children, Ndrangheta lived with his family in an expensive apartment on Park Avenue. After seven months and two weeks, the CIA investigation was discontinued. Reasons: nothing incriminating and a lack of manpower.

Salech (or) Salich Bokker: It is possible that this individual could be Seleh Bakr, 41-years of age, another Algerian national. Bakr is a member of the Algerian Finance Committee and a member of the United Nations' World Intellectual Property (WIPO) agency.[9] Bakr has an apartment on Park Avenue in New York City. He and Ndrangheta are not close friends, as far as the Agency can detect.

We are placing Ndrangheta and Bakr under immediate intensive surveillance. I will meet you at Applecart D-3KK.[10]

The Death Merchant reflected on another problem. How severe it was at present was a moot question. Company specialists had not been able to black-bag Verlin Dragg in his office in New Bedford. The four agents had arrived at 10:07 A.M. Dragg was not there. He had slipped in the snow at his home while going to

---

[9] An organization that seeks to protect, through international cooperation, literary, industrial, scientific, and artistic works, that is, "intellectual property."

[10] See Death Merchant #48, *The Psionics War.*

his garage to leave for the office and had broken his left leg and fractured his left elbow. He was in Saint Agatha's Hospital in Acushnet, a suburb east of New Bedford, where he made his home.

The Company men had quietly checked to make sure. Uh huh. Dragg was in Saint Agatha's, in room 309.

At this altitude the sky was clear, and since there wasn't any moon the stars shone with laser brightness. There was Cassiopeia and giant Altair; to the east, Boötes and sinister Markab; toward the plane of the ecliptic, Antares.

Looking out the window of the airplane, the Death Merchant saw another star, this one in the constellation Perseus—Argol, whose name meant "demon" in Arabic.

The realization made him uncomfortable. If he failed to stop Qaddafi and his insane scheme, these stars would very shortly look down on millions of American corpses—*Including my own!*

Chapter 10

Amityville, Long Island. An imposing-looking mansion built of limestone and surrounded by graceful sycamores, black oaks, and rock elms, the Flechter Rest Home and its grounds sat back off Route 41, which branched from Amityville Road. To the people of the area the rest home was an expensive sanatorium whose patients were corporate executives who had lost the battle against modern business pressure.

The sanatorium did blend well with the rest of the countryside, even if the large grounds were surrounded by an eighteen-foot-high cyclone fence. The fence was somewhat of an eyesore, detracting from the quiet atmosphere. But only in the rear. During the warm months the front fence, facing Route 14, and both sides were covered with fast-growing clinging vines—yellow trumpet, red trumpet, and bittersweet vines in which honeysuckle tried to hide itself.

Although the Central Intelligence Agency secretly owned the small mental hospital and much of it was not as it appeared to be, the twenty or so patients were very real. They weren't, however, executives from American companies and conglomerates. They were career employees of the Agency, mostly from the clandestine division, "spooks" who had cracked under the constant strain of leading double and/or triple lives and had suffered mental and/or emotional breakdowns. Some were alcoholics. Others, sick with severe depression, had attempted suicide. None were actually psychotic; yet all had to be treated and restored to normalcy. Every patient had knowledge of secrets that had to remain secret.

Flechter Rest Home was much more than a small sanatorium, much more. It was not only one of the main safe houses on the East Coast but was also a special research laboratory in which scientists, including parapsychologists, conducted experiments in mind control and in the paranormal—ESP and related subjects.

In the CIA files the rest home was coded Applecart D-3KK.

Wearing a camel's hair three-button blazer, a blue madras shirt with white collar and cuffs, and gray wool flannel trousers, Courtland Grojean studied the alabaster eagle resting on the right corner of the desk behind which he was seated. Exquisitely proportioned, with an eighteen-inch wingspan, the eagle rested on a black marble base.

At length, the chief of the CIA's Covert Action Staff turned his sharp-featured face toward the Death Merchant.

"In view of what happened at the salvage yard, the East Germans and the Libyans now are positive that we have a tremendous amount of raw data regarding their plans," Grojean said, speaking distinctly. "They are therefore faced with three choices: Mischa Wolf will either call off the operation, put it on hold, or he'll risk a go-ahead, on the assumption that the nerve gas can be brought in and spread before we can intervene." His gray eyes silently probed Camellion, asking for his opinion.

"Wolf is too clever to take unnecessary chances; we both know that." Camellion shifted position in the tufted chair in front of the walnut desk. "At the same time, he can hardly cancel the operation without placing himself in the gravest of danger. It would not sit well with the East German government if it had to return Qaddafi's millions—and the blame would fall on Wolf."

Grojean began toying with a silver letter opener. "Then you believe Wolf will push the project forward?"

"Why shouldn't he? As far as Wolf and the Libyans are concerned, their plan hasn't been compromised. Griesbeck and the two other American businessmen didn't possess any truly dangerous information. Griesbeck didn't know the name of the vessel and the time of its arrival. It might be arriving at any port, all the way from north Maine to the Florida Keys; and we still don't have idea one how the East German agents are going to bring the gas into the U.S. I'd say by launch. Aircraft would be the logical choice for dispersing it into the air."

"I disagree completely." Grojean's tone was firm, as if he had made up his mind. "Wolf is extremely circumspect. To judge from his past operations—at least the ones we know about—I can't conceive of his pushing ahead when there's a clear danger of discovery, not when he knows we're aware of what East German intelligence intends to do." He shook the letter opener at Camellion, using it as an extended finger. "Our files are crammed with information on that sauerkraut head and his intelligence apparatus, which is probably the best in Europe."

"A lot of that information could be incorrect," Camellion said dryly. He slipped a hand into the right pocket of his suede sweater so that only his thumb protruded. "The Agency has pulled some bones in the past. Twenty years ago with Lee Harvey Oswald, for example. The CI [1] boys in the Company goofed when they sent Oswald to the Soviet Union. When he returned from Russia, they lost control of him and he began thinking he was a 'super James Bond' who could outwit the KGB on this side of the oceans. In the—"

"That was sixteen months before I took over the covert section!" With an angry motion, Grojean threw the letter opener on the desk. "I wasn't involved with those idiots in CI and the smooth-over. [2] I had nothing to do with it."

Camellion's smile was slightly sardonic. "You shouldn't take any of this personally. I was merely pointing out that the Company has made serious miscalculations in the past. We know now—you and I—that Oswald should have been terminated months before the Kennedy hit. Instead, to cloud the waters, the CI nitwits send a double of Oswald running around Texas and Mexico, even after they had learned he had gotten involved with the

[1] Counterintelligence.
[2] CIA jargon for "cover-up."

Mafia and was going to be used as the fall guy for the Kennedy hit. This was gold-plated stupidity!"

"The Agency couldn't be positive about the Kennedy assassination until after it happened!" Grojean said quickly in defense of the CIA. "We wouldn't have permitted President Kennedy to be terminated."

The Agency certainly would! Camellion went on, "After the hit the Company found itself in a position of damned-if-we-do-and-damned-if-we-don't. It couldn't let the truth be known, that it was the Cosa Nostra that knocked off Kennedy. It couldn't without letting the world know about all the little plots it had made with organized crime to kill Castro." Camellion uttered a small, gleeful laugh. "On the other hand, the Company covered its tracks pretty well, a lot better than headline-grabbing J. Edgar Hoover did.[3] The big-shot union leader who acted as the original liaison between the CIA and the Mafia vanished.[4] The two mobsters involved were terminated.[5] Lesser lights died of 'suicide' or had 'strokes' or 'heart attacks.'[6] Neat, my friend. Very neat and efficient."

Grojean's face had darkened and his eyes were filled with storm clouds. Even though there was not one piece of lint on his clothes and every crease was in place, he appeared tired. He was. He had arrived the previous day at noon, five hours after Camellion's plane, and the Beech Baron that had carried the

---

[3] Hoover was more concerned with his own personal image and the image of the FBI than he was with the truth. Hoover totally ignored the rumor that a very big Mafia don had threatened to have President Kennedy killed, this stemming from the fact that John F. Kennedy and Bobby Kennedy were determined to smash organized crime. Even when Ed Reid, a Pulitzer Prize-winning reporter who heard about the rumor while researching a book about the Mafia, told the FBI about the threat, Hoover responded by casting aspersions on Reid's professional ability and integrity.

[4] Jimmy Hoffa.

[5] Sam Giancana, one-time head of the Outfit, the Chicago crime syndicate. He was shot once in the back of the head and six times in the mouth—with a .22 pistol. John Roselli, a Las Vegas mobster. He was found floating in an oil drum, his legs cut off.

[6] Lesser mobsters who were connected with Hoffa-CIA-Castro plots were Salvatore Granello, Charles Nicoletti, and James Plumeri. All were found shot.

other members of the Blue 15 Network to New York had landed, and he had had little sleep.

Abruptly, Grojean's manner underwent a transformation, his demeanor becoming jocular. "I think you're attributing too much power to the Agency. After all, even the CIA respects Presidents."

"Naturally," Camellion said with mock seriousness. "But when Presidents start to interfere seriously with the activities of the Agency, they leave the Oval office, don't they?"[7]

To Grojean there was no one more irritating than someone with less intelligence and more sense than he had! He leaned forward, folded his hands, put them on the desk, and scrutinized Camellion, his eyes full of fire.

"I'd cut the throat of my own mother to protect this nation from the Communists," he said in a voice that was slow and quiet but firm. "And so would you! You of all people know that it's impossible for us to operate efficiently if we stay within the law. I suggest you quit playing games, Death Merchant. I'm sure that's what you're doing."

Camellion didn't show any anger at Grojean's use of the term *Death Merchant*. Despising the sobriquet, Camellion knew that Grojean had used it to rankle him. He merely said in a voice that was infuriating to Grojean, "The only thing you can be sure of is that which is happening now—today. All the rest is speculation. At the moment that's all we have with Akram Ndrangheta and Seleh Bakr, if Bakr is the man who was with Ndrangheta; and there isn't any evidence that the Algerian government is involved in the plot with Qaddafi."

"One thing is certain: if those two have a vest-pocket operation going for themselves, they're taking a big risk," Grojean said mildly, grateful that Camellion had steered the conversation away from the CIA. "If they're caught and deported, the Algerian government will take a dim view of their working for Qaddafi and East German intelligence."

"The Algerian government is not applicable to any factors at this stage of the game," Camellion said in a practical tone. "At present, our best chance for success is to obtain the necessary information from Akram Ndrangheta and perhaps Seleh Bakr. If they don't know the name of the vessel carrying the nerve gas, we'll be at a dead end. By the way, you and the other brass have already realized that Washington has to be a prime target?"

[7] Watergate!

Grojean nodded slowly and stared at Camellion for a moment. "The President and his family and his top people are leaving tomorrow in *Air Force One* for a tour of the western states."

Camellion laughed in good-humored resignation. "And the CIA brass?"

"We have special airtight shelters at Langley"—Grojean took off his glasses—"but who knows when to go into them? Who knows when the gas will be spread? Personally, I'm not counting on the East Germans and the Libyans succeeding. Which leads to one question: When do you intend to grab Ndrangheta and Bakr?"

The Death Merchant asked, "Do you have anything else in Ndrangheta's and Bakr's 201 File[8] other than what you gave over the radio?"

"I gave you all we had." Grojean sounded annoyed. "Their situation hasn't changed. Bakr and Ndrangheta didn't do anything unusual last night or the night before. It's the same with them today. Ndrangheta didn't go to the UN building until two-thirty, and it's close to four now."

"You've put a tap on their phones?"

"From the central exchange—nothing incriminating. I doubt if Bakr and Ndrangheta spring any travel arrangements on their wives until the very last moment. When they do, we won't know it. They certainly won't use the telephone. Their departure from the U.S., or at least from the East Coast, will be sudden and unexpected to even their friends. I suggest you grab Ndrangheta and Bakr tonight, or do I have to give you a direct order? Time is running out."

---

[8] A 201 File is kept on any individual in whom the CIA takes an interest. A 201 File is also kept on each career employee. There are also phony 201 Files for agents in deep cover and/or on cover assignments. Such people may or may not be case officers and/or CIA career people. The idea of cover and cover arrangements is all very basic to the Company. If an agent did work that was very classified and/or involved "Executive Action," then there will be a second 201 File whose contents will be pure fabrication. A third 201 File will be factual and tell the true facts. The triple file system is complicated, but it works well in that it gives the Agency a lot of flexibility in protecting the people in its employ.

There isn't any 201 File of any kind—phony or otherwise—on Richard Camellion.

"I estimate we have three days and three nights before we have to make a positive move," Camellion said candidly. "I suggest we continue day-and-night surveillance on Ndrangheta and especially on Bakr for that length of time."

Courtland Grojean's eyes narrowed in surprise. "Why?" he asked, his steady gaze unwavering. "And why concentrate on Bakr?"

"Time is equally as precious to the Libyans and the East Germans," pointed out Camellion. "They know what really went down at the salvage yard outside Atlanta. Griesbeck is missing. They assume we have him and that he's told us everything he knows. That means he's mentioned Ndrangheta, who now must assume he's being watched very closely—phone tap, mail cover, every way possible. Yet none of them can be sure that Griesbeck remembers Bakr's name, or that Griesbeck even attached any importance to him. He only met Bakr once."

"Get to the point, Camellion," Grojean said, his lips puckering with impatience. "What does it have to do with a three-day postponement?"

"I feel that our strikes against the ice cream plant and the salvage yard will not only force the enemy to be more cautious, but to also speed up the operation, all of it contingent upon the arrival of the ship carrying the nerve gas."

"Very well. That's a reasonable assumption."

"It's also reasonable that Ndrangheta, almost certain in his mind that he's being watched by the Company, is more or less limited in what he can do in the way of personal contact. Therefore, I have that low double-gut feeling it will be Bakr who will do the extra leg work, who might make the wrong move and give us a better lead."

"A better lead than Bakr or Ndrangheta?" Grojean, his eyes hard, fidgeted and hunched his shoulders.

"Affirmative. If a better lead doesn't develop within three days, we can always net Bakr and Ndrangheta. The decision rests with you."

Grojean looked away. A low double-gut feeling, Camellion had said. When all the nonsense that lay people associate with intelligence work is brushed to one side, one finds that hunches and intuition do play large roles in intelligence matters; and Camellion had always been right in the past—uncannily accurate in his predictions of what actions adversaries would take, almost as if he possessed some extraordinary preterhuman method that permitted him to look around the veil hiding the future.

"Let me think about it for an hour or two." Grojean glanced at the Death Merchant, pushed back his swivel chair, and stood up. "Let's go to the assembly room. There should be some word about Dragg by this time. They've had all day to do him in."

They left the office. Grojean locked the door and, turning to the left, they walked down the thickly carpeted hall toward a door on the right, toward the end of the corridor. At the opposite end of the hall, in the direction from which they had come, was another door, this one, while appearing to be of wood, of sheet steel. It separated the actual mental hospital from the Applecart D-3KK part of the station.

Not all of the Blue 15 network members were present in the assembly room. Wally Chatters and Duane Halverson were playing chess. H. L. Kartz, sitting Indian style on the floor, was working a crossword puzzle in the *New York Times*. Pini Hilleli was reading Brooklyn's Hebrew-language newspaper *Israel Shelanu* ("Our Israel").[9]

Roland Marissa, a Company career employee, was seated on a folding chair in front of the radio table on which was a Yaesu FRG-7 transceiver and a FRG-7700. Black boxes and scramblers were attached to both sets, and the code pickup could be tape-recorded for double analysis.

A wide-shouldered man, built as square as a box, Marissa smiled enthusiastically at Grojean as the chief of the covert section and the Death Merchant walked into the room.

"The report came in five minutes ago, Mr. Brent," he said to Grojean. "Verlin Dragg has been put to sleep. They used a method that was suggested by Mr. Chatters."

"I recommended chlordane,"[10] Chatters said to Grojean, look-

[9] The main paper in the United States through which transplanted Israelis make contact with one another. In New York, they can tune in every night to radio station WEVD for news from Israel.

[10] An insecticide and an extremely poisonous volatile oil. With thirty grams of chlordane in a 25 percent solution in an organic solvent, a target will be dead in forty minutes.

107

ing up from the chessboard. "It was a simple matter to visit Dragg during lunchtime at the hospital and put the poison in some of the food on his tray."

"A man-and-woman team did the job," Marissa commented, looking at Grojean, who, sitting down, was carefully pulling up the legs of his trousers. "They posed as Mutual of Omaha insurance agents. Dragg had a major medical policy with Mutual of Omaha."

"The only policy of benefit to him now is his life insurance," H. L. Kartz said in his usual gloomy voice. He was still unhappy that Grojean and Camellion had not accepted his plan to kill Eugene Dusenbury. Verlin Dragg had been terminated because Griesbeck had confessed that "another man is to arrange to make five airplanes available to Ndrangheta. That's what he told me. He didn't give me that name of the man and he didn't say what the planes would be used for."

That man had to be either Eugene Dusenbury or Verlin Dragg. Kill Dragg and, if he were the man, the Libyans and East German Intelligence could not replace him on short notice. Should Dusenbury be the man, he had been rendered ineffective by constant FBI surveillance. The Company was positive that the Feds were watching him very closely, night and day, and that the FBI suspected he was more than merely a major stockholder in Farrell's Forty Flavors. The CIA could be positive because it had a highly placed contact within the FBI.

Accordingly, Camellion and Grojean had calculated that with the FBI watching Dusenbury, it would be too dangerous to terminate him. A stink with the FBI was all the CIA needed to complicate a situation that was already elaborately complex.

Always wanting to kill someone, Kartz had suggested any number of methods in an effort to convince Grojean and Camellion that Eugene Dusenbury should be sent "to the next world."

"We could use sodium morphate," Kartz had said. "It tastes something like apple pie. Take it from me, one hundred milligrams is fatal to the target. Heart failure is usually diagnosed as the cause of death. Or we could use digitoxin. It's a medical drug used in the treatment of heart failure. It's delivered by injection and it only takes three to five milligrams to do the job. Or we could blow him up in his car. We

108

could use iodine crystals[11] to confuse the explosive experts."

Grojean and Camellion had been firm. NO. Dusenbury would not be touched.

"So far the luckiest guy is Farrell," Pini Hilleli said. "Wherever he's hiding out, he's safe." He folded "Our Israel" and frowned. "What I'd like to know is when we're going to do the number on Akram Ndrangheta and Seleh Bakr?"

"Right on. We've already lost a day and a night and almost another day," Merwin Boradus said crisply from where he sat on an upholstered chair. Pleasant featured and narrow chested, he took out a pack of Winston Ultra-Lights and began removing the cellophane. "So far I haven't heard anyone mention plans for grabbing those two."

"What's to plan?" intoned Barry Newheart. "Our people are watching their every move. We know where Bakr and Ndrangheta live. All we have to do is go to their apartment houses, flash phony FBI ID, and announce that they're under arrest. By the time their families make a call to the Feds in Manhattan for information, we'll have vanished with our two prizes."

"I agree," murmured H. L. Kartz. "With the two choppers out back, our transportation is excellent. The Konnorso Building is on Fifth Street, almost smack in the heart of Manhattan. We land on the roof, do the job, take off again."

Duane Halverson wrinkled his nose and stared directly at Camellion and Grojean. "If it's a matter of voting, I say we should grab those two while the grabbing is good. Who knows? Suppose they try a run-out? Then what?"

"Then—nothing!" The Death Merchant's voice was deep and savage. "Those two aren't going anywhere until all the arrangements for the delivery of the gas have been made. I do not mean the actual spreading of the VXB. It will never come to that, not

---

[11] Mix one teaspoon of iodine crystals in one cup of ammonia and stir well. When this is mixed, make a paper filter and shape it like a cone. Pour the mixture into the filter and keep the residue that is left in the filter. This is the contact explosive and is safe while wet, but active when dry. Place the wet explosive in the target's automobile lock cap, in the key slot. After drying, the explosive is active; when the target stops at a gas station and inserts the key in the gas cap slot, the contact explosive ignites, causing the gasoline in the tank to explode. One gallon of gasoline equals thirty sticks of dynamite.

if we use our heads and have some patience. Three days is still within the safety range; and, like Newheart said, we can grab Bakr and Ndrangheta anytime.''

Grojean sounded weary. "Just one thing. When you do net them, there won't be any leaflets scattered implicating the *Movimiento de Acción Revolucionaria*. The State Department's had the Mexican ambassador on its back. He's still insisting that the men responsible for the trouble in the salvage yard were not members of the MAR.''

Kartz snickered loudly. "We wouldn't want to give the Mexicans a bad name, now would we? Maybe we should drop handbills labeled 'Martian Resistance Movement?' ''

"There won't be leaflets of any kind," Grojean said, looking first at Kartz, whom he disliked intensely, then at Camellion, of whom he was not very fond. "We can't implicate MAR again. And to point a finger at another revolutionary group would make it obvious that the perpetrators were only trying to conceal the truth by blaming another group.''

"Well and good, but when do we grab Ndrangheta and Bakr?'' asked Wally Chatters.

The Death Merchant turned to Courtland Grojean, who was rubbing his hands together. "I want three days, Mr. Brent. The decision is yours.''

"You have the three days and that's all you get," Grojean said stormily. "At the end of three days, I want those two grabbed.''

Thinking that a conviction is that splendid quality in ourselves that we call bullheadedness in others, Camellion merely nodded— *And if I'm wrong, we won't have lost anything.*

Chapter 11

Incredible as it seemed, seventy-four men and women (sixty-four men and ten women) were required to keep track of the movements of Akram Ndrangheta and Seleh Bakr. The main reason for such a large number was that one or two or a dozen agents could not possibly keep up with the targets without Bakr and Ndrangheta spotting them; and because of traffic it was not always feasible for two or three Company street men[1] to tail the individual targets. Yet the agents were always in contact with each other—"hearing aid" attached to a walkie-talkie, mike under a lapel, the frequency open and locked.

Even so, such a cross-tracking system was not infallible. For one thing, it was impossible to keep sight of Bakr and Ndrangheta in the UN building and/or offices. Many meetings were behind closed doors. The only thing the Company people could do was to position themselves close to strategic outside entrances and wait for the subjects to appear. The general area—Manhattan—while perfect for losing oneself in a crowd, also worked against the CIA people in that it was not always possible for them to park their cars where they could watch the cabs at the United Nations, which Bakr and Ndrangheta consistently used. The same situation prevailed at the apartment houses where the two men lived.

On the first of the three days that the Fox had given Camellion—no developments, including that night. Bakr stayed home with his family. Akram Ndrangheta and his family dined out and returned home early.

Early the next morning, Camellion had a talk with Courtland Grojean. An hour later, Grojean put out the order that the wives of Ndrangheta and Bakr be placed under intensive surveillance.

That afternoon Seleh Bakr left the United Nations after lunch (at 1317 hours) and, by taxi, went to the public library on the corner of West Forty-second Street and Fifth Avenue. An hour later, he left the library and took a bus—transferring once—to Rockefeller Center between Fifth Avenue and Avenue of the Americas.

"He suspects he's being followed and is trying the duck-and-dodge method," the report came in by radio from the street man in charge of the trailing operation, a man named Larry Kosgriv. "When he took the bus on Forty-second, he got off even before the rest of the people were on. Then he took another bus and got off a block from Rockefeller Center. He hailed a cab and had the driver take him all over the place before dropping him off at Rockefeller Center. He's been getting in and out of elevators ever since, in Rockefeller. You know why. He wants to see if the tail gets out with him."

[1] Such operatives are called street men whether they are men or women. Even feminists would frown on the term *street women*.

111

"Where is he now?" Camellion spoke into the mike attached to the radio.

Back came Kosgriv's voice. "In a cocktail lounge on West One Hundred Sixth Street, west of Central Park. He's talking to some foreign-looking man. Both are in a booth."

"Do you have enough people handy to tail the newcomer, the man that Bakr is talking to?"

"We can try."

That same afternoon, Mrs. Bakr and Mrs. Ndrangheta rented cars from Avis and parked the vehicles in the underground garages of their respective apartment houses.

H. L. Kartz, Virgil Lindsey, and Duane Halverson urged Camellion to move in on Seleh Bakr and Akram Ndrangheta, maintaining that the two Algerians were about to make that vital move.

"We wait," the Death Merchant said.

At 1642 hours that afternoon Bakr left the Parrot Lounge, got on a bus, got right off again, hailed a cab, and went home.

Taking up the trail of the man that Bakr had met, agents tailed him first to the General Post Office, then to the N.Y.U. Medical Center—and there they lost him. Nor had agents been able to photograph the man. He was heavyset and "about fifty."

Bakr did not leave his apartment house that night.

Mr. and Mrs. Akram Ndrangheta also remained at home.

Neither couple had guests.

Wally Chatters suggested that it was possible that either Seleh Bakr or Akram Ndrangheta—or both—would try to slip out a rear entrance and that the "rented cars are only a blind to throw us off track."

"It really doesn't matter," the Death Merchant said. "Our people are watching all the entrances. Men are also stationed close to the garages of the two apartment houses."

Nothing of value took place the next day. Bakr went to the United Nations. So did Ndrangheta. Both men went straight home after work. That evening, Mr. and Mrs. Ndrangheta went out to dinner and were home by 11:30. Mr. and Mrs. Bakr gave a small dinner party attended by eleven couples—people from the United Nations. Not a single couple was from the Deutsche Demokratische Republik, the German Democratic Republic (East Germany).

112

"One more day, Camellion," Grojean reminded the Death Merchant.

Fate smiled sweetly on the Death Merchant during the early afternoon of the third and final day. Seleh Bakr attempted to slip away from UN headquarters—tried by leaving through an entrance he seldom used, this move alone making the agents extra suspicious. He took a cab to Flower Hospital on Fifth Avenue and again did his best to outwit anyone who might be following him, getting in and out of elevators and making quick exits. He finally left the hospital through a rear door, hurried a block by foot, took another cab, and went to the World Trade Center in lower Manhattan, where he again indulged in any number of duck-and-dodge methods. Another Yellow Cab. North on Broadway. Then north on the Avenue of the Americas. West then on Forty-second Street to Times Square. A quick switch to another cab and on to Grand Central Station.

It was all the experienced Company street men could do to keep track of him.

Luck burst all over the place! It was at Grand Central Station that Bakr met the man he had met previously in the Parrot Lounge on West 106th Street. The two men didn't linger; instead, they took a taxi—this time through the Queens Midtown Tunnel underneath the East River.

Another report came into Applecart D-3KK at 4:45 P.M.

"They've gone to Brooklyn," Kosgriv reported in a voice that was excited. Not only had Bakr and the unidentified man gone to Brooklyn, but they had picked up a car at the public garage in South Brooklyn and had then proceeded to drive to the Bay Ridge section. Finally they had parked behind the Chalmer Brick Works near Fourth Avenue and Eighty-sixth Street. They had then gone inside the building.

"The place looks pretty run down," Kosgriv reported by radio. "We know there are people inside. We can see heat coming from the chimney. We can see a fuel-oil tank to one side of the main building."

"What kind of section is it around Fourth and Eighty-sixth?" Camellion inquired of Kosgriv. "Industrial? How about other businesses in the vicinity of the brickyard?"

"I'd say a small, run-down industrial section," Kosgriv's voice came through the transceiver. "There are quite a few deserted buildings in the vicinity of the brickyard. To the east is a lumberyard. There's no sign of activity around it. West of the yard is a large lot. It's filled with a lot of junk. It's difficult to tell what's there because of the snow. There are five old wrecks of cars. More empty lots are in the rear. Any special orders?''

"Stay put," said Camellion, who then surprised even Courtland Grojean by shutting off the radio and announcing, "Now is the time to strike, to move in on Bakr and the man with him. At the same time, we can have the FBI pick up Akram Ndrangheta."

"Strike?" H. L. Kartz echoed. He stared in disbelief at the Death Merchant. "You mean right now, this very minute?"

The very practical Grojean merely looked at Camellion and asked, "Why now?"

"Why not now?" Turning, the Death Merchant went to a wall and pulled down a rolled map of Brooklyn and the surrounding area. He then swung around and raked Grojean and the other men with an icy stare. He addressed himself to Grojean. "You were going to pick up Bakr and Ndrangheta tomorrow morning. Why wait? By moving now, we can grab the man with Bakr, plus the others inside the building. Bakr and his friend didn't go there to talk only to each other. I'm gambling that we've hit some kind of jackpot."

"Can we do it? Do we have the time?"—from Duane Halverson, who was so engrossed in the recent development that he had let his cigarette burn down to his fingers. He said, "Damn!" when the heat reached his fingers and quickly snubbed out the butt.

"We'll need luck," Pini Hilleli said, his face serious.

"It's only a ten-minute flight by chopper from here to Brooklyn," offered Virgil Lindsey. "But we can't land in the street or in one of the empty lots. We'd attract too much attention."

Grojean, who was also studying the large wall map with the Death Merchant, tapped a large green area with a slim finger. "We can land here. This is a U.S. government reservation—right here, west of the Dyker Beach Golf Course, in south Bay Ridge. The reservation is slightly more than a mile from the brickyard. All I'll have to do is make a few phone calls."

"I'll look up Roy and have him warm up one of the choppers." Barry Newheart looked at Grojean for a moment, then started to hurry from the assembly room.

"Tell him we'll use the Westland Lynx," Camellion called after him. His eyes turned to Grojean. "You might also arrange for two or three cars to meet us at the reservation. We'll need quick transportation to the brickyard. But not U.S. Army cars."

"I'll get on it right away; you work out the details," Grojean said, a calculating note in his voice. With the sure tread of a sleepwalker, he strode from the room.

Kartz touched Camellion lightly on the arm, after which he tapped a small red square on the map. "This police station is only nine blocks from the brickyard. We fire one shot, and those blue bulls will swarm all over us. How do we get around that?"

Merwin Boradus laughed nervously. "We can't go around gunning down police in the streets." He laughed again, louder this time. "Think of the publicity!"

"Not to mention the danger to us," Wally Chatters said dryly.

"Considering what's at stake"—Camellion's blue eyes were as hard as diamonds—"we can, and if it comes to that, we will."

Kartz tilted back his head, his expression mocking. "Big deal. Let's say we put to sleep a dozen or so cops. Fine. How do we get out of the area? All the streets will be blocked within minutes. And we can't use an eggbeater the way we did in Atlanta. Both the Lynx and the Choctaw are full of identification and both birds are registered to the rest home. I doubt if this safe house has any special paint around." He turned around and looked at Roland Marissa. "How about it, Rolly?"

Marissa, still at the radio table, shrugged and said casually, "We have some paint, but there isn't anything 'special' about it."

Kartz moved closer to the Death Merchant, who was still studying the large map. "Okay. Assuming that we do get to Seleh Bakr and whoever else is in there with him, how do we get away clean from the area?" He snickered. "There's too damn much snow for us to roller-skate!"

Fighting an urge to let Kartz have an old-fashioned right hook to the mouth, Camellion turned and glanced at Marissa. "Seriously, do you have enough paint to coat one of the choppers?"

"Sure." Marissa's face underwent a series of surprised expressions. "But as cold as it is, you know what the job would look like! It would be piss poor!"

By now, Kartz and the others had realized that Camellion was dead serious about using a helicopter to escape from the brickyard. None were looking forward to such an exceedingly dangerous operation.

Duane Halverson was blunt in making known his opinion. "It's a harebrained scheme," he said, sounding disturbed. "How

115

can we land in a painted-over chopper at the government reservation? Hell, there's a veterans' hospital there and Fort Hamilton. Those army boys will talk."

"Mr. Brent will veto the plan," Virgil Lindsey said smugly. He stared accusingly at Camellion and added as an epilogue, "There's also the problem of our being seen and identified after we lift off from the brickyard. Crap! We'd have to fly clear across Brooklyn and then come back here to Applecart D. Can you picture the police swarming all over this place? I can tell you right now that Mr. Brent can't!"

"The plan could work!" Wally Chatters stood up and stretched. "But we'd have to use both helicopters, one to go to the reservation, the second one to pick us up at the brick works."

"And especially to hold off the police," finished the Death Merchant, speaking with the sharpness of a construction boss rebuking a steel riveter who complains he's afraid of heights. "What you're forgetting, Lindsey, is that by the time we grab Bakr and get out, it will be pitch dark. You've also forgotten that helicopter traffic is common over Brooklyn and Long Island. At this time of day and as cold as it is, who's going to remember a helicopter flying high overhead—and landing here?"

"Then we're going to use only one?" Chatters thick brows moved with his frown. "Impossible! It can't be done."

"Patience, my boy. Let me finish," Camellion said cheerfully. "We'll use the Lynx to fly to the government reservation. While we're on the way, the boys here can give the Choctaw a quick coat of paint. When we're ready to leave the brickyard, we'll contact the Choctaw back here and it can fly in and pick us up. Wohlwend can fly the Choctaw. One of the regular bird pilots here at the station can fly the Lynx."

"I still say it's all academic," insisted Lindsey. "Mr. Brent will never permit such a wild scheme to be put into action."

"I didn't hear him protesting a little while ago," Pini Hilleli said soberly. "He didn't stop Newheart from going after Wohlwend!"

"Go kiss a hair brush," snapped Lindsey. A few minutes later, he grinned like the Cheshire cat when Courtland Grojean returned to the room, strode purposefully across the thick rug, and scowled at the Death Merchant. "What plan have you worked out? There's one thing—you can't endanger this station."

The Death Mercant outlined his plan, finishing with, "I estimate the danger factor to the station at less than ten percent." He made a sweeping motion with his left hand. "Of course, if you cancel, the danger factor will decrease to zero; however, our chances for finding the nerve gas will have decreased."

There was a long pause, no one speaking. At length, Grojean said in a low, cold voice, "Do it. All the arrangements have been made with the army at Fort Hamilton. You'll land on the parade ground. Major Don Gress, an aide to Colonel Seebley, will meet you."

1809 hours. Richard Camellion, H. L. Kartz, and Pini Hilleli were in the first car, a Firenza SX hatchback, which was being driven by Sergeant Burns. A half block behind was the four-door Buick in which rode Wally Chatters and Virgil Lindsey, both of whom were the Communications Contact. The Death Merchant would contact them by walkie-talkie. In turn, they would contact Applecart D-3KK on a portable shortwave with a band secure against intrusion.

The Buick was driven by another soldier from Fort Hamilton.

Barry Newheart, acting as "Mr. Brent's" deputy, and Henry MacNeill, who had piloted the Westland HAS 2-Lynx, had remained at Fort Hamilton, where Newheart had sworn Sergeant Burns and Corporal Ritter to secrecy, warning them in severe tones that if they ever discussed driving the two cars to anyone— "Even among yourselves or with your families"—they would be little old men by the time they were released from a federal penitentiary.

"We should be there in another five minutes," muttered H. L. Kartz, who was sitting in the rear seat, to Camellion's right.

The Death Merchant didn't reply. Huddled in a gabardine greatcoat with a thick alpaca collar, a felt hat pulled low over his forehead, Camellion reached into a right inside pocket of the coat, pulled out a TEL-6Y walkie-talkie, extended the antenna, turned on the set, and contacted Larry Kosgriv. "Are the subjects still in place?"

Back came Kosgriv's voice. "No change. They are still inside the main building."

Earlier, while still in the Lynx chopper, the Death Merchant had apprised Kosgriv of the situation and of the operation that was about to take place. Camellion now said, "We're in a Firenza hatchback. The others are behind us in a Buick sedan. When you see us, you and the others pull out. Keep in touch with the fruit-of-the-tree base. Confirm, please. Over."

117

"Understood."

Camellion switched off the walkie-talkie, pushed the antenna into its well, and returned the set to his inner coat pocket. He glanced outside. The darkness was complete, the headlights of oncoming cars almost a constant series of large yellow white eyes, the vehicles driven by men and women coming home late from work—driving carefully over the road slick with snow packed as hard as steel. On the narrow parkways, on each side of the road, were tremendous mountains of snow, shoved there by numerous city snowplows. In many places the snow had been piled so high that it partially hid the houses to the rear of the small yards, giving him the weird feeling that he was driving through a tunnel cut through solid snow. The New York City summer and the fall had been extra wet; the winter was now extra cold.

To the right, a streetlight flashed by. Underneath the light, a metal street sign projected from the post—87th Street.

"Sir," Sergeant Burns said nervously to the Death Merchant. "You want me to make a right and go east on Eighty-sixth? Or do you want me to take another route?"

"Right on Eighty-sixth," ordered the Death Merchant. "Drive at normal speed. We don't want to attract attention."

Sergeant Burns then surprised Camellion and the two other men by advising them in a fatherly tone, ". . . to be very careful. That section of Eighty-sixth is run-down and tough. Gowanus Expressway is only five or six blocks to the east and there's some tough bars in the area."

Camellion smiled in amusement. "Thank you, sergeant. We're prepared to give a good account of ourselves in case of trouble."

"Like blow up the sons of bitches," growled H. L. Kartz.

The flow of traffic was heavier on Eighty-sixth Street, but thinned considerably past Fourth Avenue, most of the vehicles either going north or south on Fourth. Past Fourth Avenue on Eighty-sixth, the area was run-down, although the buildings were a far cry from the abandoned wrecks one found in large sections of the Bronx. The commercial buildings, as well as the private dwellings, on the north, or left, side of the street were of a bygone era and of an architecture so common in the 1890s, decorated with a lot of fretting now faded and eroded. In many houses windows on the first and second floors were boarded up. Railings were broken on porches, sidewalks broken and filled with potholes. Fences were in a state of disrepair.

Lombardi's All Night Garage was on the right side of the street, on the corner of Fourth and Eighty-sixth—an old structure as brightly lighted as a Christmas tree. East of the garage was an empty building—low and long—that had once been a restaurant, its front boarded up, drifts of snow piled up around it like dirty whipping cream.

East of the one-time restaurant was the large lot that Larry Kosgriv had described, a dreary place filled with piles of snow-covered junk, including five old automobiles.

Then came the Chalmer Brick Works, a business that was still in operation, even though it was closed during the cold months of the year. To the west was a small building made of concrete blocks and painted what could be gray. The main building was to the east. Shaped like an enormous 7, this building was long, with the horizontal arm facing Eighty-sixth Street, the long rear strung out behind it. West of this long building were square stacks of bricks sitting on wooden pallets and covered with snow. In back of the brickyard was a large open area—a plain of snow, the wind having sculptured the snow into various shapes. In some places the snow was taller than a man; in other sections the wind had blown away the snow so that the hard, frozen ground was almost bare.

Still further east on the right side of Eighty-sixth was the deserted and abandoned lumberyard—an office and display building and three long sheds, the snow piled high on the slanting tin roofs, icicles hanging crookedly from the rusty gutters.

Sergeant Burns was driving the SX hatchback past the brickyard as Camellion switched on the TEL-6Y transceiver and contacted Wally Chatters in the Buick.

"We'll go all the way around the block, and then go east again on Eighty-sixth," Camellion said. "The second time around, we'll get out on the corner of Eighty-seventh and Fifth Avenue—on the northwest corner. We'll wait for you two."

"Why not go down the alley and get out in back of the brickyard," Chatters suggested. "If the snow is too deep for the cars, we can go on foot. It's too risky to go in from the front."

"That's how I have it figured, old buddy—on foot," Camellion said quietly. "The cars might get stuck."

A thin, cold wind blew snow around their legs, and there was an uncanny suggestion of invisible pipes playing an evil tune, one that suggested the terrible sadness that could only come from a city of lonely corpses. Chatters carried the shortwave enclosed in a hard plastic case; it was slightly larger than an attaché case. The Death Merchant's gloved right hand was filled with the handle of a leather case that contained a Noctron V infrared night-vision viewer. Kartz carried a black nylon case filled with two MAC M-10 Ingram submachine guns and eight magazines, four for each SMG. Virgil Lindsey also carried a Noctron V device. Only Pini Hilleli's hands were free.

The five trudged down the alley, moving west, the darkness cloaking them. Yet they could see fairly well, due to background light being reflected from the snow. Walking wasn't all that difficult, only tricky. Large city trucks had been through the alley, and the Death Merchant and the other men walked in the deep ruts. The only danger was that they might slip on the slick, icy surface.

After a time, they paused at the rear of the abandoned lumber-yard and stared at the dark, forbidding buildings that loomed several hundred feet away.

"We can be positive that there aren't any tramps holed up in those sheds," whispered Pini Hilleli, his breath coming out in a fog. "It's too cold." He tightened the hood of his Gore-Tex parka and sighed loudly.

"It's twenty-one degrees above zero," Kartz said. "There was a large thermometer in front of the gas station on the corner. Let's get the damn show on the road, Camellion."

"Yeah, we're going to," Camellion said. "Wally, you and Virgil hole up in one of the lumberyard's sheds. We'll contact you on the walkie-talkie. Just in case we get burned, use your own judgment with calling in the chopper."

Kartz, who had opened the nylon case, took out one of the Ingram SMGs and handed it to Chatters. He then handed the four magazines to Lindsey, who shoved them under his gray Malone pea coat.

"Camellion, you fellows do what you have to do in a hurry," murmured Chatters to the Death Merchant, "or you'll find us nothing but two frozen corpses. It's going to be frigid in that empty lumber shed."

Without another word, Chatters and Lindsey turned and started moving through the snow to the dark lumberyard sheds. Camellion, Kartz, and Hilleli headed northwest toward the rear of the brickyard.

"There must be a watchman," Hilleli said. "In this kind of neighborhood the owners wouldn't leave the buildings unguarded."

"Yes, I've thought about them," Camellion said. "First we have to find them; then we'll do a slip-up-on-them deal."

The three of them stopped halfway to the rear of the main building and Camellion removed the Noctron V night-vision viewer from its case. He put the rubber cup of the instrument to his right eye, adjusted the 25mm/fl. 4 lens and inspected the landscape ahead. Bleak! As lonely looking as an unkept graveyard. Nothing but the wind blowing tiny clouds of snow around the bottom of the buildings and from the roofs.

There's the car that Seleh Bakr came in!

A Ford wagon, the vehicle was parked to the rear of the office.

There weren't any lights in the office.

Something is missing! Something doesn't add up!

"They couldn't be sitting inside in the dark," whispered Hilleli. "Where do you think they are?"

The Death Merchant continued to study the buildings through the Noctron-V device.

H. L. Kartz, who had taken out the other Ingram SMG and had tied the case with its three magazines to his full-length quilted coat, tapped Camellion on the left shoulder. "We're at the wrong angle to see the west side of the long building," he said gruffly. "We'll have to move another eighty feet or so to get the right perspective."

"Keep as low as possible," Camellion advised.

They reached the desired spot five minutes later and snuggled down by the side of a ten-foot square of bricks. Once more the Death Merchant put the Noctron V tube to his eye. *Praise the Lord and kick the Devil!*

A light! A very dim glow to the right of the office, in the front section of the long portion of the building that was perpendicular to Camellion and his two companions.

"We see it," Kartz said, sounding almost human. "If it's where the watchman is, we have it made. We can get in through the office and creep in on him from the west."

"Why the four large chimneys?" inquired Pini Hilleli of no one in particular. "And what're those contraptions on top of them?"

The chimneys, protruding from the roof of the long building, were eight feet square and topped with what appeared to be a kind of metal box.

"Those are the chimneys of the kilns." Camellion didn't remove the night-vision device from his right eye. "Those gizmos on top are smoke filters. We can't have air pollution in the clean, sacred city of New York." Then he quickly lowered the Noctron V tube and carefully shoved it into its case. "Let's get to the rear door of the office."

The Death Merchant was still bothered, burdened with a sense of that which was unfinished. *What did Pini say—'They couldn't be sitting inside in the dark!'*

Cautiously Camellion and the two men with him crept forward, a cold wind blowing the snow around them.

Chapter 12

If the wind blows, it will enter at every crevice!

Thinking of the Arabian proverb, Seleh Bakr felt with a sick heart that the evil wind was blowing directly toward him, and bringing with it a destruction that would shatter his world. For the past few weeks he had often asked himself why he had let his greed overpower his common sense. But he had done just that—months ago, when he had agreed to become a courier for Colonel Qaddafi's people stationed at the United Nations in New York. By the holy breath of Allah, he should never have listened to Akram. Only later had he and Akram learned that the deadly SSD—East German intelligence—was helping Qaddafi accomplish whatever it was he wanted accomplished in the United States.

Bakr knew it was now too late. He knew too much. So did Akram. Neither man knew exactly what the plan invovled. They only knew that something that was extremely destructive was to be smuggled into the United States—and used! An atomic bomb? Bakr and Ndrangheta didn't know. They did know what would happen to them if American intelligence trapped them! They'd be deported. Then their own government would have them shot!

Hot, ill at ease, and uncomfortable in the clay diggings, Bakr was careful to appear relaxed and not to show his fear and resentment of Peter Hinnerich, who had come with him to the brick works, or of the two other East German SSD officers who had arrived earlier in the afternoon. Bakr was positive that all three Germans had demons in their heads. They had to be crazy, as insane as Qaddafi himself! American intelligence was closing in; yet Qaddafi and the East German agents were determined to continue the operation, using the Libyans who had been smuggled into the United States months ago and who had taken refuge in the clay diggings underneath the main building of the brick works. A score of East German agents scattered throughout the eastern and the southeastern portions of the United States would help them. Even at this moment, in this enormous, gloomy cavern of a place, Hinnerich was speaking an insanity that could only lead to the worst kind of destruction. Bakr was convinced that he would be in the center of the catastrophe.

"In spite of the setbacks, we can still achieve success," Peter Hinnerich was saying aggressively. "Within three days the vessel will be close enough to American shores for us to meet her and relieve her of her vital cargo."

Sitting close to an electric heater, Hinnerich turned to Werner Junge, who was seated next to Major Jamsid Anill, a member of the Libyan State Bureau of Security. "Werner, your cover as a French businessman is perfect; and you speak English without any accent. Tomorrow you will make arrangements to fly to Columbia, South Carolina. From Columbia, you can charter a small airplane to take you to Charleston, South Carolina. In that coastal city it will be your job to rent a cabin cruiser large enough to take us out into the Atlantic to meet the vessel."

"When will we know the name of the ship?" asked Major Anill. Dressed in a rumpled gray suit, he was tall for a Libyan, almost six feet.

Hinnerich frowned slightly. Werner Junge and Otto Grotewoll eyed Anill closely—with obvious distaste.

"Major, realize that our first rule, always, is security," Hinnerich said mildly. "Only five persons know the name of the vessel at the present time—Colonel Qaddafi's personal representative, his assistant, and our own two top agents, who are in charge of the operation."

"It's all on a need-to-know basis," interposed Otto Grotewoll smoothly. "There isn't any need for you and the others here to have the name of the vessel. I'm sure you understand."

For a short moment the square-jawed Anill stared at the smooth-faced Grotewoll, who always seemed to be smiling as though he were enjoying a joke that was eternally amusing. The Libyan didn't get a chance to reply. He was getting ready to speak when Werner Junge said, "Major, your job is to supervise the Libyan pilots who will fly the aircraft." He smiled charmingly. "Why ask for information that could endanger that supervision. I'm sure your superiors wouldn't appreciate your curiosity."

Major Anill was positive that Suleiman Maghrabi and Abdullah al-Mansour will take a very dim view of his conduct should the damned East Germans report that he was asking curious questions; and Maghrabi was Qaddafi's representative! Officers who displeased Qaddafi had a habit of vanishing in the desert.

"Very well," Anill said stiffly. "However, where are those planes? Who will obtain them, now that the American CIA is watching the American who was to arrange for us to have them?"

"They might even arrest him while he is still in the hospital," said Abu Akkcam, another Libyan.

"Or kill him!" Azourin Bab, another Libyan, offered.

Seleh Bakr listened to the men talk. He could detect that the Libyans in the underground "cavern" were as uncomfortable as he. They had every right to be. For nine weeks they had been confined in this enormous hole in the ground, taking their rest in sleeping bags, eating their meals out of cans, and sickened with boredom and anxiety.

Nervously, Bakr looked around the mammoth cavity that had been dug from the earth over the years. As a boy in Algeria he had worked at the monotonous task of making bricks, using a method that had been ancient in Africa before the pyramids had been built. Mud and plant fibers were packed into wooden forms and the soft mud baked in the hot sun. That was all there was too it.

Modern methods were different and more efficient. Lumpy clay was dug from the earth and fed into a large crushing machine that broke it up, after which a moving belt carried the crushed clay to another machine that ground it into a fine dust. This dust, properly mixed with water (and sometimes with coloring matter) was then used to make the bricks (the Chalmer Brick Works made four different sizes), which were then put into kilns and heat-hardened for days at a temperature of 2,500 degrees Fahrenheit. Different kinds of clay produced different kinds of color. However, red clay was the most common.

Bakr looked at the uneven walls of the chamber—forty feet

deep, eighty feet long, and sixty feet wide. The upper sections of the clay walls were braced with planks held firmly in place by long iron rods that, crisscrossing each other, stretched from wall to wall, with an iron framework, beginning in the center of the floor and moving upward, supporting them. Only an area ten feet from the floor on three sides, exposed raw clay.

Toward the center of the chamber was the large crusher and its huge "mouth" of a bin. From it a five-foot wide "V" conveyer belt moved upward to the long building above. To the north, or the front of the chamber, wooden steps spiraled upward around a central column constructed of iron rods. On each side of the twisting staircase hung ropes used to raise and lower various pieces of equipment. In the center of the ceiling was the screened, six-foot square air shaft.

Only three Primus propane lanterns were burning, their flames, behind rounded glass, flickering and throwing off monstrous shadows that crawled over the walls and slithered silently into invisibility, making Bakr feel that he was in the bowels of a breathing mausoleum.

Werner Junge was saying to Major Anill, "We'll solve the problem of the aircraft after we meet the vessel—which reminds me!" He turned his attention to Peter Hinnerich. "When will I receive the funds to fly to Charleston and to rent the cabin cruiser? The cost will be considerable. We'll need a large cruiser, one that can withstand the waves of the Atlantic this time of the year."

"I'll turn the money over to you tomorrow at—"

A loud buzzing cut Hinnerich short, the sound coming from a boxlike device fastened to one side of the large clay-crushing machine. A red Christmas-tree-size bulb was also a part of the alarm—and it was blinking on and off.

In that instant, time seemed to suspend itself. As all heads turned to the buzzing and the flashing red light, every man knew that the impossible had happened. An intruder, or intruders, had entered the building upstairs.

Peter Hinnerich jumped to his feet, apprehension skidding all over his fleshy face. "We couldn't have been followed to this place, Bakr and I! We took too many precautions!"

"*Ach*! It's probably some of those black savages who do what they please in this filthy city of mixed races!" hissed Junge, pulling a Walther P-38K autopistol from underneath his suit coat and looking at Major Anill. "Major, have some of your people go upstairs and investigate—hurry!"

Instantly, a worried-looking Jamsid Anill began jabbering in Arabic to the Lybians around him, many of whom understood English only poorly.

Otto Grotewoll, taking a HK PSP autoloader from his over-coat pocket, bit the side of his lower lip and said, "If it's only one or two men the three watchmen should be able to handle them."

"We can't take any chances," Hinnerich said in a small voice. He turned and stared at the spiral stairway.

Seleh Bakr had one thought, and he knew that the other men were thinking the same thing—*Suppose the intruders weren't burglars? Suppose he and Hinnerich had been followed?*

Chapter 13

Those things that can be postponed usually are! Getting into the office of the brick works was another matter. Speed was essential. Speed and expertise is what the Death Merchant used. Using No. 6 lockpick, he opened the Yale lock of the office door in only two minutes and fourteen seconds. Just the same, neither Camellion nor Kartz nor Hilleli felt like dancing a jig of joy. The reason was that Applecart D-3KK had not had any electronic equipment for detecting and "defusing" any possible alarm system.

Acer Scriggs, the chief case officer at Applecart had explained that "This is a special safe house and research center, not a supply depot for your dirty-tricks boys!"

The necessary equipment could have been obtained from a supply unit in Manhattan, but there hadn't been time, unless Camellion & Co. wanted to risk losing the targets at the brick works. The Death Merchant had decided to gamble that the point of entry, either door or window, would not be wired.

Camellion heard the slight click. With Kartz and Hilleli standing behind him—Hilleli with a Star M-PD double-action .45 pistol in his right hand, and Kartz with two Heckler &

Koch VP70Z pistols—Camellion returned the lockpick to its aluminum tube, dropped the tube in the left pocket of his greatcoat, pulled a Safari Arms 81 BP Super MatchMaster autopistol from a left side shoulder holster, then very slowly turned the knob and pushed open the door. A lot of darkness—but no bells rang, no sirens screamed. This lack of sound didn't mean that they were safe. The alarm could be of the "silent" variety.

There was some light in the office, in the form of light reflected from the snow and filtering through the dirty windows. Across the room, to the east, was another door dimly outlined in the semidarkness.

Hilleli whispered, "If there are any watchmen, they have to be beyond that door. If it's locked, how are we going to take them?"

"First things first," replied the Death Merchant. They were only six feet into the office, and Camellion, wanting to make sure he knew exactly where they were going, took out the Noctron V night-vision viewer and casually surveyed the room. He didn't see anything unusual. The office was exactly that—an office. There were desks, filing cabinets, etc. There wasn't sign one of an intrusion detector. He looked at the hardwood floor for signs of a carpeted switching mat. None. He slowly searched the walnut-paneled walls. Nothing. He could not possibly know that high up on the north wall, toward the ceiling, a portion of the paneling had been cut out and cleverly covered with walnut-grained paper filled with holes and that inside the opening was an R7-001 passive infrared motion detector that covered a twenty-five-by-twenty-five-foot area; it was the R7-001 unit that had activated the alarm in the clay-digging chamber.

Down on one knee by the corner of a desk, Camellion put the Noctron V in its case, pulled up his left pant leg, and unstrapped the nine-inch noise suppressor from the back of his leg.

"Where in hell did you get the silencer?" Kartz's whispered voice sounded as if it had been chiseled from granite with grenades.

"I had it in my own kit," Camellion replied, screwing the silencer onto the extra-long barrel of the special 81 BP Super

MatchMaster.[1] "I have two more, but they'll only fit Auto Mags."

Hilleli was breathing heavily from tension. "If it's not the watchmen behind that far door, it could be Seleh Bakr and the man who came with him," he said fiercely, watching Camellion tighten the noise-suppressor tube to the muzzle of the MatchMaster.

"Damn it," snorted Kartz. "We don't even know if there are any watchmen. Take it easy and play this second by second."

"We'll know in a minute or so," the Death Merchant said. "This is just like hunting big game. We either get the target first or it gets us."

Kartz's hard face remained impassive—as usual. Almost never did he reveal his true feelings. Hilleli, however, glanced curiously at the Death Merchant; and he wondered: had he detected a note of enjoyment in Camellion's firm voice?

Getting up, Camellion moved to the door at the east end of the office, Kartz and Hilleli creeping purposefully behind him. Reaching underneath his greatcoat with his left hand, he pulled an air-force type penlight from his leather vest and then—then he remembered, the burst of recall solving the problem of the unfinished business that had been pinpricking one side of his mind. He remembered that one time in Baytown, Texas, he had visited a brickyard with Juan Ortega, a good friend. Juan, the manager of the brick works, had explained that while the clay didn't have to be dug in the yard, it did have to be in close proximity to the works.

There aren't any clay pits or fields in Brooklyn! Camellion told himself. *The clay isn't being dug in the yard. There's only one answer. The diggings are under the building—and that's where Seleh Bakr and the other man are. Whom did they meet?*

[1] The regular MatchMaster has a five-inch barrel for greater accuracy. The Model 81 BP Super has a six-inch barrel. The weapon is built around the frame of a Model 81 BP, but uses a Safari Arms Enforcer slide, this giving even faster cycling than a five-inch slide and allowing more forward weight because of the longer barrel weight and shape. Furthermore, the six-inch barrel utilizes a special screw-in bushing rather than barrel-to-slide fittng. Also, the Super uses an Enforcer recoil spring, which removes all the pressure from the bushing.

The MatchMaster Camellion is using is also special in that it has a seven-inch barrel, permitting the use of a silencer.

He switched the lens of the penlight to red and turned it on. Well now! In the reddish beam he could see that the lock was a heavy-duty electrical lock, a cylindrical lock that operated by an internal electrical solenoid. When the solenoid was released by a switch, the knob could be turned and entry was possible.

"There's only one way to do it," Kartz said hollowly. "If there are guards on the other side, you had better be fast."

"I'll be faster than a hound dog running to his honeymoon!" Camellion said, then did what he had to do. He stood back, lowered the Super MatchMaster, and fired three times, confident that the KTW bullets[2] would almost tear the lock from the wood. At least they would wreck the electrically controlled mechanism.

The noise suppressor made only three *Phyyyttts*. Two of the slugs went into the wood on either side of the lock. There was a loud *CLANG* as the third .45 slug tore through the lock and blew out its center.

The Death Merchant kicked open the door almost as fast as the wrecked tumbler and slide bolt from the lock shot east and narrowly missed Melroy O'Keefe, one of the three watchman who was walking across the room with a mug of coffee in his hand.

Don Barro and Wilford Boyle were at a small table playing checkers.

It was Camellion's third slug, tearing through the lock, that warned the three men, not that it really mattered. Before they even had time to fully comprehend what was happening, the Death Merchant was raising the Super MatchMaster and sighting in on O'Keefe, whom he could see clearly, due to the shaded light above the checkerboard.

Phyyt! The silencer whispered, the MatchMaster jerked, and O'Keefe's thirty years (two months and one week) of life came to a sudden end from the .45 projectile that tore through his chest and heart and streaked out his back. The mug fell from his hand, and O'Keefe started the final fall at the same time that Willy Boyle, starting to push back his chair, his wide eyes on Camellion, caught a KTW bullet in the left side, the slug slicing through his stomach and a portion of his liver, then going bye-bye out his right side.

Don Barro had turned and was halfway to his feet and reach-

---

[2] Armor piercing. A one-piece bullet, either brass or bronze, coated with Teflon.

ing for his holstered Smith & Wesson .38 revolver when the MatchMaster went *Phyyt* again. Instant annihilation! The .45 projectile hit him high in the chest, cut through his esophagus, shattered one of the cervical vertebrae, cut the spinal cord, and flew out his back. Dropping like wet rubber, the dead man crashed onto the table, then rolled to the left to the floor, taking many of the red and the black checkers with him.

By then, Camellion, Kartz, and Hilleli were almost to the center of the room and could see that it was a supply room filled with office supplies, odds and ends, and two toilets, both little rooms to the east. The oil heater was to the north.

Two other doors were in the supply room; they were on the south side. While Kartz went to one door and Hilleli to the other, the Death Merchant reloaded the Super MatchMaster he had just used, then pulled the second MatchMaster from its right-side shoulder holster.

Camellion motioned to Kartz. "Open it," he whispered. He stood to one side as Kartz, on the other side of the door, turned the knob and pushed against the wood with his right foot. Beyond was a shower room, no doubt for the workers of the yard. The shower room possessed two doors, one to the west, the other to the south.

Kartz closed the door, after which he and Camellion stood to either side of the second door that Hilleli shoved open. Darkness! Apparently, beyond the door was the main section of the brick works.

"And now for a newscast from the Near East," whispered Hilleli, the sound of his own voice giving him assurance. "There will not be a plague today in Egypt, although a swarm of locusts were sighted. Some slight fire and brimstone will fall on Sodom and Gomorrah. There will be a parting of the Red Sea tomorrow at promptly four-thirty in the afternoon. Joshua and his jazz band will practice their trumpets before the walls of Jericho this evening—"

"Pini—shut up!" Camellion said easily. "Voices carry. Speak as little as possible." He shoved the MatchMaster without a silencer into an outside pocket of the greatcoat, took out the Noctron V, and carefully searched the area ahead of him. Out on the floor, to his left, were hundreds of wooden forms into which the wet clay was poured. Row upon row, these forms rested one above the other on long shelves made of rods. Between the forms and Camellion and his two men were lift trucks and a variety of jitneys that were used to carry the newly shaped bricks to the four large kilns farther down the floor, to the south. South of the last kiln, he could see the front of some kind of machine. Like everything else, it was covered with clay dust.

Let me see—how are bricks made? How did Juan explain the process to me?

He remembered and realized then that the machine was used to crush the raw clay into a fine powder. That meant a conveyer belt had to be connected to the machine—*And the other end of the belt has to start where the clay is dug.*

He had been right. The diggings were underneath the building. Under this very floor, to the south of the crushing machine!

The Death Merchant suddenly realized that he and Kartz and Hilleli were standing just inside the main work section of the brick works and that since the door was still open, the light from the supply room was behind them. He was about to say, "Close the door," when he saw what he had seen scores of times in the past. Four men came from around the south side of the crushing machine and started to creep north. All four had weapons, with the lead man carrying what appeared to be either an SMG or an assault rifle—a noise suppressor attached to its barrel.

A few moments later, the enemy spotted Camellion, Kurtz, and Hilleli as Camellion yelled, "Down! To the left!"

Kartz and Hilleli reacted instantly—just in the nick of time. Simultaneously, as the Death Merchant threw himself to the left, he snapped off a single shot with the silenced Super MatchMaster, knowing he hadn't hit the man with the SMG when he heard a loud clang. Neither he nor his companions could hear Mahid L'Habisi's Heckler & Koch MP5 SD3 submachine gun[3] spitting out 9mm slugs, most of which shot through the still-open door of the supply room, narrowly missing the oil heater. H. L. Kartz, however, did detect some of the projectiles. He had been standing to Camellion's right and, consequently, was still moving to the left when the Libyan fired the long burst. Yet none of the slugs touched his flesh; they did rip across his back—three of them—and zip through the thick lining of his quilted coat so that cotton padding stuck out from the long cuts.

Two projectiles passed close to Hilleli, between his right arm and his side, but he never knew it. He was too busy seeking safety.

[3] The HK MP5 SD3 comes with silencers built around the barrel.

Camellion got down behind the rear end of a lift truck while Kartz and Hilleli took cover by the sides of large iron pouring pots mounted on rolling frameworks.

"Like the dairyman said," mumbled Hilleli in disgust, "one day it's pure butter, the next day stale margarine."

"No use crying over spilt milk," Camellion said sardonically. "The light in the door, behind us, gave us away. But now they can't see us. We'll be able to see them with the Noctron. We can—"

As if to make him a liar, light suddenly flooded the entire area, coming from dozens of 200-watt bulbs at the end of long twisted cords hanging from crossbeams in the wide ceiling.

Kartz made a disgruntled sound with his mouth. "That does it!" he spit out pessimistically, a dark look falling over his almost gaunt face. "It's a Mexican standoff and we don't have the time to stick around for the outcome."

"You have my permission to leave." There was an amused lilt to the Death Merchant's low voice. "You might get halfway to the door before that music box plays its notes and chops you apart with its quaint melody."

"Screw you, Camellion," Kartz replied caustically. "This was a screwball scheme to begin with and you know it."

The Death Merchant didn't bother to answer. Cautiously, he looked around the rear edge of the lift truck. Kartz and Hilleli peeked from around the sides of the pouring pots. They didn't see any Libyans. They did see that while Camellion's .45 slug had missed Mahid L'Habisi, it hadn't missed three of the steel drums of coloring matter stacked in front of the four kilns against the west wall. The brickyard made bricks of different color that were sold in the spring and summer for patios, barbeque pits, and what-have-you.

Camellion's armor-piercing KTW bullet had bored all the way through both sides of two drums—one filled with blue coloring fluid, the other with bright green—and one side of a third drum, the latter filled with Chinese red liquid. Its power spent, the .45 projectile had dented the inside of the opposite rounded side of the third drum, then had fallen to the bottom. Now, blue and green fluid poured from four holes in two drums, and Chinese red from one opening in the third drum, the colored mess spreading over the floor and glinting oddly in the bright lights.

Hiding among the drums, three of the Libyans cursed in dismay as the liquid flowed around their feet.

Pini Hilleli whispered in a dry voice, "Unless they've retreated, they must be down in those drums. We can't retreat and we can't go forward. Hell! This is as bad as living in Israel!" He pulled the second .45 M-PD Star autopistol from underneath his Gore-Tex parka.

The Death Merchant was quick to notice that while the metal doors of the kilns were open, one seemed to move slightly, the right side door of the kiln at the north end, the one closest to them. The bottom edge of the door was only a few inches from the floor, and Camellion wasn't able to see from the position he occupied if anyone was standing behind the door or if an enemy was there.

He soon found out!

Mahid L'Habisi, guessing that the three Americans had taken refuge in the lift-truck area—where else could they go?—had raced behind the door, to his right, near the first kiln. He and the three other Libyans knew they had surprised the three men to the north and further assumed that killing them would not be difficult.

L'Habisi leaned out from the edge of the door and started to spray the lift-truck area with streams of 9mm projectiles. At the same time, the three other Libyans jumped up from behind the drums and, with their feet sloshing in the colored fluid, started to race forward, keeping to their left to avoid the rain of metal death from L'Habisi's MP5 SD3 submachine gun.

Truncated cone-shaped 9mm slugs popped all over the lift truck behind which Camellion was hunkered and behind two large pouring kettles protecting Hilleli and Kartz. Slugs chipped Bakelite from the steering wheel of the lift truck and thudded into the tires. Ricochets screamed and wailed and made the two kettles ring with loud deep sounds. Besides striking the kettles and the lift truck, slugs passed over and around them, boring into the walls, chopping through thin metal. One 9mm projectile hit the bolt head of a hand truck, glanced off, hit the side of the lift truck protecting Camellion, ricocheted again, and struck Hilleli in the vicinity of the hip. Fortunately, the bullet had exhausted 99 percent of its power, and the parka the Israeli was wearing did the rest. The flattened-out slug ripped through the parka and trapped itself in Hilleli's wool pants. At the time, he didn't even know it was there.

After eight seconds, the Death Merchant got what he wanted:

lag time from Mahid L'Habisi, who had to regroup his thoughts, relax his finger on the trigger of the SMG, and realign the weapon. To Camellion's right the three Libyans—Nihat Orim screaming curses at the Americans (and the one Israeli)—charged forward.

"Now—smoke the dummies!" Camellion snarled at Kartz and Hilleli.

He leaned out from behind the end of the lift truck, to his right, raised the silenced Super MatchMaster, and began firing at the edge of the kiln's door, squeezing the trigger rapidly and placing the slugs six to eight inches apart, four to five feet above the ground.

Phyyt! Phyyt! Phyyt! The first three KTW .45s tore through the door, which was constructed of sheet steel welded to a steel framework. *Phyyt! Phyyt!* The fourth and fifth slugs struck the outside edge of the steel framework and were not able to reach the opposite sides. *Phyyt! Phyyt!* The sixth and seventh projectiles bored through the door as easily as a hot poker burns through a piece of toilet paper. They also burned into Mahid L'Habisi. He was getting ready to lean out and fire around the door when one bullet hit him in the right hip, the slug lodging in the bone, since it had lost a lot of its power cutting through the sheet steel. The other slug caught him just above the belt line and came to a bloody halt in the left end of his spleen. The first five projectiles had missed him.

His world growing dark around him, L'Habisi started to fall forward, the Heckler & Koch submachine gun slipping from his stiffening hands. The Death Merchant was forty-nine feet to the north and, seeing a part of L'Habisi, didn't wait to see whether the man was going to fire or try to fly.

You're a dead man, you damned dunce! Camellion pulled the trigger of the Super MatchMaster at the same instant that Hilleli and Kartz began tossed slugs at the three other Libyans.

Camellion's .45 bullet struck the dying L'Habisi squarely in the right side of his neck and made his head wobble violently as it tore through his throat and rocketed out the left side.

The other three Libyans were in as bad a situation as L'Habisi.

H. L. Kartz had put one of his VP7OZ autopistols on full automatic, and a full clip of 9mm Hornady projectiles, traveling at a standard NATO 1200 fps muzzle velocity, chopped into Nihat Orim, a big Libyan with a long, drooping mustache. Orim let out a short, loud cry, dropped the Czech CZ M 75 pistol, and stopped as though he had crashed into an invisible steel wall. Resembling a broken pretzel, he started the last fall of his life—to the left of Bayin El Korl'l, whom Pini Hilleli had just popped with one of his Star M-PD autoloaders. Like an iron fist, the .45 flat-pointed bullet had banged the Libyan in the chest, the impact pitching him backward.

A happy Kartz terminated the last Libyan, killing Samoud Alaziz with the VP7OZ autoloader in his right hand—two 9mm hollow-pointed slugs that sliced into Alaziz's chest and stomach folded the dying man over and slammed him to the dirty floor—the loud echo of the shots ringing throughout the building.

Instantly, the Death Merchant was on his feet and reloading the MatchMaster to which the silencer was attached. "We have to do it fast," he said calmly. "If those shots were heard and reported, the police will be on their way."

"We're not going to get out of here?" Hilleli's dark eyes went wide.

"I don't like doings thing halfway," said Camellion, his voice as cold as his eyes. "We came to grab Seleh Bakr, and we'll either leave with him alive, or we'll leave him here dead. I'll go first. Keep at least six or eight feet apart."

Time being a precious commodity, the Death Merchant didn't stop to retrieve the Heckler & Koch SMG that Mahid L'Habisi had used. Neither did Kartz. Hilleli did, first rolling over the corpse of L'Habisi to see if the dead man had a spare clip. The Libyan had, stuffed in his belt. Only then, after he pulled out the magazine, did Hilleli pick up the submachine gun. By then, the colored liquid was only three feet from the SMG. Running after Kartz and the Death Merchant, Hilleli pulled out the empty magazine, thrust in the fully loaded one, pulled back the cocking knob, and sent a cartridge into the firing chamber.

Camellion, a fully loaded MatchMaster in each hand, was geared for battle. He raced past the fourth kiln and came to the tall, dirty machine that was a Venderbix Nine Cycle Grinder, whose job was to crush the broken-up clay into a fine powder. Fifteen feet to one side of the machine—to the south—was the north end of the diggings, the ceiling composed of boards laid loosely over a framework of rods. There was, however, a six-foot space between the four edges of the diggings and the first boards of the ceiling. In the center of the loosely boarded ceiling was the metal air shaft that rose up to, then through, the ceiling of the main building.

From the top of the south side of the Grinder the wide "V" conveyer belt moved steeply down through the roof over the digging chamber, the belt disappearing into a square hole thirty-five feet from the side of the tall grinding machine.

Camellion didn't really have time to see any of this. He had raced past the last kiln and was moving east when he almost collided with three Libyans hurrying west who had just come off the stairs whose top was below the slanting conveyer belt.

Only Faruk Khalelli, slightly to the Death Merchant's right, had a weapon in his hand, a 9mm Beretta Brigadier pistol. Suleyman Dimirrel and Ahbu Zehdi, not expecting trouble to pop up in front of them, still had their sidearms holstered, although Zehdi carried a Czech Samopal Skorpion SMG.

Mercy, mercy, Mother Percy. I have a problem! Very quickly Camellion swung the Super MatchMasters. He succeeded with only the silenced autopistol because Faruk Khalelli was still six feet away from him and was too astonished to think clearly. The silencer whispered once and an even greater look of surprise crossed Khalelli's broad face. He blinked once, his eyes rolled back, and his knees started to buckle. A normal reaction! A .45 bullet had zipped through the aortic arch, above the heart, and had then zipped out his back.

Ahbu Zehdi and Suleyman Dimirrel were closer to the Death Merchant than Khalelli, who lay on his back, blood flowing slower and slower from his slack mouth. Dimirrel, almost directly in front of the Death Merchant, grabbed the rounded tube of the noise suppressor with his left hand while the fingers of his right hand closed around Camellion's right wrist. He then did his best to twist the MatchMaster and its noise suppressor from Camellion's firm hold—and his best was very good. Dimirrel weighed 194 pounds and was as strong as two young camels in their prime.

Crooked-nosed Ahbu Zehdi (he had once been kicked in the face by a goat) reacted even faster than Suleyman Dimirrel. His huge left hand shot out, his strong fingers becoming a vise around Camellion's left wrist, and, as he began to twist the Death Merchant's wrist to his right, he succeeded in turning the muzzle of the MatchMaster away from him. At the same time, Zehdi started to bring the Skorpion SMG around; in a few more seconds he'd be able to shove the muzzle of the short barrel against Camellion's left side and excavate part of his torso with 9mm projectiles.

The pressure of Zehdi's left hand forced Camellion's finger against the wide trigger of the MatchMaster and the weapon roared, but the big solid slug missed Zehdi by almost three feet. Grunting like an excited pig, Zehdi stopped swinging up the Skorpion and concentrated on the MatchMaster, twisting with all his might. He became more confident when he succeeded, when Camellion's fingers were forced open and the pistol fell to the floor.

Zehdi's elation, however, vanished when the Death Merchant, doing the unexpected, let him have a Tang Soo Do karate left-legged front thrust kick, Camellion's foot crashing into the Libyan's solar plexus with such force that the toe almost touched the backbone.

It's impossible to hold onto a man's wrist when your liver, stomach, and thoracic ganglia have been mashed to a bloody pulp. Shock raced up Zehdi's spinal cord and exploded in his brain, his body rigid as though it had just been sprayed with liquid air. He gasped loudly. The Czech submachine gun dropped from his hand and fell to the floor. The fingers of his left hand relaxed around Camellion's left wrist. Instantly, the Death Merchant jerked his arm away and speared Zehdi in the throat with a *Yon Hon Nukite* four-finger spear stab—so fast that his hand and arm were only a blur. Gasping and gurgling, Ahbu Zehdi started to go down, unconscious and dying before his body hit the floor.

Suleyman Dimirrel twisted the silenced MatchMaster from Camellion's right hand, but he didn't have time to be happy about it. All he had done was free the Death Merchant's right hand, which was every bit as deadly as his left hand.

Dimirrel didn't even have time to formulate a new plan of attack. The Death Merchant attacked with a double motion—a right-handed Shito-Ryu karate *Seiken* forefist that crashed against the bridge of Dimirrel's nose at the same time that the left-handed *Ni Hon Nukite* two-finger spear stab caught the Libyan below the Adam's apple. The forefist had dimmed Dimirrel's consciousness and the two-finger stab smashed the trachea. With great choking sounds sliding from his mouth, Dimirrel started to sink to his knees, dropping the MatchMaster with its noise suppressor.

Camellion, about to reach down and pick up his two MatchMasters, heard H. L. Kartz's frantic voice—to his left rear, from the vicinity of the southwest corner of the fourth kiln:

"CAMELLION! *DROP!*"

Kartz had seen what the Death Merchant—his eyes down toward his MatchMaster on the floor—had not seen: three Libyans had just come off the spiral stairs whose top opening, under the conveyer belt, was in the north center of the clay-digging chamber.

Labib Mogazbi, the first Libyan, was raising an East German example of a Soviet Makarov self-loading pistol and about to put several 9mm slugs into Camellion. He didn't succeed. Kartz cut loose with his two Heckler & Koch VP7OZ autopistols, the two weapons roaring and spitting out 9mm hollow-nosed projectiles.

At the exact time that Kartz fired, Mogazbi's finger pulled the trigger of the Makarov, the sharp crack of the weapon blending in with the louder reports of Kartz's VP7OZs. Yet Mogazbi's 9mm bullet was wasted. Camellion had dropped the instant he had heard Kartz's voice and the bullet whizzed four inches over his head.

Kartz didn't miss. Like Camellion, he seldom did. His first two hardball slugs hit Mogazbi in the chest and slammed him back, his feet and legs doing a rapid little dance as Beniel Kibir and Lakhdar Saherin tried vainly to pull their pistols, Kibir armed with a SIG-Sauer P230 autoloader, Saherin with an Egyptian Tokagypt autopistol. Kartz's 9mm projectiles rained all over Kibir and Saherin, killing the two Libyans before their fingers could close around the butts of their weapons.

Now realizing what had happened, the Death Merchant didn't bother to pick up his two MatchMasters. Instead, while on one knee, he reached over to his left, grabbed the Czech Skorpion that Ahbu Zehdi had dropped, and swung the submachine gun toward the opening of the top of the steps that led down into the digging chamber. There was always the possibility that more Libyans were coming up. More than a possibility! It was fact.

Camellion caught sight of the side of a man and fired, the little Skorpion chattering, the blast of slugs catching Azourin Bab, whom Major Jamsid Anill had sent upstairs with orders to assess the situation. The short burst was more than effective. Nine projectiles popped Bab in the left side of the chest and blew him apart. With bits of his coat fluttering to the floor, the corpse fell backward and came to a halt—eight feet later—when its feet and arms became wedged inside the wide metal mesh of the railing on the outside of the stairway.

Only when Kartz was beside him and covering the steps with his two VP7OZ pistols did Camellion put down the Skorpion and pick up his MatchMasters.

"I owe you one, H. L.," Camellion drawled good-naturedly. "Shucks, you're good enough to take up police work, or"—he chuckled—"maybe be a 'private contractor' and work for the Company."

As usual, Kartz was a total stranger to humor. Reloading his two Heckler & Koch pistols, he glanced at Pini Hilleli, who had reached him and Camellion, and said to the Death Merchant, "They're down there. How do we get them to come up? Don't even hint that we might go down those steps. I'm not being paid to commit suicide."

The Death Merchant looked past Kartz at Hilleli. "Pini, get on your TEL and contact Wally and Virgil. Have them call Applecart and get the chopper in here. Tell them to have Roy Wohlwend contact us when he gets here—say, when he's still a thousand feet overhead."

Hilleli nodded and reached inside his parka for the TEL-6Y walkie-talkie.

Still facing the steps to the clay-digging chamber, Camellion, from the corner of his eyes, saw Kartz holster his VP7OZ pistols and unclip the little MAC M-10 Ingram SMG from the nylon case tied to his quilted coat.

"Time is pressing," Camellion said in a practical voice. "All I can think of is to frighten them into coming out. We've already put eleven to sleep forever. There can't be that many more down there. Bakr and the other joker have to be among them. Any suggestions?"

He listened to the subdued conversation between Hilleli and Wally Chatters and heard Chatters say, "We have it—over. And damn! We're frozen!"

Kartz sounded as mournful as he looked. "Negative. We don't have grenades. We sure as hell can't get them out with just this." He held out the MAC SMG. "This single chatterbox won't help us any with the police, not against the high-powered rifles of the SWAT boys. Let's face it. We've failed. Whoever is down with Bakr can tell us to shove it."

"How about fire, say gasoline?" Hilleli's question took the Death Merchant and Kartz by surprise. Having finished contacting Chatters and Lindsey, Pini was shoving the walkie-talkie into his parka.

Camellion became alert. "What do you mean?"

Hilleli burst into agitated speech. "I noticed a hundred-gallon drum of gasoline by the drums of colored stuff. The drum was

139

marked GASOLINE. I don't know if there's any gas in it. There were also some gallon cans stacked close by, the kind with the pull-out spouts.''

"The lift trucks run on gasoline," the Death Merchant said thoughtfully, turning over possibilities in his mind. "Tell you what, Pini. Go see if the large drum has gas. If it has, fill two of the gallon cans—and bring two empty cans."

"As good as done," Hilleli said cheerfully. Turning, he ran toward the rows of coloring drums to the north.

"And if the drum is empty?" Kartz was totally pessimistic. He had lighted a cigarette and smoke curled upward from his nostrils.

"Then we do the only thing we can do—leave!" Camellion intoned. "And God help the American people. This is the last chance we've got."

"You know how it is," Kartz growled. "Cast your bread upon the waters and you'll get a soggy sandwich every time."

Pini Hilleli returned a very short time later, two empty gallon cans under his arms, pressed against his sides, two red metal cans in his hands. From the way he carried them, Camellion and Hilleli could see that they were full. They could also see that he had stuffed oily rags into the side pockets of his parka.

A self-satisfied smile on his sharp-featured face, Hilleli put down the four cans. "If we had some oil, we could make some genuine Molotov cocktails."

"We want to frighten them, not fry them," Camellion said, thinking that one quart of exploded gasoline—*Should have the force of about nine sticks of commercial dynamite. But we'll have to allow for air space. Two quarts to each gallon can should be about right!*

Each gallon can was almost half full of gasoline. The screw-on spouts had been taken off and the openings stuffed with oily rags, a foot-long "wick" hanging down from the top of each can. With Hilleli and Kartz in secure positions by the Venderbix Nine Cycle Grinder, where they could easily terminate anyone who came up the stairs, the Death Merchant went to work. If his plan failed, there was a good chance that 20 million Americans would be dead from VXB nerve gas within several weeks, perhaps even sooner.

If that happens, I'll personally kill Qaddafi, provided I'm not one of the corpses!

140

Seleh Bakr and the three East Germans, crouched by the clay-crushing machine, knew that everything was wrong upstairs. But they didn't know the source of the trouble. Other than Bakr and the three German *Staatssicherheitsdienst* intelligence agents, there were only three Libyans left in the clay-digging chamber— Major Jamsid Anill, Abu Akkcam and Ahmed Behir, all three as nervous as a college freshman on his first visit to a house of ill repute. They were positive in their own minds that all the other men were either dead or prisoners of—who? All that firing— and then Bab had been killed! There he lay, sprawled out dead, thirty feet up on the stairs.

Major Anill's low voice broke the strange silence. "Better to die than to let them capture us!" He stared toward the stairs. "We'd be in disgrace in the homeland."

Peter Hinnerich looked long and hard at the grim faces of Werner Junge and Otto Grotewoll, whose faces were dotted with sweat. All three knew that Major Anill might have been speaking for them too. Yet the prospect of dying did not appeal to them. Even so, what could they do? The only way out was surrender— unthinkable!

A harsh voice suddenly called down from the northeast corner of the ceiling: "EITHER SURRENDER NOW OR WE'LL BURN YOU TO DEATH. YOU HAVE TO THE COUNT OF TWO TO DECIDE. ONE! TWO! WHAT'S YOUR ANSWER?"

Cursing in Arabic, Major Anill raised the Skorpion SMG and sprayed a long burst in the direction of the voice, the loud chattering of the weapon reverberating through the large chamber.

Anill and the others were still smelling burnt gunpowder and listening to the echoes of the exploded cartridges when they saw something on fire drop through the opening in the ceiling to the north, from the northeast corner. Whatever it was, the blazing object struck the floor and exploded with a roar that sounded like one hundred shotguns going off. There was a rolling ball of bright flame, some twenty feet in diameter, followed by burning gasoline splashing over a large area of the east and north walls and an even larger section of the floor. None of the fire, however, touched the stairs.

"*Mein Gott!*" gasped Peter Hinnerich, holding the barrel of his SIG-Sauer pistol upward. "The swine meant what he said. We must do something."

"We can only surrender," Otto Grotewoll said in a small,

resigned voice. "We are the rats in a hole in the ground. The Americans are the catchers."

With some of the other men, he looked fearfully around the chamber, which now was dancing with more dark shadows generated by the burning gasoline.

Seleh Bakr said nervously, his voice trembling, "Enough fire down here, even if it doesn't touch us, will eat up the oxygen. We'll smother to death."

Bakr jerked slightly when Camellion again called down, this time from the southeast corner of the eighty-foot-long chamber.

"WE HAVE ALL NIGHT AND PLENTY OF GAS. AND GRENADES ARE ON THE WAY. HERE'S ANOTHER BIG HOTFOOT FOR YOU QADDAFI-LOVING SONS OF BITCHES!"

Automatically, Bakr, Peter Hinnerich, and the two other East Germans moved from the east side of the crushing machine, stepping to the west side with the three Libyans.

Nothing happened. No can of gasoline and its burning greasy-rag wick fell toward the floor.

Several minutes passed. Major Anill, constantly scanning the ceiling, walked slowly back and forth. Ahmed Behir and Abu Akkcam had moved away from the three Primus lanterns, somehow feeling that there was safety in distance from the lights. Constantly looking upward, they had moved to the vicinity of the southwest corner of the chamber.

"ABOVE YOU!" yelled Seleh Bakr.

"WATCH OUT!" shouted Otto Grotewoll.

Akkcam and Behir caught only a glimpse of the flaming can as it fell, and tried to run, strange animal sounds pouring from their throats.

Time for their final dream time! Neither man had a chance to escape the half-gallon of gasoline that the Death Merchant dropped. Wanting to confuse the enemy, he had hurried around to the southwest, had lighted the rag, and without a word of warning had thrown the can downward . . .

WWEEEERRROOOOMMMMMMM! The burning ball of gasoline expanded, part of it splashing over the heads and backs of Abu Akkcam and Ahmed Behir, both of whom shrieked in hideous agony and began frantically beating at themselves with their hands, all the while screaming. The fire soon pulled the air from the lungs of the two Libyans and they stopped screaming and fell to the floor. By now, their clothes were blazing fiercely, and the fire giving off the familiar odor of burning cloth and the sweet pork smell of flesh being barbecued.

His hands trembling only slightly, Major Anill lowered his Skorpion SMG and put a three-round burst into each corpse. Purposefully then, he strode to Peter Hinnerich and the two other East German agents and a terrified Seleh Bakr.

Hinnerich, his SIG-Sauer hanging loose in his right hand, felt appalled at the look of fierce hatred on Major Anill's sweaty face. He had seen that look before—the maniacal look of a fanatic, the look of a man who was more than willing to commit suicide and take everyone else with him. *Nein*! Not this day!

For the past ten minutes, Hinnerich had been thinking along purely practical lines. Remaining in the clay-digging chamber was nonsense. To remain meant certain death. The only way out was to surrender. All three Germans had diplomatic immunity. They would be sent back to East Germany. And Mischa Wolf would promptly demote them and have them charged with treason as punishment for their failure, or else make their lives so miserable that they would wish they had died in the chamber. Would it not be better to obtain political asylum in America? Hinnerich further reasoned that with the information he had about the nerve gas, plus his knowledge of the East German intelligence service, he could be an asset to the Central Intelligence Agency. Junge and Grotewoll? Hinnerich knew they were survivalists whose thinking was similar to his.

"We will charge up the steps!" announced Major Anill in a loud voice. "We will die fighting for our cause. I will lead the way."

Peter Hinnerich raised his SIG-Sauer autopistol and shot Anill twice in the chest. Anill blinked in total astonishment at Hinnerich for a single moment, then dropped.

"That idiot! What 'cause'?" mumbled Otto Grotewoll.

His face expressionless, Hinnerich turned the SIG-Sauer to Seleh Bakr, who threw up his hands, a look of horror on his face. "W-Wait! I—"

Twice the SIG-Sauer cracked, the 9mm slugs hitting the Algerian in the chest, the impact pushing him back against the side of the clay-crushing machine. Slowly, his eyes still open, he started to slide to the floor. His hind end hadn't touched the floor before Werner Junge was yelling at the top of his lungs—"AMERICANS! WE GIVE UP! WE SURRENDER!"

*   *   *

Right behind Hilleli and Kartz, the Death Merchant watched them escort the three East Germans out the office entrance of the brick works, the three SSD agents holding their hands on top of their heads.

At least we won't have to snuff any innocent bluecoats.

Roy Wohlwend had contacted H. L. Kartz by radio while the Death Merchant was throwing cans of gasoline into the clay chamber, and advised him that he and Camellion, Chatters and Lindsey would not have to concern themselves with the Brooklyn police—that "Mr. Brent has seen to it that there won't be any interference from the police."

Grojean must have pulled a hundred big wires to get the High Brass to even hint to 'civilians' that a national security operation was taking place!

Outside the office building the cold stung his face and the wind, which had quickened, blew snow around his feet. Ironic! They had crept in like burglars, but now were leaving as conquerors!

A hundred feet ahead and to the right the Sikorsky S-58 Choctaw helicopter rested in an area the wind had swept clean of snow, Wohlwend idling its rotor. Spotlights from the chopper illuminated the area, and he could see Wally Chatters and Virgil Lindsey waiting by the port-side door.

Camellion smiled. The men at Applecart had painted the chopper *pink!*

Chapter 14

It is said than an individual can never develop his full potential if pressure, tension, and discipline are taken out of his life. On this basis, the Death Merchant and the members of the Blue 15 network were rapidly developing their latent talents.

Ever since Richard Camellion had returned to the safe house outside Amityville, Long Island, and the three Germans had talked their heads off, there had been frantic planning. At the time, Courtland Grojean and the Central Intelligence Agency were not interested in the internal structure of the East German *Staatssicherheitsdienst*. CIA specialists would question Hinnerich,

Junge, and Grotewoll for months at Langley; the three would be given a series of polygraph tests and subjected to narcohypnosis.

Now it was the information divulged by Peter Hinnerich that was of prime importance. The name of the vessel carrying the deadly VXB-2L6 nerve gas was the *Prinz Rupert*, a cargo ship of East German registry. Her next port of call was New York City, then on to Halifax in Nova Scotia. But the plan of the SSD was not to remove the nerve gas from the *Prinz Rupert* in New York or, for that matter, while the ship was docked in Halifax. Mischa Wolf and Qaddafi's plan called for a method that was far more secure. A cabin cruiser would meet the *Prinz Rupert* two hundred miles southeast of Charleston, South Carolina. The canisters of gas would be transported to the cabin cruiser, which would deliver the canned death to American shores. The helpful Hinnerich, who flatly stated he wanted political asylum, had even written down the coordinates where the cruiser would meet the *Prinz Rupert*.

Question: Would the *Prinz Rupert* continue on its way or turn back for East Germany?

Problem: The vessel was legally on the high seas. Therefore, the vessel was legally outside United States' jurisdiction. To attack and board the vessel would be an act of international piracy. The United Nations? Forget it. It was either board the *Prinz Rupert* or let the vessel go on its way.

The Higher Authority in Washington, D.C., would have to decide.

By 2100 hours of the following morning that Higher Authority had made its decision. A TP[1] coded message was flashed from Langley Central to Applecart D-3KK: *Find the Prinz Rupert, board the vessel, obtain the canisters of nerve gas, and bring them to the United States. Terminate everyone on board the ship, then sink it.*

"I'll be a dirty name," Camellion said half under his breath when Grojean gave him the message within the privacy of a small, soundproof conference room. Only Camellion and Grojean were in the room. "Here we have murder by the throat; yet the President of the United States wants us to bring back the gas—great!"

"Don't blame the President," Grojean said, somewhat hesi-

---

[1] Top Priority.

145

tantly. "He and his political hacks don't know about the *Prinz Rupert*." The spy chief got up from the corner of the desk on which he had been half sitting and stepped closer to Camellion. "You know as well as I that there are some situations too vital, too important, to be entrusted to politicians, even to the President of the United States. After you cut past all the hoopla, the reality is that our President is nothing more than an elected executive whose first duty is to his political party. He'll be told when it's over with. If he had been told last night, he'd still be discussing it next week. This decision had to be made by trained people."

"The military—the Joint Chiefs" Camellion said, a knowing look in his odd blue eyes.

Grojean gave the Death Merchant a mock frown of disapproval. "You didn't hear me say that!"

"I didn't have to. Two and two always add up to four."

"Let's go and give the others the news," Grojean said and turned toward the door.

Hannibal Llewellyn Kartz, hunched over a table, pouring blackberry brandy into a mug half full of hot coffee, shook his head. "I think it's doing it the hard way," he said in his flinty voice. "Why board the ship and try to get the gas when the navy could sink the Kraut boat?" He looked up from the table at Grojean and Camellion, both of whom were leaning over another table, studying a large nautical chart with Barry Newheart, Virgil Lindsey, and Duane Halverson. The five men didn't look back.

"It makes a lot of sense, not having the navy sink the ship." Maurice Ehlers, sitting in a big easy chair close to Kartz, screwed his face together to shift his eyeglasses into position on his small nose. "Suppose the gas leaked out before the ship hit bottom?"

"Bullshit!" sneered Kartz. "Five or six missiles would blow the ship and the gas to kingdom come and back.

"Oh, it should be comparatively easy to board the ship from a chopper," remarked Pini Hilleli, leaning back comfortably on a couch. "After all, it's not as though they had a lot of big stuff to throw at us. The choppers can blow it half apart before we get aboard!"

Kartz stirred the coffee and brandy. "The Chinese have a saying: All the flowers of tomorrow are in the seeds of today.

That means that tomorrow on the Atlantic is going to be all stinkweed for us. Wait and see, my Israeli friend."

Hilleli turned his attention to the table where Virgil Lindsey was tapping a spot on the chart with the tip of a pencil. "Right here is where the *Prinz Rupert* should be at 1000 hours tomorrow morning. That will place the *Prinz Rupert* exactly one hundred ninety-six miles[2] southeast of Charleston. I mean exactly!" He straightened up and looked from Grojean to Camellion. "Of course, that's predicated on the assumption that she will hold her present course and that the vessel the *Tiger Shark* is shadowing is the *Prinz Rupert*."

"It's the *Prinz Rupert*," Grojean affirmed. "Commander Pearl is an experienced submarine commander. If he says he has located the *Prinz Rupert*, he has—period."

"In that case there's no problem," said Lindsey.

"Where will the position of the ship be tomorrow morning," began Camellion, "if her captain turned back this morning?"

"Why should the captain return to East Germany?" demanded Grojean, frowning at the Death Merchant. The other men at the table glanced questioningly at "Mr. Brent." Surely, he hadn't forgotten? He wasn't old enough to be senile.

The Death Merchant knew perfectly well why Grojean had asked the question: he always thought more efficiently when he heard an answer he already knew repeated.

The Death Merchant said, "Hinnerich swears that he was to have a conference this morning with the head agent of the SSD in this country. When Hinnerich, Junge, and Grotewell didn't arrive at the New York Public Library, Gunther Flegel had to assume they'd been natted. He must now formulate plans around the dismal fact that not only have his three main agents been taken, but the Libyan pilots as well. That puts a bit X on the delivery system of the nerve gas. Flegel and Qaddafi's two head honchos have to know the mission has fallen apart."

"What does all that have to do with the *Prinz Rupert?*" Grojean looked rather grimly at the Death Merchant. "Legally the vessel is on the high seas. Flegel and Halbritter and Qaddafi's two big sand fleas know we can't touch the *Prinz Rupert* any more than we would dare attack a Soviet naval vessel."

"Flegel, all the East German agents, and the two Libyan

---

[2] The international nautical or air mile is equal to 1,852 meters, or 6,076.115 feet.

hotshots are stranded in this country—so what?'' Duane Halverson's big elastic mouth twitched. They know we'll—or rather the FBI—will be watching all the major airports and harbors. But that still wouldn't be any reason for the *Prinz Rupert* to do an about-face to Germany.''

Pini Hilleli moved in closer to the table, saying, ''I think all of you—you too, Mr. Brent—are missing Richard's point.''

Virgil Lindsey's eyes blazed. ''I suppose you haven't?''

''Flegel knows that we know all the details of the plot,'' Hilleli went on urgently. ''A plot that could cause the death of millions! And we know where the gas is—only two hundred miles from American shores! Yet we're supposed to sit here and do nothing about it! Flegel is going to think differently. He's going to reason that Uncle Sam will be going after the *Prinz Rupert*—which we are!''

A lot of eyes stared at Hilleli—and at the Death Merchant.

Hilleli moved his tongue inside his lower lip, then walked away to the Mr. Coffee machine. Camellion met the eyes candidly, saying, ''Flegel might also reason that the *Prinz Rupert* would be easy transportation back to East Germany. He can't trust the airports now that we are on to him. Other than himself and Halbritter and the two Libyans, he has thirty SSD agents to worry about; and Wolf is noted for taking care of his agents. He doesn't work by halves.''

Grojean said mechanically, ''How would you say Colonel Flegel might accomplish this task of rapid evacuation? He wouldn't dare try at Charleston. Overall, however—''

''And he wouldn't try to fly his people out!'' Barry Newheart said quickly.

''—Flegel wouldn't have much difficulty finding a boat somewhere along the northern coast,'' Grojean continued in a pleasant manner. ''Only we'll reach the vessel before he does. The navy patrol boats shouldn't have any trouble picking up him and his people.''

''I think you're wrong, Mr. Brent,'' Camellion said airily, folding his arms. ''Flegel expects us to hit the *Prinz Rupert*. He knows he can't reach the vessel in time with a motor launch. He'll fly. He'll fly out to the *Prinz Rupert* in one or two choppers.''

Grojean thought for a moment. ''I suppose it's possible,'' he remarked sourly. ''Let's think it out. We know that Hinnerich is desperate for asylum. It isn't likely that he lied to us. We can, on that somewhat fragile basis, work on the premise that there are thirty-three people, other than Colonel Gunther Flegel, who want to leave this country.''

''He could have made arrangements to fly to the West Coast or the Middle West,'' offered Virgil Lindsey. ''I don't find that a bit farfetched. He certainly has a plan of escape in mind.''

''That's reasonable,'' agreed Grojean, his steady gaze asking the Death Merchant to continue.

Camellion did. ''If I were Flegel, I'd have two escape plans laid out. One would be flights from commercial airliners leaving New York. The route could be to the Middle West or the West. But why do it the hard way. One could fly straight to Europe from John F. Kennedy International.''

''Flegel wouldn't dare try that now,'' jumped in Halverson, who was wiping his glasses. ''He knows the FBI is watching all international flights. That's standard procedure.''

Camellion held up a restraining hand. ''Exactly. For that reason he would rely on his own transportation, and not only in case something went wrong and he couldn't take commercial flights. This time of the year there's the weather to be considered. All flights could be grounded. Put yourself in Flegel's place. You'd have a couple of helicopters stashed somewhere months in advance of when you'd need them. The birds would have to be Westland Sea Kings, Sikorsky Sea Stallions, or some variant, birds that have a long range—five hundred to six hundred miles. And that, gentlemen, is how I think Flegel and Friends will get to the *Prinz Rupert*.''

He glanced from face to face, waiting for comments.

Lindsey toyed with a Navigaide Course Protractor, the tiny spinning wheels of his mind reflected in his thoughtful eyes. ''Well—let's say that Flegel had two—we'll make the copters Sea Kings. Say he had two Sea Kings stashed somewhere in the greater New York City area.'' He made some rapid calculations, using the protractor and a pencil. At length he looked up. ''We find it's from eight to nine hundred miles from New York to where the *Prinz Rupert* is right now—and that's only one way. Oh, it wouldn't be much of a problem to put down halfway and refuel. Even so, the pilots would have to make the return and—''

Lindsey stopped, realization flooding his face.

Camellion finished for him. ''You got it, sport! Who said the choppers had to return? The pilots could hover about the *Rupert*,

149

discharge their cargos, then sit down on the ocean, if the waves weren't too high. Then they could sink both birds. No problem."

Grojean peered solemnly at the Death Merchant. "We hardly have the time to check with every manufacturer of helicopters. Even if we did have the time, it would take months to uncover the chain of fronts the East Germans used in acquiring the crafts."

Barry Newheart cleared his throat. "Sir, I think we shouldn't lose track of the fact that all this helicopter business is pure conjecture. We don't have one iota of evidence. Hinnerich blabbed his head off, but he didn't say anything about any helicopters."

"Newheart, someone should put your head in a vise!"

Camellion, Grojean, and the other men at the table turned and stared at H. L. Kartz, Newheart and Lindsey glaring at him.

"By the time all you career people decide on a way to read the enemy's mind," Kartz said laconically, "the Krauts will have finished what they intended to do. I suggest you listen to Camellion and do it his way, or you're going to end up holding an empty sack and wondering why you weren't invited to the dance."

Camellion and Grojean smiled; Kartz had spoken the truth and both men knew it.

Insulted and feeling foolish, Newheart almost shouted at Kartz, who was pouring more brandy into the mug, "We 'professional people,' as you call us, don't need advice from a damned mercenary who puts money and himself ahead of the American people. Furthermore—"

Kartz actually laughed—a sort of HO-HO-HO that rolled up from his belly. "Cupcake, you got it all wrong. Because of taxes I have to think of the dear American people! As a member of the great middle class, I help feed the poor, I help pay the taxes the rich don't have to pay, and I also help educate the brats of all the millions of 'undocumented workers' who shouldn't be here in the first place."

"All courtesy of the U.S. Supreme Court," Maurice Ehlers said, a bitter note in his voice. "It's too bad that Qaddafi isn't trying to blow up those nine damned dictators. I'd wish him luck!"

Before anyone could verbally jump on Ehlers, Kartz sneered, "What Camellion is telling you dunce-heads is that Colonel Flegel was dumb enough to tell Hinnerich all the details of his escape plans."

"He did tell Hinnerich that there was a definite plan A and a plan B. the first to escape the nerve gas when it was being spread, the second for a general escape if something went wrong," Newheart said stiffly, staring angrily at Kartz.

"Yeah he did, and Hinnerich admitted it," Kartz shot back. "Any fool knows why the boss Kraut didn't tell that slimy Hinnerich any more than he had to: Flegel wasn't going to let anyone or anything endanger his own escape route. Flegel only told Hinnerich the name of the ship because it was vital that Hinnerich tell the Libyans at the proper time. It's that uncomplicated."

Courtland Grojean had opened the top of a box of Benson & Hedges 100s. "Mr. Kartz is correct, gentlemen," he said, staring down at the tightly packed cigarettes. He looked up, his gray eyes falling on Newheart and Lindsey. Both men wore expressions that reminded one of a blank granite tombstone. Duane Halverson merely looked stunned.

"We're going to proceed on the basis that Colonel Flegel and his agents are going to fly to the *Prinz Rupert* in helicopters. If Camellion is correct with his theory, we'll bag all of them at the vessel. If he's wrong, no harm done. We'll still have the ship and the gas."

"I suppose you still want the location of the vessel," Lindsey said acidulously to Camellion, "where it will be tomorrow if she turns around today?"

"Affirmative." Camellion sounded sardonic, "although it's not that important. Whichever way the *Prinz Rupert* heads, *Tiger Shark* will keep us posted." He swung to Grojean. "What's the latest on the weather. That's one enemy we can't beat."

Grojean took one of the cigarettes out of the box and called over to Kartz, "Mr. Kartz, considering what the Agency is paying you and if you're not too drunk and if it's not too inconvenient, could you find the energy to get your butt to room Six and ask Jensen for an update on tomorrow's weather in sector Eighteen C?"

"I think I might be able to accommodate you, Mr. Brent." Kartz got up and, without giving anyone a second look, left the room. He didn't stagger.

"It's unfortunate that we have to employ such discreditable mercenary types," remarked Halverson, wrinkling his nose as if smelling something disagreeable.

"Careful, my peacockish friend," Camellion warned, yet his

151

tone was pleasant, "or I might forget my extreme humility and tie your arms in a knot around your neck. I'm also one of those disreputable *condottiere*—a 'discreditable mercenary.' "

Halverson glared furiously at the Death Merchant, his eyes burning with smoldering resentment; finally he looked away.

H. L. Kartz returned shortly, handed Grojean a folded sheet of green paper, and remarked, "It's all bad news. Like I said, it's going to be one big crop of stinkweed tomorrow."

Grojean spread the sheet on the table and, with the other men, leaned down. The sheet was from a Teletype and was a report direct from the U.S. Weather Bureau. The report did not make anyone's heart jump with joy.

A cold front was rapidly approaching from Canada. Prediction for the polar maritime[3] in sector 18C: from thirty degrees to forty degrees longitude: scattered high cumulous clouds within six hours, followed by low stratus over land and water—all within a five hundred-kilometer fan sweep from Charleston, South Carolina. A low temperature from five to ten degrees Fahrenheit. Wind-chill factor of forty to fifty below zero Fahrenheit. The waves of the Atlantic would be rough—Beaufort Scale Force 6. Speed: twenty-two to twenty-seven knots.

It was the last line of the weather report that annoyed the Death Merchant: An 80 percent possibility of snow mixed with sleet.

Halverson drew a deep breath, his sun-flecked eyes staring at the sheet of paper. Newheart cleared his throat and fumbled for his pipe and tobacco pouch in the left side pocket of his blue hopsack blazer.

At length, Virgil Lindsey commented, "Getting aboard the *Prinz Rupert* from a helicopter is going to be rather sticky-wicket under such conditions. If the deck of the vessel is coated with ice . . ." He let his voice trail off and looked from Newheart to Halverson and Grojean.

"Sleet or sunshine, it won't make any difference to you," the

---

[3] Has to do with air masses. Weathermen who were searching for traits in weather found in their records great periodic flows of certain kinds of air. By comparing their qualities and sources, they were found to be cold from the north, warm from the south, wet from the sea, and dry from the inland; and they were tagged P for *polar* (cold), T for *tropical* (warm), M for *maritime* (wet), and C for *continental* (dry).

Death Merchant said. "You won't be there. Only men trained in firefight operations will be visiting the *Prinz Rupert*. That means the SF-One[4] boys, Kartz, Chatters, Hilleli, and I. The rest of you can stay here and hope—and pray, if you're so inclined.

Neither Newheart, Halverson, nor Lindsey said anything. All three tried to keep their faces expressionless; yet Camellion detected that all three were relieved. He didn't blame them. No man in his right mind wanted to grab a tiger by the tail—*Unless he's being paid plenty of tax-free dollars to do it, is a bit nutty, and loves to play chess with Fate.*

Camellion then let them have an unexpected verbal right cross.

"You see, gentlemen, we 'discreditable mercenary types' do earn our money."

Courtland Grojean chuckled and snubbed out his cigarette in an ashtray on the table. Halverson, Lindsey, and Newheart were saved from looking too foolish by Roland Marissa, who got up from the radio table, walked over to Grojean, and silently handed him a slip of paper.

"Excuse me, men." Grojean read the message that was from Langley Central. It had been black-boxed, triple-scrambled, and the computer had silently decoded it. After reading the message, Grojean smiled and handed the paper to Camellion. It read:

Flippers and four birds have arrived at designated point. Long John waiting at naval base. Reply time of your arrival with crates.

Camellion handed the paper to the man closest to him—Virgil Lindsey. *Flippers* were the twenty-man force of SEAL commandos. *Four birds* were the attack helicopters. The *designated point* was the U.S. Naval Base in North Charleston, six miles northwest of Charleston, South Carolina. *And we're the "crates!"*

"Gentlemen, we'll take off for Charleston in exactly six hours," Grojean said exuberantly, moving back from the table.

"It's too bad that such a thing as Communism exists in the world," Virgil Lindsey said philosophically, starting to fold the nautical chart. "If it weren't for Marxism, there would be peace in the world."

"You've forgotten the Arabs and the Israelis," Newheart

---

[4] Seal Force 1.

reminded him. "There will never be peace between them; the hatred is too deep, too ingrained."

Duane Halverson shrugged his shoulders. "Look at it another way. If it weren't for the Commies, we'd be out of a job. We wouldn't know the difference because we'd be doing something else. Personally, I can't imagine a United States without the Agency."

"You're missing the most important point of all," Camellion put forth. "The Communists are a vast help to the forces that shape history and civilization."

Even Grojean, sensing that Camellion was serious, gave him an odd look. "I fail to see the logic of that statement," he said.

The Death Merchant gave him the answer. "A vital factor of civilization is that it moves forward because of those who oppose it." He stretched to relieve the tightness of the muscles in his neck. "I'm going to catch up on my sleep. Wake me when it's time to go to Mac Airport."[5]

Camellion turned and left the conference room, hoping that the navy technicals had followed his advice with three of the attack helicopters.

Chapter 15

Through the porthole of the upper deck, Colonel Gunther Flegel saw that the swells were heavy. A hard northwesterly wind had come up only several hours ago and the sky was overcast, a solid sheet of dirty, dull lead. The temperature had dropped rapidly, and with the decline had come snow, large flakes, so that the *Prinz Rupert* seemed to be stuck in a universe of cotton. Then had come the sleet. The spray froze upon the ship and gave bow, sides, and decking a heavy coat of mail. The water ceased to drop and trickle from the cargo booms and the windows of the superstructure, and the spray came in solely at the well in the afterpart of the ship. Flegel could see through the late-afternoon twilight that the large whitecapped waves, stung by the wind, rolled and tumbled as if angry, as if trying to decide what to do. The water pounded the cargo ship, increasing its roll and pitch so that every

---

[5] Long Island MacArthur Airport in South Central Long Island.

154

now and then, objects on tables slid a few inches, first one way and then another. The *Prinz Rupert* carried a cargo of leather hides, textiles, and pipe fittings—all securely braced in the holds.

Letting his body go with the movement of the vessel, Flegel felt almost happy as he watched the rough waves rise and fall and the wind pick up and scatter the water. *Ja!* Such weather would make the *Amerikaner* have second thoughts about attacking.

Flegel turned from the porthole and made his way unsteadily up the steps of the boat deck. It was only 1630 hours, but lights burned in the superstructure because of the heavy gloom outside the ship. Once on the bridge deck, the SSD officer hurried past the generator room and started for Captain Smoelter's office, thinking of how fortunate he and Manfred and the others had been. The instant he had realized that American authorities had closed in on the brickyard, he had sent the emergency order to the SSD "illegals" scattered throughout the greater New York City area[1]—Collect at point b-z, per arrangement of escape plan. By chartered aircraft the SSD men, including Flegel, Halbritter, Abdullah al-Mansour, and Suleiman Maghrabi, had flown to Columbia, South Carolina. Then on to Dentsville, only a short distance away, to where the two Sikorsky Sea King helicopters, with their oversized fuel tanks, had been stored on a farm owned by an American but rented by one of the SSD agents. Even as they had started flying out over the Atlantic, afraid that they might be forced down by either U.S. Coast Guard or U.S. Air Force choppers, the wind had quickened, the wind that had preceded the cold front that was arriving earlier than expected. It was all that Heinrich Reinner and Karl Bergner could do, using every ounce of their piloting skill, to hover the Sea Kings over the more than slightly pitching *Prinz Rupert* as the men crawled down chain ladders to the deck below. It had been an even greater risk for the seamen of the vessel to pick up Bergner and Reinner after they had set down the two birds in the rough water. Once the two men were away from the helicopters, small explosive charges in the crafts were detonated by remote control and the two choppers sent to the bottom.

In spite of the total failure of Plan Y, Flegel felt that he and

[1] The New York City area is perfect for "illegals" from other nations. We use the term *illegals* to refer only to foreign agents. NYC is truly the ethnic melting pot of the nation.

the others had been blessed with exceptional luck, fantastic fortune. *Ach!* To have reached the two helicopters with such speed, and in such weather, although the elements in South Carolina had not been tempestuous. There had been half-clear skies and only moderate wind. The truly rough weather hadn't started until they were in the helicopters and headed out over the Atlantic.

Damned Americans! It had all been very costly, the American pilots, feeling they had the "foreign businessmen" at a complete disadvantage, charging triple for the chartered flights from New York to Columbia.

Flegel came to the captain's office, knocked on the door, and soon was inside, seated in a comfortable chair and drinking English whiskey with Captain Smoelter, who was worried and didn't try to conceal his deep concern for the safety of his vessel. Only forty-four years old, he nevertheless had a very wrinkled face and small brown eyes that seemed to be set too far apart in his long head. While not a member of the East German intelligence apparatus, he was, on this voyage, under the control of Marcus "Mischa" Wolf, the deadly chief of the *Staatssicherheitsdienst*. He had not had a choice. In East Germany no one ever has a choice. When the State screams JUMP, the good citizen shouts HOW HIGH?

"Herr Flegel, this is an extreme situation," insisted Ludwig Smoelter. "I myself can't conceive of the Americans attacking us on the high seas. Such an act would be total piracy." He leaned forward on his chair and did not put the glass in his right hand on the desk, afraid that if he did, the movement of the vessel would spill the contents. "Yet the Americans know that this vessel carries the nerve gas—the means to kill millions of them. At best, they are an ill-mannered, arrogant people. I tell you, they will attack!"

Flegel took a sip of whiskey, leaned back, and, holding the glass with both hands, lowered it to his lap. To Captain Smoelter he presented a face of confidence he didn't really have.

Now that he had reached the *Prinz Rupert* and was safe—for the time being—Flegel had time to think about Director Wolf's reaction and whom he would blame for the failure of Plan Y. The answer was obvious. Colonel Gunther Flegel was in charge of Plan Y. Colonel Gunther Flegel would get the blame—unless he was very lucky. One thing in his favor was that he and Mischa were good friends. It might not be too difficult to convince Mischa that the failure involved nonhuman factors—a chain of unforeseen circumstances that had enabled the American Central Intelligence Agency to drop the net. After all, it was Qaddafi's own "Protective Bureau of the Sacred Nation" that had generated the major mistake. It was not Flegel's fault or the inefficiency of the SSD that has placed Quamar Boutesi, the assistant chief of the *Al Naqui-zam'i Mir-iza*, in the pay of the CIA!

"Captain, I don't feel that the Americans will bother us," Flegel said with vast cordiality. "They realize that the plan has failed, that we no longer have the means to deliver the gas."

Captain Smoelter frowned. "How can you be certain?"

Flegel laughed bitterly. "The only reason the Americans would come after us now would be revenge. Fortunately for us, the Americans aren't that practical. They are too wrapped up with fair play, human rights, and all the rest of the nonsense that has turned their society into a jungle of self-interest groups. *Nein*, I do not think the Americans will bother this ship, captain."

Far from being convinced, Captain Smoelter finished his whiskey with a quick, nervous gulp. He got up, went over to a filing cabinet, opened the top drawer, took out a bottle of whiskey, and, moving back and forth slightly with the sway of the ship, refilled his glass.

Turning, he looked questioningly at Flegel and said, "Our course must be changed. To dock in New York would be a mistake. The Americans would impound the vessel."

"*Ja*, that's true," Flegel said heartily. "We're not going to make the port in Canada either. I suggest you call the chart room and tell your officer there to plot a course that will take us back to the homeland. What was the last report from radar?"

Captain Smoelter sat back down at his desk. "There's another vessel forty-eight kilometers ahead of us. Otherwise, we're alone in this section of the ocean."

While somewhat relieved that the *Prinz Rupert* would be turning back, Smoelter still felt uneasy. Before the vessel had begun its voyage a large number of weapons had been brought aboard, scores of Soviet PPS *Machinenpistoles*[2] and even several ShKAS light machine guns—". . . as a preliminary measure," the SSD agent who had come aboard with the weapons had

---

[2] This is the Soviet submachine gun *Pistolet-Pulemyot Sudaeva*, which takes a 7.62mm round. The magazine holds thirty-five rounds.

explained. And if Flegel was actually positive that the Americans would not attack, why had he ordered the guns distributed to his men and to the members of the crew?

"I'll contact the chart room," Smoelter said. He turned for his left and reached for the button of the communicator attached to the wall. Before he could press the button the speaker gave a loud BEEP and the agitated voice of Kurt Meninger, the first officer, said, "Captain, answer, please."

"What is it, Kurt?"

Meninger replied, "You had better get up here to the wheelhouse, captain. We might be in for serious trouble. Radar has picked up four objects. One is a vessel. It's twenty-four kilometers to the northwest. The other three are aircraft. They're moving too slow to be American fighter jets or commercial aircraft. They're thirty-six kils away to the northwest. All four are coming straight at us. What are your orders—in case they attack us?"

Captain Smoelter, feeling as if someone had hammered a bolt into his skull, turned and, stunned, glared at Colonel Gunther Flegel, who had paled.

Chapter 16

With the deep throbbing of the RH-53 Sea Stallion's two turboshaft engines beating in rhythm against his ears, the Death Merchant mused that everything and everybody had some use— *Even the dime! It's not worthless in spite of inflation. In an emergency it makes a good screwdriver. H. L. has a big mouth and no tact, but on missions like this one, he's invaluable. And an expert killer is what it takes.*

Ever since the Sikorsky Sea Stallion had lifted off from the naval station, Kartz had been in a heated debate with Daren Givens over Israel, Kartz maintaining that the Israelis were ruthless assassins who murdered innocent Arabs, men, women, and children—that "There are many thoughtful Jews—in Israel and in the U.S.—who feel that the wrong damn bunch is running Israel these days, whipping up hatred for the Arabs that is more typical of the most primitive political systems of the Middle East and not at all characteristic of the hopes of the majority of Zionists who struggled to establish and build Israel.''

Sergeant Givens, a young, husky blond who was pro-Israel, maintained stoutly that the Israelis—''They're three million surrounded by one hundred million—had a moral right to defend themselves, that ''What the hell do you think we Americans would do if the Mexes were firing at us from across the Texas border? You know what we'd do! We'd go into chili-land and make short work of the greasers!''

Neither Camellion nor Captain Glen W. Griffith, the commander of the ten SEAL Force 1 antiterrorist commandos, intervened. Why should they? Kartz and Givens were grown men. Besides, the loud discussion—with Kartz moving his arms like the blades of a windmill in a strong wind—within the partially soundproof chopper took the minds of the other men off the deadly danger into which they were flying.

''You don't seem to consider what Yasir Arafat and the PLO have sworn to do!'' Givens yelled at Kartz, who was sitting across the aisle. ''Push every Israeli into the sea. And that means kill every Israeli! It was the PLO that blew up a busfull of Israeli children. What the hell do you expect the Israelis to do, send the sonsabitches a thank-you note?''

''Don't worry! The Israelis got even,'' sneered Kartz. ''Last summer when they invaded Lebanon, they killed ten thousand civilians and created more than half a million homeless refugees. They even used cluster bombs on civilians. This doesn't surprise anyone who knows Ariel Sharon, who led the Israeli force. He's a tyrant who intimidates even that little runt Begin!''

''I think Sharon is a damned good general,'' ground out Givens. He sure beat the piss out of the PLO and the Syrians.''

''He's also a sadist. He's the joker who ordered his troops to snuff twelve Arabs in retaliation for the murder of an Israeli woman and her two children. After twelve were gunned down, Sadist Sharon still wasn't satisfied, so he had forty-six Arab houses blown up while the Arabs were still inside. Sixty-nine Arabs were killed, most of them women and children.[1] Need I say more about Israel's defense minister?''

''Make your point! Make your point!''

''I'm saying that what happened months ago in Lebanon can easily be understood when one realizes that Begin and Sharon

[1] True—this took place in 1953

159

believe that pure violence can destroy an idea and terrorize a people—in this case the Palestinians."

Sergeant Givens thought for a moment and hooked his thumbs over the pouched cartridge belt around his waist. Then he said, "I suppose you'll say next that the PLO hasn't been killing innocent Israelis! What about that?"

"I didn't say that," growled Kartz. "Hell yes the Arabs knock off Israelis—and that's murder. But they don't kill on the scale that the Israelis kill. Killing is Menachem Begin's trademark! His savage record goes all the way back to the 1940s, when a group of prominent American Jews wrote a letter protesting Begin's visit to the U.S. He was then the leader of some Jewish party in Palestine. I forget the magazine the letter appeared in.[2] But it was Begin and his terrorist group that blew up the King David Hotel—almost a hundred people were killed—and ordered terrorist assaults on Arab villages, including the massacre at Dar Yasin."[3]

All this time, Pini Hilleli had stayed out of the discussion

---

[2] True. On December 4, 1948, the *New York Times* ran a letter signed by twenty-eight of America's most respected Jews, including Albert Einstein, Sidney Hook, and Rabbi Jessurun Cardozo. The letter protested the visit of Menachem Begin, then leader of the Herut party, described as *"closely akin in its organization, methods, political philosophy and social appeal to the Nazi and Fascist parties."* The signers were worried that Begin would collect money and support, thus creating the impression that *"a large segment of America supports Fascist elements in Israel."* The signers cited Begin's terrorist acts and espousal of *"ultra-nationalism, religious mysticism and racial superiority."* (Italics mine.)

[3] True. The massacre occurred April 10, 1948. Dar Yasin was an Arab village whose residents lived on good terms with Jews. But Begin's Irgun terrorists wanted to occupy Dar Yasin for strategic purposes. The terrorists, led by Begin, attacked with rifles, machine guns, grenades, and even cutlasses—later seen dripping with blood.

Some 241 men, women, and children were butchered. Twenty men were led off in chains and actually paraded like cattle through Jerusalem's Jewish sector, then lined up against a wall and shot.

Begin later bragged that the horror at Dar Yasin caused seven hundred thousand Arabs to flee Palestine. British historian Arnold Toynbee had something else to say. He said the mass murders were "comparable to crimes committed against Jews by the Nazis."

between Kartz and Sergeant Givens. Now he said, unexpectedly, "As a former Israeli, sergeant, I can tell you that he's right about Begin. Only several years ago, Begin wrote in an Israeli magazine that the slaughter at Dar Yasin was not only justified but necessary, that without it there would never have been a state of Israel!"

"Exactly," Kartz said with satisfaction. "And now Begin and Sharon—his chief 'hit man'—are slaughtering thousands of Arab civilians to crush the Palestinian spirit, the same kind of spirit that fires up Zionists like them."

"Begin's logic is really fascinating," Hilleli said, grinning as if he were about to tell a joke. "If an Israeli shoots up Jerusalem's Dome of the Rock Mosque and kills Arabs—well, he's crazy. But no nation bombed Israel for it! On the other hand, if an Arab gunman kills an Israeli, then U.S. supplied Israeli bombers rain cluster-bomb death on Lebanon. No insult intended toward you men, but the biggest suckers are you Americans!"

Kartz's grin was from ear to ear.

Sergeant Givens made an angry face. "How do you figure that?"

"Look what Begin did right after his army finished with blowing hell out of Lebanon. He flew to Washington and demanded that the record 1980 two-and-a-half billion-dollar aid to Israel be upped to three billion. Begin makes you American taxpayers pay twice—first for Israel's brutal assault on Lebanon and then for the relief of Lebanon's suffering people. You should ask your Congress who runs this nation—Begin or the Reagan administration?"

Kartz leaned out and looked down the aisle toward where Camellion was sitting on the starboard side. "Camellion, you've been strangely silent the past ten minutes. Surely you must have an opinion—or do you consider yourself a good friend of the Israelis?"

The Death Merchant was far too clever to permit Kartz to pick an argument with him. He merely said, "When I reflect that three million Israelis are surrounded by one hundred million Arabs, I think of what a wise Chinese said when China was invaded by Japan. He said that the more populous China would win. He explained that in the first month, ten thousand Chinese would be killed and only one thousand Japanese. Soon it would be one hundred thousand Chinese and ten thousand Japanese.

After some years, after millions had died on both sides, there would be no more Japanese and the Chinese would have survived."

The pilot's voice ended the possibility of Kartz jumping into the act again—"Eleven minutes to the target."

"I'll be glad when we're down and aboard that Kraut tub," mumbled Oscar Hyink. "I always get half airsick on flights like this."

Captain Griffith didn't have to remind the ten SEAL Force 1 commandos to check their equipment. The ten commandos in the chopper, plus the other nine commandos in another Sea Stallion, were all pros; all ninteen had been ready since the moment they had stepped into the two birds—and so had the Death Merchant, Kartz, Hilleli, and Chatters. Nonetheless, each man gave himself a brief inspection—Colt (XM177E2) Commando submachine gun (actually a shortened AR-15 rifle with a telescoping butt), 9mm Browning Hi-Power autopistol, spare magazines and clips were where they should be. There were no grenades. Camellion and Captain Griffith had decided that within the closed confines belowdecks, grenades could be as dangerous to their own men as to the enemy.

Not this day! The Cosmic Lord of Death is with me, not against me!

As calm as old concrete, Camellion leaned back and relaxed against the padded rear of the bench and calculated the chances for success. The odds were all with SEAL Force 1—*At least for stopping the Prinz Rupert. Finding the special canisters of nerve gas is another ball of bitter butter.*

Thus far, everything had worked out well, better than he had even expected—*Considering the dumb ding-dongs we have in the services these days!* One of the problems with the Sikorsky Sea Stallions had been their total lack of armament. The three helicopters were training craft for rescue-at-sea operations and as such did not need or carry weapons. The three choppers were equipped with IR selector heads that picked up infrared light, this accomplished, in part, by a low-light TV camera that picked up background light and amplified it.

There were no pods containing Vulcan gatlings or miniguns, not a single weapon controlled by a silent electronic brain presided over by the pilot.

While still at Applecart, Courtland Grojean had used the shortwave to contact his special projects officer at the North Charleston, South Carolina, Naval Base. The reply was that the armament outfitters would do their best, provided the weapons arrived in time from Andrews AFB, California. If the weapons did not arrive in time, the Death Merchant's suggestion would have to be ignored. The three choppers would then be armed with .50 caliber heavy Browning machine guns.

Success! Arriving at the naval base, the Death Merchant and the rest of the men were pleased to find that they would have more than .50 calibers with which to attack the *Prinz Rupert*. Originally, there had been four helicopters, but weapons had arrived for only three. The two Sikorskys that would carry the force had a six-barrelled XM 134 7.62mm minigun that could be fired from the starboard cargo opening. The third Sea Stallion had a minigun on the port side. The 7.62mm was a light machine gun, but it fired at 6,000 rounds per minute. The third chopper also had a 40mm cannon mounted starboard. An awkward, graceless-looking weapon, it could fire one hundred per minute and could make junk out of anything it hit.

The plan of attack was simple, based on gunship[4] tactics used in Vietnam, flying around and around the target and blowing hell out of it. The three choppers would first clear the decks of the *Prinz Rupert* and demolish the superstructure as much as possible, after which two of the birds would hover as low as possible over the forward decks and discharge its cargo of commandos.

Diesel powered, the *Prinz Rupert* was a cargo ship, her basic design of the full scantling type, with a raked stem, cruiser stern, a single screw, and a balanced rudder. The second deck was continuous throughout, the nine bulkheads all extending to the upper deck and dividing the vessel into five cargo holds, fore and aft peak tanks, and three deep tanks. The two diesels and the rest of the propelling machinery were located in a single mid-ships compartment. The fuel-oil tanks were located in the sides

---

[4] The first of the gunships in Nam was Puff the Magic Dragon, also called SPOOK. This was a C-47 transport. SPOOK was followed by the improved SPECTRE, a four engine AC-130A cargo plane. It carried a 105mm howitzer that poked out of the left fuselage—port. The biggest gun ever mounted in any aircraft anywhere, the 105 was a terrible weapon. A round for it weighed forty-seven pounds. Further forward was a 40mm cannon. Still further forward was a pair of seven-barrel 20mm Vulcan Gatling guns firing 2,500 rounds per minutes. Last were two 7.62 miniguns.

of the ship. Number of the crew: seamen and officers—seventy-two.

Again the pilot's voice came through the speaker: "The approach will be in two minutes."

By then, U.S. Air Force gunners, borrowed from Edwards AFB, had opened the starboard cargo doors on all three Sea Stallions and had swung the miniguns into firing position. On the third chopper a gunner in protective harness had opened the port door and was at the long-barrelled 40mm cannon, ready to start throwing armor-piercing projectiles at the superstructure and the main deck of the *Prinz Rupert*. Two of the helicopters had flexible steel-cable ladders—sixty feet long—in boxes bolted to the floor on the port side, two ladders per bird.

"It's damn near time to do it," muttered one commando, securing his helmet.

"I'll be happy when we're on deck," said another man. "Getting down the ladder is going to be more difficult than a Sioux manhood ritual." He zipped the collar of his all-weather nylon-polyester coveralls as protection against the bitter cold blowing in through the open cargo doors, the piercing chill intensified by the strong wind and the forward rush of the gunship. He was, however, grateful that the flight had been short and that the altitude hadn't been any higher than fifteen hundred feet. At high altitudes there were all sorts of things to worry about—hyperventilation, nitrogen narcosis, hypoxia, and other ailments.

Through the small windows of the three Sea Stallions—what there were of them—and the open cargo doors, the Death Merchant and most of the men could see the swirling dark waters of the Atlantic, four hundred feet below, a maelstrom of water that was a giant surging plain of agitated swells breaking into smaller waves with white-topped crests.

They saw the *Prinz Rupert*. Her bow pointed northwest, she rode well in the water, well but sluggishly because of the ice that coated her masts, decks, hull, and superstructure. Due to the background light and the phosphorescent content of the water, the vessel appeared to be a ship of ice, an eerie kind of glistening ghost ship from some demented half-world.

While the two Sikorskys containing the SEAL Force 1 commandos hung back a fifth of a mile from the vessel, the gunship with the 40mm cannon went in for the first run. The pilot crossed the bird a thousand feet astern of the ship, then came in fast to rake the *Prinz Rupert's* starboard side. The gunner began firing when the chopper was horizontal to the after deckhouse, the 40mm cannon roaring, each projectile flashing when it struck the vessel.

Zing! Whump! Whang! Clonk! Scores of 40mm rounds stabbed into the starboard side of the after deckhouse, the two stern booms, and the smoke pipe.

Zrump! Zrump! Zrump! The wide funnel quivered and vibrated from the impact of the big projectiles. A lifeboat hanging from davits on the boat deck was reduced to instant kindling. Windows on the boat deck, the upper deck, and the bridge deck exploded into millions of pieces of ice-covered glass.

After going through the windows and the thin metal sides of the superstructure, the armor-piercing tungsten-carbide-cored rounds, traveling at a velocity of 2,330 fps, achieved incredible destruction in the interior of the ship. The chief engineer's office, the chief mate's quarters, the second and third mates' spaces, showers and toilets were ripped by the big slugs. Yet not a drop of blood was spilled. Captain Ludwig Smoelter and Colonel Gunther Flegel, anticipating such action, had ordered all the men below—except those in the wheelhouse.

On the bridge deck the chart room, radio room, and captain's office and quarters were wrecked by the armor-piercing projectiles.

The wheelhouse was turned into a slaughterhouse.

In the wheelhouse there was only the helmsman, Kurt Meninger, and the two SSD men who were among those "illegals" who had come aboard with Colonel Flegel, each intelligence agent behind a Soviet ShKAS light machine gun that protruded forward from several open windows of the wheelhouse.

There could be only one place where any helicopter could hover and let down troops—over the foredeck, to the rear of the forecastle. Accordingly, the two light machine guns in the wheelhouse were positioned so that they could sweep the foredeck and the chopper with hundreds of slugs. The only thing that Colonel Flegel hadn't counted on was the terrible firepower of the Americans.

Half a hundred 40mm projectiles hit the top and the starboard side of the wheelhouse. It took only 29.2 seconds—and it was all one long, loud, disagreeable sound. The shattering of glass, the projectiles tearing through the openings, the walls, and the ceiling, then slaughtering the two SSD agents behind the light MGs; another series of thid-thid-thid-thids as the helmsman was chopped apart; and loud WHANGGGGS as projectiles struck the LMGs and spun them crookedly on their makeshift mounts. Then the rain of death was past and 40mm projectiles were bombarding the forward masts and the booms and zipping through the covers of the first and second hatches.

First Officer Meninger got to his knees, looked around, and felt his stomach turn over in revulsion. The compartment was blood splattered. Globs of the helmsman's brain were plastered over the magnetic steering compass, hanging there like some invader from space. The two SSD agents had been cut apart, their blood slowly creeping across the floor.

The Sea Stallion gunship crossed in front of the bow of the *Prinz Rupert* and began raking the port side of the cargo vessel. Projectiles slammed into the winches of the booms and almost demolished the winch-operator platform of the second boom. Once more the wheelhouse and the port side of the superstructure were subjected to the torment from hundreds of 40mm projectiles. Again the stern booms and the after deckhouse were bathed in metal rain, the gunner paying particular attention to the after deckhouse, in which was the after steering station.

Finishing its run, the gunship veered to the right and revved up to several hundred feet, making room for the second helicopter. Since its XM 134 minigun was starboard, the chopper went in on the port side of the vessel, which, while still moving, was off course, its bow starting to move in a wide circle.

Watching, the Death Merchant was quick to realize that if the waves had been hurricane size, the vessel would have rolled over, since she was riding in the troughs instead of crossing them. As it was, the waves were only rough and the troughs were small, weather that was perfect for the Death Merchant— *Only slightly stormy. Then again, if the waves were being lifted and tossed back by a hurricane, we wouldn't be here!*

Camellion felt excellent, like a man who had just won a million-dollar lottery. And for more reasons than one. The *McCall*, a U.S. Navy PCER,[5] had made radio contact and reported that she was standing by a mile and a half to the west.

There was another reason, the biggest of all: he immensely enjoyed what he was doing. He was not alone in his love of excitement. Kartz and Chatters, Hilleli and—to a certain extent— the SEAL commandos were the kind of men fascinated by death-dealing machinery. All very normal—for them. Normal because

[5] A rescue escort vessel.

166

there are those men and women who love danger, who find violence and death fascinating. Some become professional mercenaries. Or stuntmen. Or drive racing cars. Always they live in the fast lane, skating barefooted on the cutting edge of life's razor blade.

To the Death Merchant it was the same kind of feeling as fighting a chopped Harley, a death bike with a suicide stick because it has an overbore and too much cam—*And that's what a chopper gunship is—the ultimate outlaw bike.*

Courtland Grojean would not share such a feeling. He was of a different type. Grojean was of the breed who pry and probe, who are dominated by a passion to discover hidden secrets. Those people number in the millions. Most are just plain gossips. Others become involved with law enforcement.

Or become executives in intelligence organizations.

The Fox was also a natural-born worrier and pessimist. At the moment, he would be pacing the floor at the naval station, where he and the other professional spooks were waiting. Raymond "Buster" Dyye, the pilot of the chopper in which Camellion was riding, had reported to Grojean when the three Sikorskys had arrived at the scene. An "independent operator," Dyye would again report to the Fox after the operation was completed.

The second gunship began firing, its minigun making one long *BRRRRRRRRRRRRRRRRRRRRRRR*, the six barrels revolving rapidly and vomiting 7.62mm projectiles at the rate of 6,000 rounds per minute. It was a fire stream so incredibly rapid that pilots in Vietnam referred to the flow of steel from a minigun as a "death ray."

That ray now swept the port side of the *Prinz Rupert*—main deck and superstructure, the gunner being very attentive as to where he fired, making sure that the tidal wave of death flowed only through already shot-out windows and portholes. The 40mm stuff could easily pierce the light metal sides of the superstructure; 7.62mm projectiles could not. Thus, the gunner directed his gush of metal only at openings. After all, why waste precious ammo?

Then the gunship, having raked the port side, crossed the bow of the *Prinz Rupert*, banked, turned, and began directing the death ray at the starboard side.

"Sort of beautiful, isn't it?" said Wasil Rid, one of the commandos seated to Camellion's right. "When you think about

167

it, it kind of makes you think you're chipping away at colored ice!''

Camellion smiled faintly at Rid's comparison. Rid was accurate. Each gunship carried a powerful searchlight, mounted under the cockpit, the light controlled by the pilot or copilot. As the gunship moved slowly around the *Prinz Rupert*, the powerful white beam made the ice coating the vessel glisten with color, with radiating whites and blues and quick flashes of reds and greens and gold, tossed out from prisms formed within the thicker portions of the ice.

The gunship completed its brief run and lifted away, to wait as the third and the last Sea Stallion did its job.

Buster Dyye's voice bounced out of the speaker of the intercom. ''Hang on. We're going in. Enjoy the show.''

Down went the Sea Stallion, rapidly losing altitude and banking steeply to starboard, the gunner at the minigun bracing himself, the commandos gripping handholds extra firmly.

Hanging on for dear life, Camellion and the men who could see through the starboard side cargo opening saw the *Prinz Rupert* growing larger and larger, as if rising up to meet them. They knew that the gunship was moving from the sensation of pull, of the ''tug'' that made them feel they might be lifted from the bench and shoved to port.

Quickly Dyye had the big bird at an altitude of only 75 feet and 300 feet to the port side of the *Prinz Rupert*, which was still slowly turning in a circle—but now with a difference. Now it was without purpose, as if she were drifting—*Which means that her engines could have been shut down—maybe!*

The stern of the vessel loomed large and the gunner at the minigun opened fire, one long, roaring *BBBRRRRRRRRRRRRRR-RRRRRRRRRRRRRRRRRRR*. The vibration of the exploding cartridges making the gunship shudder slightly.

''Well good God, Gertie!'' said one commando, shouting to make himself heard above the roaring of the terrible weapon and the *clank-clank-clank-clank* of shell casings hitting the floor, dozens a second. ''At least we don't have to worry about any Triple-A[6] when we board the target.''

It was the same old story all over again, with thousands of 7.62mm slugs hosing both sides of the ship. But after the bird had completed spraying the starboard side, it did not lift off and

---

[6] Antiaircraft and artillery.

hang back with the two other choppers. Instead, Dyye swung up, turned around, and—at 400 feet to starboard and only 50 feet above the thrashing waves—headed toward the bow. Again he turned the bird so that its nose faced the port side of the ship and the port side of the helicopter was toward the length of the vessel. Slowly—carefully—Dyye began to steady the gunship over the forecastle.

The gunship was getting ready to discharge the Death Merchant and the first batch of SF-1 commandos to the deck of *Prinz Rupert*.

Chapter 17

It was a delicate balance between success and catastrophe, between life and quick, explosive death. Buster Dyye carefully began to rev the chopper down over the forecastle of the *Prinz Rupert*, his task complicated not only by the brisk wind, but also by the movement of the vessel, which was now drifting helplessly and at the mercy of the waves. The 40mm cannon projectiles had wrecked the steering column of the wheel in the after steering station in the after deckhouse; in turn, the wrecked column had partially jammed the steering system in the wheelhouse on the bridge deck. The chief engineer had then been forced to shut off the engines.

Only the Death Merchant thought about the danger facing the helicopter as it descended over the forward deck of the ship. The diameter of the main rotor was seventy-two feet three inches. From the forepeak of the bow to the first cargo boom the distance was eighty-one feet six inches. This meant that the distance between the tip of the blade and the boom was only slightly more than nine feet—a very narrow margin of safety, considering that a hard gust of wind could blow the bird sternward, in spite of Dyye's expertise with the controls.

"Throw out the ladders and get the hell out!" shouted Dyye through the intercom. "We're down to fifty feet and I'm not going any lower. It would be too dangerous."

By the time Dyye had finished speaking, two of the SEAL commandos were dropping the ends of the two steel-cable ladders through the port cargo opening. At each end of the opening another commando stood to one side, watching the main foreward deck and the front of the wheelhouse, their Colt CAR SMGs shouldered and ready to fire at the slightest sign of activity. Each man wore a night-vision device over his face, a single-tube Cylops binocular goggles, ideal for night observation or in deep twilight.

No sooner had the ends of the ladders touched the high ice-covered deck of the forecastle than the two other gunships that had moved in began a terrible firing, thousands of projectiles striking the sides of the superstructure. The gunship with the 40mm cannon and the minigun was on the port side of the ship. The second bird, it's starboard side facing the vessel, directed its rivers of steel at the starboard side of the *Prinz Rupert*.

Going down the cable ladders was not an easy task, and not only because of the icy wind cutting against one's face. Each man wore a pair of ice creepers, and the sharp points had a tendency to slip on the metal rungs. Several of the commandos and Camellion slipped more than once, but always managed to catch themselves in time.

There was one consolation. They realized that it was very unlikely that they would be fired on. Only an idiot would expose himself to such unbelievable lines of projectiles pouring from the two miniguns, rounds that found every window and porthole, every tiny opening.

The first unit of SF-1 crept down the ladders, the metal point of the ice creepers clanking against the rungs, the large helmets of the commandos making their heads seem swollen from some unknown but terrible malady. Above them the Sea Stallion shuddered unsteadily, moving from side to side, like a mechanical monster testing its chains—but never more than four or five feet to either port or starboard, now and then slightly from bow to stern or vice versa.

Richard Camellion and Pini Hilleli were the sixth and the seventh men to set foot on the deck of the vessel, which was covered with ice an inch thick. Keeping low and jabbing each foot down firmly on the deck, they hurried sternward and snuggled down by the twisted remains of a ventilator cowl that had been chewed up by the 40mm cannon. The smell of burnt paint and warm air drifted from the mouth of the cowl and was quickly lost in the raw and fresh smell of the sea and the wind. Close by, the five other commandos, who had been ahead of Hilleli and the

Death Merchant, were lying flat on the icy deck, their protection another ventilator cowl and the anchor windlass.

In short order the last commando was on deck, and Captain Glen W. Griffith, a TEL-6Y walkie-talkie in his gloved right hand, was reporting to Buster Dyye that all the men were down safely. In the cargo section of the helicopter, Robert "Jazbo" Wesholt, the copilot, pressed the RECALL button on each cable container; with humming sounds, the winches in each box began to retract the cable ladders. Two minutes more and the ladders were folded and snug inside the two containers. Dyye lifted off and headed the bird northwest. All three gunships would return to the naval station, leaving the task of picking up SEAL Force 1 to the *McCall*, the navy PCER vessel.

The second gunship moved in, the pilot carefully guiding the eggbeater over the deck of the forecastle. The cable ladders were lowered from the starboard side and the remainder of the commandos began crawling down on the steel webs.

"If that bird comes down, it will take us with it." Wally Chatters looked up fearfully at the Sea Stallion. He and H. L. Kartz had taken positions close to Camellion and Hilleli and, unlike the commandos, carried automatic weapons similar to the Death Merchant and the Israeli—super sleek M-10 MAC LIST[1] submachine gun, or machine pistol. Each M-10 had a specially long magazine that held fifty-two .45 cartridges. Each round was a KTW cartridge.

For sidearms, Chatters, Kartz, and Hilleli carried Safari Arms BP Super .45 autopistols; so did the Death Merchant, Camellion's in shoulder holsters. In addition, Camellion had snuggled in a hip holster a Custom Model 300 Alaskan .44 Auto Mag.

The last commando stepped from the ladder onto the deck. Almost three minutes passed, then the second gunship revved up, cleared the masts, and zoomed off toward the coast. The third Sea Stallion followed.

Captain Griffith made his way over to the Death Merchant, who had unhooked his MAC-10 from a chest cross-strap and was rubbing his lips with a Chapstick. Griffith was twenty-nine, slight of build, and had a trace of Tampa, Florida, in his voice.

Griffith said to Camellion, "We could get into the guts of this

[1] MAC-Military Armaments Corporation LIST-Lightweight Individual Special Purpose.

tub by blowing one of the cargo hatches and dropping down. That way we could bypass the mid-deck housing."

Camellion shoved the Chapstick into a top pocket of his all-weather coveralls. "No good. We'd have to slide down on lines. Our Kraut chums could be expecting such a move and be waiting for us. We have to neutralize the superstructure. If we don't, the East Germans might sneak back into it. That would only complicate our work."

Griffith exhaled loudly. "I figured we'd have to trot the length of this deck to the superstructure," he said in disgust.

"As well as the after deckhouse," Camellion added. "The hatch to belowdecks in the after steering station has to be sealed. Once we have the enemy on the run, we don't want him slipping above decks."

"What's the difference?" asked Chatters. "There's nothing up here but ice and wind. So let them come up here and freeze their butts off!"

"How are we supposed to 'seal' a bulkhead?" Kartz's granite visage congealed visibly. "We can jam the lock wheel with a bar or some object, but who's to say the Krauts won't blow off the locking mechanism or the lugs with explosives?"

"I still maintain that we should have brought grenades," Pini Hilleli said to no one in particular.

The Death Merchant let his eyes settle on Kartz. "The East Germans on this ship didn't think they'd ever have to fight. They probably have enough weapons—Mischa Wolf never leaves his knots untied. But I doubt if they brought explosives with them. To their way of thinking, why would they need explosives? Surely not to use against their own vessel."

Pini Hilleli remarked, "The logical place for us to enter is through the bulkhead in the superstructure. We can split up. One group can head to the stern, the other group to the bow."

"We're going to do it somewhat that way," Camellion said with a grin. He turned from Hilleli to Captain Griffith. "I have a suggestion. My boys and I—"

"I'm not your 'boy'!" growled Kartz.

"I and Chatters and Hilleli and *Mister* Kartz, along with Sergeant Givens and seven commandos, will hit the mid-housing. We'll head toward the bow. Captain, you take the rest of the boys and go in through the after deckhouse. Then you work your way to the bow. Jam the bulkhead stern as soon as you're belowdecks. Don't forget to check the steering-gear compart-

ment in the stern on the second deck and the void space in front
of the rudder; there's the after peak in back of the rudder. Unless
you can think of a better method of attack?"

Hilleli gave a low laugh. "You've been on ships before,
haven't you, Camellion?"

"A few."

Griffith loosened the chin strap of his Racal Amplivox EOD
helmet.[2]

"Mr. Camellion, I think that now is the time to tell me what it
is we're after. Mr. Brent said that once we were on board, you'd
let me in on the secret."

"The most deadly nerve gas in the world," Camellion said
bluntly. "There's six hundred forty pounds of it on this vessel,
in liquid form, probably in twenty-five-pound container tanks. I
haven't the slightest idea where the tanks could be hidden."

A dark cloud floated across Griffith's face. "How are we
supposed to find the gas—or do you CIA people have some sort
of electronic crystal ball?"

"We have to take one of the big shots prisoner and make him
tell us," Camellion said simply. "We'll have to have a lot of
luck."

"And if our luck's all bad?"

Camellion smiled at Griffith. "Shucks, there's no use to shock
the stalks before the corn is off. First things first. Let's split up
and get inside this pile of steel. Who knows when the sea might
get rougher. Captain, the commandos are your men. You do the
choosing."

Nodding, Griffith called out to Sergeant Givens.

In a very short time the two groups were moving toward the
stern, the points of their ice creepers digging into the ice.
Moving his men at a pace faster than Captain Griffith, the Death
Merchant and his group of eleven paused only briefly under the
winch-operator platform of the first cargo boom. They then
hurried to the second platform, on their way pushing aside small,
jagged pieces of metal that had been torn from the steel-mesh
platform by the 40mm projectiles. From underneath the half-
wrecked platform, Camellion and the others could see the front
of the mid-deck housing. The front of the superstructure looked

---

[2] Manufactured from antiballistic material, the helmet provides
protection from blast and fragments and is fitted with Sonovalve
acoustic valves to protect against explosive noises.

as if it had been caught for a week in the center of World War III. Every window had been shot out and there were hundreds of holes, a foot in diameter, in front of the superstructure on all three decks. The bridge in particular had received the most damage, the hundreds of holes grim testimony to the effectiveness of the 40mm stuff.

"Nothing could have lived through that," said Wally Chatters with satisfaction. He turned and looked for a moment at Captain Griffith and his group, who were approaching.

"Who said that anyone did," remarked Sergeant Givens, bracing himself as the vessel rolled slightly to port.

The Death Merchant pulled down the visor of his helmet. "Welllll, if no one has a question of a spiritual nature, shall we proceed?" Camellion remarked teasingly.

"Let's get on with it," Kartz growled reprovingly. "We're not here to preach sermons."

If all human wisdom can be summed up as waiting and hoping, then Gunther Flegel had become a "genius" within the space of twenty minutes. Manfred Halbritter, Abdullah al-Mansour, and Suleiman Maghrabi weren't far behind.

With the majority of the SSD agents, Colonel Flegel, Halbritter, and the two Libyans had taken refuge on the first deck of the vessel, toward the bow. The East Germans and the Libyans entertained no illusions about their ultimate fate, although, secretly, most wanted to surrender. Yet none wanted to be the first man to speak aloud his thoughts.

Colonel Flegel had hoped that the attacking Americans would take the path of least resistance and attempt to reach the holds through the first cargo hatch. The Americans had not accommodated Flegel.

Abdullah al-Mansour, an HK 5A3 9mm submachine gun in his hands, looked up at the large room-sized hatch cover. "They'll have to come through the bulkhead in the superstructure," he said hoarsely, wiping sweat from his long mustache. "If the captain and the crew can cut down some of their number . . ."

Flegel and Halbritter turned and looked at the Libyan with contempt.

"Don't be a fool." Suleiman Maghrabi proceeded to put into words what Flegel and Halbritter were thinking. "The ship is wrecked. It cannot be steered, and we are in American waters. We could kill every man who dropped from the helicopters. The

U.S. Navy would still never permit us to leave. Face it. We will be dead in a short while, or worse, prisoners. We can never surrender; we would be disgraced forever."

Alfred Groner Heine, one of the SSD agents, snickered loudly, then turned away when he saw Flegel glaring at him.

Colonel Flegel picked up his Skorpion SMG, cleared his throat, and looked challengingly at the men. Ever since the American helicopters had been sighted, he had searched desperately for an answer, for a way out, for some means of escape, all the while knowing that he was seeking the impossible. Trapped! Like bugs in a bottle with a tight cork, he and the others were totally imprisoned.

"Let's move to the cargo hold directly below us," he said, his undertaker's tone businesslike. "We can make a better defense from lower in the ship."

"What about the gas?" Halbritter asked in a whisper, looking perplexed. "Are we going to leave the tanks where they are?"

There were times—concluded Colonel Flegel—that Halbritter could ask a question that centered around complete stupidity.

"Tell me, what would you have us do with the gas?" fumed Flegel. "Throw it in the ocean—if we had access to the water—or would you release a tank or two and commit suicide, taking the Americans with us and having the damned stuff reach the American coast. Such madness would result in a catastrophe for our own people!"

"*Nein, Herr* Colonel, I didn't mean that at all and you know it!" Halbritter defended his position angrily. "I realize that the Americans no doubt know the role we played in the conspiracy. I'm also aware that if the gas now killed any of the American swine, our country would be blamed for it and that war would result. But why should we let the Americans find the gas and add it to their supply of chemical weapons?"

"It took almost a year to produce that special nerve gas," Suleiman Maghrabi said sternly, "and rightfully it belongs to my nation."

"You're outvoted," Colonel Flegel told him. "The gas remains where it is. We have enough to worry about without risking any of the gas escaping."

Without another word and still surprised that Halbritter had spoken to him in such an impolite manner, Flegel started toward the bulkhead that led to the No. 1 hold. He was walking into his own coffin and knew it.

The oval door to the officers' mess on the upper deck level had been securely locked. Several 40mm projectiles had not only torn off the lock, but had blown off the top hinge as well. The Death Merchant pushed aside the door, darted into the long room, and saw that it was empty. Chatters, Kartz, and Sergeant Givens crept in after him; behind them came Hilleli and the SEAL commandos, all eleven prepared to kill on a split second's notice.

Outside, Captain Griffith and his eleven commandos made their way to the after deckhouse.

"Camellion, this is an exercise in futility," Kartz said defiantly. "To have stayed up here, the Krauts would have had to have a death wish that would leave Freud flabbergasted!"

"I'm inclined to agree with him," Chatters said. "But I guess we have to do it room by room?"

"And deck by deck!" Camellion said in admonitory tones. "We don't need speed. This ship isn't going anywhere and the Germans won't be getting reinforcements." He looked around a doorway into a hall. The narrow passageway was empty.

Room by room, deck by deck—the lamp room and deck lockers, spaces for the cooks and messmen, the oilers and seamen's rooms on the upper deck—all were empty. So was the bos'n's office. It was as if the mid-deck housing were part of a ghost ship—*We know where the "ghosts" are! Waiting down in one of the holds, or maybe in the engine and steering compartments!*

The majority of the force waited impatiently on the upper deck while the Death Merchant, Kartz, and Sergeant Givens crept up a narrow gangway to the bridge deck. The chief engineer's office and quarters, the rooms of the first assistant engineer, chief mate, second assistant engineer, third assistant engineer, second mate, third mate, chief steward—as empty as a politician's promises, the furnishings covered with a thin layer of dust that had fallen from the ceilings and bits of metal and wood and other material that had been torn from the walls and furniture by 40mm projectiles. Through shot-out windows and rips and tears in the outer walls, the terrible wind whistled a dirge.

Camellion and his two companions were in the engineering department, a room facing the starboard side of the vessel, when Sergeant Givens said, "Look at that!" and motioned with a swing of his Colt CAR SMG toward the windows and several large rents in the thin aluminum walls. The wind was blowing snow into the room.

"We don't have time to make snowballs," Camellion said. "Let's bob along to the bridge."

Surprise! They found a corpse in the battery room in the bridge deck. The fat crewman had almost been cut in half by a 40mm projectile. The corpse lay sprawled on its back across a row of smoking batteries that were giving off a terrible, throat-clogging stink. The mouth of the dead dummy was wide open.

Oddly enough, the generator was still running in the generator room, and the floor was almost clean. It was a different state of affairs in the captain's office and living quarters. The walls of all three rooms had received thirteen hits by 20mm projectiles, and snow blowing in through the jagged rents already lay thick over the floor and the furnishings. A propaganda poster on the wall of the Captain's office—*Unsere Liebe Unserem Kommunistischen Vaterland*—looked ridiculously out of place, its red coloring and bold black letters meaningless. Totally useless—like a tea cart parked in the middle of a cemetery.

Three torn-apart dead men in the bloody wheelhouse—blood frozen slick and gruesome on the floor and over the walls and equipment. Here the snow was blowing fiercely through the row of high windows in front, those openings facing the bow, the cloud of white flakes scudding in all directions.

Kartz suddenly gave a loud giggle that was positively obscene; it was the first time the Death Merchant had ever heard him make a sound that even remotely resembled mirth.

"Heh, heh, heh—I guess we could call that a real 'brainy' compass," he smirked, staring at the magnetic compass covered with the large blob of now frozen brain material.

Sergeant Givens gave Kartz a long look but didn't say anything.

The Death Merchant strode over to the chart room, to the right of the wheelhouse. Nautical charts lay on the floor, snow piling up on them. Other charts, fastened to the chart table, continued to be tortured by the wind, their ends flapping monotonously.

The Death Merchant saw the world and all that man had built within the wreckage of the chart room. In less than seventeen years the great cities would lay destroyed—most of humanity dead, the fields and air intensely radioactive—*Why am I here? Why am I doing this? Why not?*

It would have been so easy if the big brass hadn't wanted the containers of VXB. The navy could have simply moved in. If the

East Germans refused to surrender, the vessel could have been sunk with small charges placed by SEAL frogmen. No good. Uncle Sam wanted the nerve gas to add to his own chemical stock, which was already estimated at 50 millon pounds and was scattered in ten army arsenals. Not enough! The Army was preparing to buy enough chemical feedstock to manufacture 2.9 million pounds of conventional nerve gas[3]—enough to kill at least 10 million people. Already a chemical factory was being built in Pine Bluff, Arkansas, a complex that would produce nerve gas ingredients such as methane phosphonyl dichloride, which was chemically similar to some commercial pesticides. At the Pine Bluff factory, batches of the substance would be chemically combined with hydrofluoric acid to make a rare compound known as methyl phosphonic difluoride, nicknamed DF. DF was one of the two ingredients that would be packed inside 155mm artillery shells. The second ingredient was called isopropyl alcohol amine, or QL.

Ironic! If we don't blow up the world, we can poison it! Ah—it's vital to our "national security!" Ho-ho-ho-ho-ho-ho! Sic transit gloria mundi! So be it!

Camellion turned, walked back into the wheelhouse, and followed Kartz and Givens into the radio room, to port of the wheelhouse. The shortwave transmitter—a West German Tenkenheimer—and navigation instruments had been shot to pieces and turned into junk. The radio direction finder, echo sounder, sonar and radar screens shattered. Not only had many of the instruments been struck by 40mm metal, but also by scores of 7.62mm minigun slugs.

There wasn't any value in rubbernecking at the rubbish. The three men hurried to the upper deck and, with the rest of the tiny force, prepared to move to the level of the second deck, that is, the first deck inside the *Prinz Rupert*.

Camellion took out his TEL-6Y transceiver and contacted Captain Glen Griffith, who, with his eleven commandos, was in the after steering compartment in the stern housing. The bulkhead door was locked and—"We're going to have to use the B stuff and blow it," Griffith reported. "After that, there won't be any way we can seal the opening. We'll have to risk that the Germans won't slip through to the main deck."

"Affirmative," Camellion said. "Blow it. No doubt we'll

---

[3] Tabun, sarin, soman.

have to blow the bulkhead midships. "Good luck. Meet you in the bow."

"Anything else?"

"Shoot to kill but—I know this sounds silly—if you run into anyone who looks important, try to keep him alive. Out."

The Death Merchant switched off the walkie-talkie, shoved the set into its case, picked up the Ingram SMG, and glanced at the men. "Let's go below."

Their senses on high alert, they moved onto the gangway in a stern passage, went down the steps, passed through an ordinary doorway on the main deck level, went down another flight of steps, and came to a small rectangular area. The bulkhead to the second deck was at the end of the area.

"We'll have to blow the locking mechanism and the two hinges," Kartz said, studying the bulkhead with its rounded swing-in hinges and spin wheel that controlled the locking mechanism.

A poor relative to the door of a bank vault! The Death Merchant walked over to the wheel and tried to turn it to the right. He couldn't, the door was locked.

"I'll do it," offered Sergeant Givens. "Three one-pound charges will blow that door six feet on the other side."

"Only if they're placed right," said Wally Chatters.

"They will be!" Givens looked at Camellion, who nodded and motioned to the rest of the men with his Ingram SMG. "Go on up to the main deck level," Camellion said. "I'll ride shot-gun with Givens while he places the B charges. And take your ice creepers off. We don't need them down here."

The other men went up the steps, their ice creepers clanking against the metal. Camellion sat down on the bottom step and began unstrapping his ice creepers as Givens took out three one-pound blocks of Composition B, and explosive composed of 52.2 percent RDX, 40 percent TNT, and the rest beeswax. Between the three of them, Camellion, Givens, and Griffith carried thirty pounds of the powerful military explosive, each block containing a detonator that could be timed, and a magnetic plate.

"I'll set each one for sixty seconds," Givens said. He placed the first block in back of the lock wheel, the magnetic plate grabbing the metal of the bulkhead. The second and the third block went against the massive hinges. Givens set the timer on the block against the lock to sixty-four seconds, the timer on the top hinge to sixty-two seconds, the one on the bottom hinge to

179

fifty-nine seconds. Then he and the Death Merchant hurried up the steps and got down with the other men.

No sooner had they snuggled down than there was a rather loud yet muffled *BLAMMMMM* from the stern. Captain Griffith and his boys had blown open the bulkhead in the after steering compartment.

BERRRRROOOOMMMMMMMMMM! The thunderclap explosion of the three Comp-B blocks placed by Sergeant Givens made the vessel shudder violently. An instant later there was a loud, final thud as the blasted bulkhead door crashed to the floor. The way to the holds of the *Prinz Rupert* had been opened.

"The landing down there is narrow," Camellion said sagely. "We can't bunch up down there. Better that two men go first and secure positions inside, three at the most. Who'll volunteer?"

"You know I'm not going to sit here and twiddle my thumbs!" Kartz said pompously. "It's bad for my toenails!"

"Count me in," said Clyde Wolfsob, one of the commandos. "I don't have anything better to do."

"You going to call us on the walkie-talkie, Camellion?" Sergeant Givens's hard eyes stared at Camellion.

"Affirmative." Camellion glanced at Kartz and Wolfsob. "Keep to the side of the steps and do it fast," he said. He then turned and headed for the steps.

Camellion raced down the steps, keeping to the left. Slightly behind Camellion were Kartz and Wolfsob, to the right. In no time at all the three were on the landing, on either side of the smoking opening.

The three pounds of Comp-B had done its job, had ripped the steel door from its heavy hinges and the lug bolts of the lock and had tossed it ten feet inward. It lay on the floor, tilted at an angle. Beyond the opening was blackness. Either the enemy had turned out the lights or else the bombardment of 40mm projectiles had wrecked a vital part of the system.

"Lightsticks first," said Camellion, a crooked smile on his face. "I'll cover you."

Kartz and Wolfsob pulled three Cyalume lightsticks each from their oiled canvas shoulder bags and shook each seven-inch-long plastic Flex tube violently until each tube was glowing with brilliant yellow white chemiluminescence light that would "burn" for three hours. The two men looked at the Death Merchant, who then leaned around the oval opening and sprayed the darkness with a long burst from the MAC-10 SMG, moving the little

180

machine pistol from side to side. An instant after he stopped firing, Kartz and Wolfsob tossed the six lightsticks through the opening, throwing them as hard as they could without exposing their bodies to any of the enemy who might be hidden in the darkness. The sticks were very light, and one zoomed seventy feet before falling to the wooden decking. The darkness vanished. Now it was intense yellow light.

"I'll go in first," Camellion said and shoved a full magazine into the MAC-10 machine pistol. "One man can do a better job of securing a position. Slugs are more likely to catch one of us if we go in together."

"Why you?" Kartz looked hurt—almost. "I can run as fast as you, maybe even faster."

The Death Merchant shrugged. "Be my guest. Have a happy suicide."

Kartz had not exaggerated. He could run—fast. He streaked through the opening at a zigzag, a Super MatchMaster in one hand, the M-10 machine pistol in the other hand.

The enemy was there. Captain Ludwig Smoelter had scattered his heavily armed crew throughout the second deck and the five holds of the doomed ship. Working at a frantic pace, crew members and the SSD men had filled empty steel drums with slabs of cork (taken from the refrigeration section of stores) and had scattered the drums throughout the length of the second deck, both fore and aft. Behind each drum waited a member of the crew, armed with either a Skorpion machine pistol or a Soviet PPS submachine gun. In addition, many of the crew carried pistols, Walther P-38s, and East German versions of the Soviet Makarov. There were also three SSD agents forward on the second deck. It was they who began firing at a darting and weaving H. L. Kartz.

Skorpion projectiles burned air dangerously close to Kartz, three 9mm slugs cutting through his coveralls, two at the left inner thigh, one through his right collar. His life was saved by speed and his talent for ducking and dodging, plus the lighting factor. The lightsticks were on the floor, the intenseness of the light, shining upward, confusing the East Germans.

Kartz was only ten feet from a drum to his right when a desperate Ernst-Josef Barthe, an SSD agent, reared up to fire another burst with his Skorpion. Kartz was much faster. The M-10 Ingram in his right hand chattered—*burrrppppp*—spitting out six .45 Teflon-coated KTW slugs that did a Grade-A job on

181

the East German intelligence officer, turning his heart and lungs into bloody jelly before knocking him to the floor. A few seconds later, Kartz was down behind the drum, snuggling close to the wall.

Enemy slugs started coming rapidly through the steel barrel—*Zip! Clang! Thuddddd!* But the projectiles were stopped by the cork. Somehow, one 7.62mm from a Soviet PPS stabbed through one side of the drum and by a fluke missed all the cork. The projectile bored through the side facing Kartz and stabbed him in the right side of the chest. However, the bullet had lost the majority of its power, and the NATO/SWAT Class III Military vest[4] worn by Kartz did the rest, stopping the round before it bored even half an inch into the vest. All the slug did was increase Kartz's anger, already at white heat.

"*Kraut* sonsabitches!" he snarled, then raised the MAC-10 over the top of the drum and began spraying the area from side to side at the same time that the Death Merchant—who had already called Sergeant Givens on the walkie-talkie—and Clyde Wolfsob charged through the bulkhead, zigging and zagging and firing at two drums to the left of Kartz and twenty feet ahead of him—drums they had spotted the instant they had stormed onto the second deck.

The seaman behind the drum Camellion had marked died almost instantly, the steel-penetrator KTW .45 loads boring through the steel barrel with the ease of a .22 slug stabbing through window glass. The crewman didn't have time to realize he was hit. With his entire face, part of his neck, and part of his left shoulder shot away, the corpse slumped, blood spurting like a red-water fountain.

This engagement was Clyde Wolfsob's first; yet he acted like a vet body counter, spraying the area ahead with his Colt Commando SMG, the 5.56 X 45mm projectiles zipping through the Muzzle Mizer,[5] or muzzle brake, at the end of the barrel.

Werner Kessler, another SSD agent, would have blown Wolfsob into Foreverness if it hadn't been for Camellion. Behind the

---

[4] The vest, with a steel ProtectoPlate, defeats rounds of 7.62mm NATO ball ammo, and all lesser threats, including .41 and .44 Magnum loads.

[5] Designed by Charles A. "Mickey" Finn, the Muzzle Mizer effectively controls both vertical and horizontal muzzle turbulence while the weapon is in full and semiautomatic fire.

barrel that Wolfsob had targeted, Kessler had not been taken out of the action by the eleven 5.56mms that had come his way. The layers of cork had absorbed the slugs. All the time, Wolfsob was getting closer.

In desperation, Kessler leaned out from the side of the barrel to fire, and that's when the Death Merchant popped him with the BP Super MatchMaster in his left hand, the .45 ACP semiwadcutter bullet banging the man in the forehead, opening his skull to the extent that a portion of his brain could have been seen—if anyone had stopped to look.

Then Camellion and Wolfsob were down behind protective barrels, alternately firing and throwing Cyalume lightsticks forward. Behind them, two more SEAL commandos charged through the bulkhead and raced ahead as Camellion, Kartz, and Wolfsob raked the forward area with streams of submachine gun slugs.

The fourteen East Germans were not a match for the Death Merchant and his people, who kept up an almost constant firing, two or three men reloading while the others sprayed the area with streams of slugs. The KTW bullets were another deciding factor, the armor-piercing slugs slicing through the drums as though the barrels weren't even there!

It required only seven minutes to whack out ten Germans. The remaining four tossed out their weapons, three shouting in English, "Americans. We surrender. Don't shoot."

Camellion lined the four against a wall and demanded to know if any men had boarded the *Prinz Rupert* recently, either by launch or by helicopter.

"Thirty or forty of them," one of the men muttered, staring at Camellion and the other hard-faced men with fear in his eyes. "W-We don't know who they are."

"In what part of the ship are they hiding—and don't lie to me!" Camellion sounded as grim as Death itself.

"I'm not sure," the man said nervously. "They're either in the first or second hold."

A calculating smile on his face, Camellion turned to Sergeant Givens and looked from him to Wally Chatters and Pini Hilleli, both of whom were on either side of the commando. "All we have to do now is blow the bulkhead to the second hold and proceed from there to the big prize in the first hold, that is if Colonel Flegel, the two Libyan sand crabs, and the rest of the trash aren't holed up in the second cargo space."

Camellion turned to go. He stopped when Kartz put a hand on

his arm. "What about them?" Kartz motioned to the four Germans with his MAC-10. "We can't leave them here or take them with us."

"They're not my concern," Camellion said equably. "I don't care what you do with them."

He motioned to the other men and turned toward the bulkhead. Behind him, Kartz's MAC-10 machine pistol chattered.

Chapter 18

A true talent will make do with any technique! is another proverb that adds up to meaningless "wisdom." The Death Merchant, the three Company men, and the Force 1 commandos had a lot of bent, bump, and faculty; yet there was only one way they could get into the No. 2 cargo hold: the hard way, the dangerous way. Only one way: explode the bulkhead and move in. The same harsh realism applied to Captain Griffith and his group. There was only one way, just one, they could reach the No. 3 cargo hold: explode the bulkhead and storm the hold.

The East Germans were waiting. In cargo hold No. 2 they were secure behind heavy wooden crates filled with bolts of woolen, cotton, and linen cloths (some of the bolts of fine, thin weave and some of heavy, thick weave). In cargo hold No. 3 the crewmen were waiting behind even heavier crates filled with brass and steel pipe fittings of various kinds and sizes.

The crates in both holds were of such a size—six by five by five feet—that even the KTW armor-piercing projectiles would not completely penetrate them, unless a KTW bullet happened to strike the end of a bolt of cloth, in which case the slug would travel between two layers of the tightly rolled cloth. If the bolt was lying horizontally, the slug would have to first bore through several feet of cloth and then stab through the next bolt and the bolt after that one.

In hold No. 3, Captain Griffith and his eleven commandos had it worse. Even KTW projectiles, used by the Death Merchant and the three Company men, could not stab through so much hard metal.

The Americans had casualties. In securing the No. 3 hold, Captain Griffith lost Wasil Rid, Wayne Huite, and Lamar Atoff.

But the force terminated eighteen of the enemy. Griffith and his eight men then prepared to explode the bulkhead between the holds and attack cargo area No. 4.

Camellion and his pitifully small group lost two men in gaining the second cargo space. Andy Seibert caught a burst of PPS 7.62mm slugs in the chest and was a cold cut before his corpse made contact with the floor. The end came for Ansel Gutridge by means of a single 9mm Czech M-61 Skorpion[1] bullet that zipped into his head through the left temple.

For a short time, Camellion and his men were pinned down in a Mexican standoff. The East Germans could not retreat because the Americans were at the bulkhead between No. 2 and No. 1 holds. Nor could the East Germans attack. Neither could Camellion. Retreat—yes. But he and the commandos had no intention of doing so.

Nonetheless, the number of the East Germans slowly decreased. The SEALS were better shots, could shoot faster, and didn't permit emotion to interfere with tactics.

"Why not use say five or six ounces of Comp-B?" Hilleli suggested.

"Not yet," Camellion said. "I think I see another way."

That "another way" involved what the Death Merchant had seen and heard during a lull in the fighting. He had noticed that the steel holding straps securing a dozen large crates to port strained and groaned loudly each time the vessel rolled to starboard. Eight carefully placed .44 Alaskan Auto Mag projectiles severed three of the straps, the expenditure of cartridges necessitated by the uneven lighting of the lightsticks. A few more rolls to starboard and two of the straps snapped. The crates began to shift, moving several feet to starboard. Then they stopped. It was the fourth strap that was preventing the first crate on the aisle from crashing to the deck and stopping all of the crates from going into a big, fast slide.

Four more .44 rounds from the Alaskan Auto Mag broke the fourth steel strap and started the catastrophe for the East Germans. WHANNNGGG! The big slug hit the strap, the strap snapped, the top crate fell with a loud crash, and the rest of the crates started to slide. With loud THUDS the top crates tumbled downward, several of them bursting open and scattering pipe

---

[1] The Skorpion usually fires a 7.65mm (or .32 ACP) bullet. However, there is also a version that fires a 9mm cartridge.

fittings. The East Germans hiding behind the bottom crates could either move or be crushed to a bloody pulp. They decided to run for it; and in so doing exposed themselves to the watching-and-waiting commandos, who fired instantly, the Colt Commando submachine guns and the MAC-10 Ingrams sounding devastatingly loud within the confines of the cargo hold.

Screaming, but only briefly, the chief engineer went down, followed by the first mate—both riddled, both spurting blood. Rudolf Essenkrautz, the radio operator, muttered *"Gott!"* and began to fall, a slug in his spleen. Pini Hilleli let him have another four rounds, and Essenkrautz's head exploded like a balloon, brains and bone splattering outward.

It was too late for the Germans. Crates weighing almost a thousand pounds began pressing against flesh. Bones snapped! Blood vessels were crushed! Muscles were ripped! A dozen blinks of the eye and six Germans were crushed, four unconscious, and dying, one with his legs pinned between two crates, the last man with his right hand imprisoned by one crate pressing his hand to another container.

Humanitarian that he was, Camellion put an end to the man's agony by shattering his skull with a .44 AMP[2] bullet. The Death Merchant, the three Company men, and the commandos then moved in, weapons roaring. Within several minutes the firing was over and so was the short battle. Twenty-one Germans had been killed, twenty-one crewmen in the No. 2 hold, now thick with drifting blue clouds of exploded gunpowder. There was the stink of sweat and the dirty smell of the hold, so common to all cargo vessels.

Don Ray Yesley, one of the commandos, slid down behind the crate, next to Camellion. "Now there's nothing between us and the first hold. Hey—LOOK!"

The Death Merchant looked; so did the other man. They all saw the door of the bulkhead to the first hold start to swing open.

"I'll be damned!" exclaimed Yesley in astonishment. "They're coming out and attacking us!"

The door had not swung a foot before the enemy was poking out SMGs and firing streams of slugs, trying to spray them in all directions, forcing Camellion and his men to stay down.

In spite of the suddenness of the unexpected, Camellion had to

[2] Auto Mag pistol.

admire Colonel Flegel, who had done the unexpected and taken the initiative. Flegel and his people were attacking.

The Death Merchant and his men fired steadily, hundreds of .45 and 5.56mm projectiles flooding over the oval door, many of them screaming off in loud ricochets. By the time the East Germans had pushed the door completely open, three of them had been butchered by the hail of steel.

Realizing that they had made a serious miscalculation, the Germans retreated, several of them making a frenzied attempt to close the bulkhead and lock it. They only half succeeded. Not only were several corpses lying across the rounded bottom rim of the opening, but Joe Kellermung and Jerrel Rhodes, two of the commandos, were behind a crate thirty feet to the left of the bulkhead, positions that enabled them to fire, at a very steep angle, between the inner side of the door and the bulkhead's rounded receiver set in the wall. Colt CAR Commando SMGs roared and three more East Germans were shot to pieces. The other Germans around the door fell back, then turned and raced to the protection of crates filled with leather hides.

H. L. Kartz and Sergeant Givens jumped up, ran twenty feet, and got down beside Camellion and Don Ray Yesley. The Death Merchant was talking to Captain Griffith on a TEL-6Y. Griffith and his group were in the fourth hold that had not contained any Germans.

"We'll come forward and link up with you," Griffith said, sounding pleased and comfortable. "How many do you think we'll be up against."

Camellion gave him the bad news. "At least forty, maybe more. We can't rush them the conventional way. We've already lost too many men."

"What do you have in mind?" Griffith sounded worried.

"Oh—it will be exciting," Camellion said with a laugh. "Come on forward."

Switching off the walkie-talkie, Camellion knew there was only one way to solve the dilemma: use Comp-B. Accordingly, he had Sergeant Givens and Clyde Wolfsob make four bombs, each one composed of an estimated ten to fifteen ounces of Comp-B molded around a detonator/timer.

The Death Merchant wasn't satisfied; instinct quietly warned him that some vital "it," some protective factor, was still missing. Detecting Camellion's subtle apprehension, H. L. Kartz said, "What's wrong? The grenades will give us the edge we need. Ten seconds' lag time is more than enough. Hell, there isn't any 'safe' way."

"We need something more positive," Camellion said soberly. "We need a surprise."

Pini Hilleli said seriously, "Why not throw a pound or two of B inside the hold? The explosions could kill the Krauts who know where the gas is hidden, which would put us back to square one."

"Or blow holes in the inner and the outer hulls," pointed out Chatters dismally. He took a cigarette from a crumpled pack.

"Tell you what we'll do . . ." A sly expression crept over the Death Merchant's lean face as he turned to Sergeant Givens. "Sergeant, take one of the boys and go to the second deck. Plant a half pound of B stuff at each corner of the hatch cover. After you blow the cover, sneak back and start spraying the interior of the hull with slugs. Don't try to hit any of the cruds or you'll have to expose yourselves too much."

Kartz growled. "A good idea. That will show the bastards where the tall grass grows."

Sergeant Givens said to Camellion, "How will we time the blowing of the hatch cover with your tossing in your B stuff? Another thing: who's to say that one of our slugs won't catch some of you?"

"When you hear our fourth bomb go off, stop firing, then get back down here," Camellion said. "Make it fast. It seems to me the seas are getting rougher."

"Good enough." Givens glanced at Sylvester Zanf, a commando who was almost seven feet tall. "Let's go, Si."

Givens and Zanf turned and hurried off. They were almost to the bulkhead that led to the steps when Captain Griffith and his eight men came through the opening. In a short time, Camellion had explained the plan to Griffith, and the entire force was moving into position and preparing for the final assault, closing in another of the partially opened bulkheads to the first cargo hold, careful not to expose themselves to the left of the oval door. Between the door and the wall was a two-foot space, and it was a certainty that the enemy had zeroed in on that space and was waiting to slug-slice any commando who attempted to slip inside. At the same time, the Death Merchant and his people had to be close enough to the opening so that when the time came, they could go in quickly, without any undue delay.

"We could go to the right and pull the door open," suggested Fernow Owner.

"No way," Camellion said. "Colonel Flegel is desperate. He might try a suicide charge. I'm counting on our B bombs to take some of them out. The only way is how we're doing it, staying to the left. I'll toss in the explosive." He looked deliberately at H. L. Kartz. "Well, Kartz?"

Kartz appeared cautious. "Well—what?"

"We know you can run faster than I," Camellion said magnanimously. "I'm surprised that you haven't mentioned how expert you are in throwing."

"Wrong, Camellion." Kartz was surprisingly frank. "I'm not so hot when it comes to tossing something."

The Death Merchant grinned. "In that case you can hand me the bombs. I'll also need a man to spray the inside, just to let the Germans know we're ready for them. We wouldn't want them trying to charge out."

"I'll do it," Pini Hilleli offered. "Things are getting a little dull around here."

Camellion, Kartz, and Hilleli moved along the wall to the left of the bulkhead, going as close as they dared without exposing themselves to the machine guns that, inside the first hold, had to be waiting to the left of the door, waiting to fire through the small space, just as Camellion and the men of SEAL Force 1 were waiting for the explosive charges to blow the top of the hatch.

BERRRROOOOORRMMMMMMMMMMMM! All four Comp-B charges roared off simultaneously. The big blast ripped off the steel covering and sent it flying upward against the ceiling, against the braces of the main deck, the thunder of the explosion traveling throughout the vessel and making the hulls and the decks shudder violently.

Weighing almost half a ton, the metal cover crashed back down and fell on one edge through the now open hatch. With a loud ringing sound, the cover smashed into wooden crates of hide in the hold below, the clanking noise accompanied by some cries of agony and more yells of fear.

"Let 'em have a spray of slugs." Camellion motioned to Hilleli, who moved around him and edged closer to the opening between wall and bulkhead, stopping just before any of the enemy on the other side could have him within a line of sight.

189

Hilleli shoved the MAC-10 SMG forward and, pulling the trigger, moved the little machine pistol from side to side.

Almost immediately several enemy SMGs replied to Hilleli's chattering MAC-10, the scores of 9mm and 7.62mm projectiles either glancing from the inside surface of the bulkhead door or else zipping through the opening at an angle that caused them to miss Hilleli by five feet.

Hilleli fired another long burst. Then, his SMG empty, he moved back behind Kartz, who had the bombs ready to hand to the Death Merchant.

Camellion put his right arm behind him, held out his hand, and Kartz handed him the first bomb composed of fifteen ounces of Comp-B, saying, ''Make damn sure they can't toss any of them back at us.''

''Not even Super Fundamentalist Man can beat ten seconds.'' Mentally, Camellion measured the width of the opening and its distance from him, thinking that if he missed, he'd blow himself and Kartz and Hilleli into the next world. He also thought of a remark that Courtland Grojean had made to him at the naval station—''I hope you like El Salvador. That's where you'll be going after this mission.''

And I don't even like the taste of chili!

He turned the small black knob of the timer on the detonator so that the arrow pointed to 12 SEC. The click-click-click started. He then tossed the explosive package straight through the opening.

BERRRRRROOOMMMMMMM! The concussion was terrific, the roaring deafening. There was more firing, but as Camellion began tossing lightsticks through the opening, he could tell it was coming from above the first hold, from Sergeant Givens and Si Zanf.

Rapidly, Camellion tossed the three other bombs through the opening, the explosions ringing in his ears, the smell of burnt TNT thick in the stale air.

Camellion drew his Auto Mag with his right hand. His left hand was filled with an Ingram MAC-10. He glanced at the line of men against the wall. They looked back. They were ready. Camellion took a deep breath, turned, and charged the bulkhead.

Streaking in low, he had time for only a transient inspection of the area, a brief vision of tumbled crates, of bodies sprawled on the deck, of desperate men prepared to kill. Behind him came

Kartz, Hilleli, and the rest of the SEAL Force 1, minus Sergeant Daren Givens and Si Zanf, neither of whom had yet had time to reach the hold.

Firing the MAC-10 as he zigzagged forward, the Death Merchant sensed enemy projectiles coming uncomfortably close. A 9mm slug ripped through his coveralls on the left side. Several more cut through the material on the inside of his right arm. He felt one of his SMG ammo bags jerk and heard a loud ZINGGGG as a couple of 9mm slugs struck one of the magazines. Several more projectiles cut to the left of his EOD helmet. For an instant he was staggered and heard subdued ZUDDDs as a couple of slugs struck him in the chest and flattened themselves against the armor plate inside the NATO/Swat Class III Military vest he wore.

The rest of the force moved in, some of the men throwing lightsticks, the others firing, Colt CAR Commando SMGs roaring, MAC-10s cracking, hundreds of slugs raking the large wooden crates, six of which had been split open by the falling hatch cover.

During those savage moments neither Camellion nor any of the men with him were the least bit concerned about capturing any of the enemy. The hell with the location of the nerve gas canisters. It was either kill or be killed.

The falling hatch cover had killed three crewmen and one of the SSD agents. That catastrophe, coupled with the four Comp-B bombs that had blown up six more men, had completely disorganized the East Germans, who were now ill-prepared to meet the Death Merchant and his force. In only thirteen seconds, Camellion and the sixteen members of SF-1 killed seven more of the enemy, so that when the Death Merchant and his men closed in, they were fighting an enemy that numbered thirty-four. Then Julian Ling, one of the commandos, caught a burst of slugs in the face, the blast sending skull bones and brain flying. It was now Camellion and fifteen men against thirty-four Commies, in a clash of bodies, of men meeting in savage eyeball-to-eyeball combat. Live or die, kill or be killed.

Darting around a crate, Camellion found Germans all around him, all of them trying to reload sub-guns, but calling it a lost cause as they rushed at him. He had used all the ammunition in his MAC-10, but he still had a full mag in the Alaskan.

"Like Raid, it kills bugs dead!" he snarled and pulled the trigger of the AMP. The Alaskan boomed and Erich Bamberger's face and head disappeared in a flash of bones, blood, and brain that tried to shoot to the sky but made it only to the ceiling. He let the empty MAC-10 SMG drop from his left hand and, at the same time he slammed Siegfried Feuermann across the face with the long barrel of the AMP, let Horst Erzkinner have a left-legged Shito-Ryu *Mae Geri Kekomi* front thrust kick, a grand slam that wrapped the German's stomach around his spine and crushed vital blood vessels and arteries in the abdominal region. There was never any redemption from such a kill kick. Looking as if his features had been frozen by a blast of liquid air, the dying Erzkinner fell back and started to sag, eyes wide, arms quivering.

Muttering oaths in German, Hans Fischer grabbed Camellion's right wrist with his left hand and tried a right-handed sword chop aimed at the left side of the Death Merchant's face. Concurrently, another SSD agent rushed in from behind Camellion, intending to turn the back of his head to mush with the barrel of an empty Czech Skorpion machine pistol. Instinct and the rush of air against his back warned Camellion of the attack coming at him from the rear. Camellion exploded into action. An *Ushiro Keage Geri* rear snap kick with his left leg caught Alfred Groner Heine five inches below where his last meal rested and made the SSD officer think his small intestine had collided with a buzz saw. Tasting the bile that jumped up in his throat, he tried to fight the waves of agony flowing throughout his body. Losing the battle, he found himself falling backward and vaguely sensed that someone was reaching out for him. Heine couldn't have fallen into worse hands.

"Stupid! You're breathing my air," snarled H. L. Kartz. His arms flashed out in the beginning of a commando neck-breaker. His left forearm went over Heine's throat, his fingers fastening to the top of his right arm. As his left arm tightened, his right hand went to the left side of Heine's head and pressed mightily to the right. *Snap! Crackle! Pop!* Heine's neck snapped a few seconds after the Death Merchant used a left-handed *Ippon Nukite* one-finger spear thrust that caught Hans Fischer in the right side of his neck, the intense agony forcing the East German to release his hold on the Death Merchant's right wrist. Camellion could then have easily put a bullet into Fischer. But why waste a bullet on a piece of slime?

"If brains were made of leather, you wouldn't have enough to saddle a flea," laughed Camellion, who then killed the SSD man by slamming the barrel of the AMP against his left temple. The

Death Merchant was also in time to see a man wearing a blue suit lean around the side of a crate. An odd-looking individual, the man was so bug-eyed he might have been suffering from colloid goiter. Camellion wasn't interested in the state of the German's health—only in what the Kraut was doing. The man was aiming a Heckler & Koch M-P5 autopistol at one of the commandos. Camellion brought up the .44 Alaskan Auto Mag and fired, the big bullet hitting Manfred Halbritter just below the hollow of the throat and first snapping his head forward then back as the impact slammed the corpse to the side of another crate.

Alarmed at seeing Halbritter snuffed, Abdullah al-Mansour, who was also behind the crate, decided his personal safety lay in another direction. A fully loaded Soviet PPS sub-gun in his hands, the Libyan jumped up, started to run to another crate to his left, and almost collided with Clyde Wolfsob, who was on the prowl. Wolfsob grabbed the Russian-made submachine gun with both hands and twisted it violently to the right, at the same time stomping on al-Mansour's right instep with the heel of his left combat boot.

Ten feet to Wolfsob and al-Mansour's left, Jerrel Rhodes and Joe Kellermug were struggling with three SSD gunmen. Both commandos were losing the battle, until Captain Glen Griffith intervened and went to work on one of the Germans with a Black Beauty boot knife, the seven-inch surgical steel blade slicing across the man's throat after Griffith had grabbed him by the hair and jerked his head back. It was doomsday for Idris Ghradeh, whose luck had run out. Blood spurting from the gaping "second mouth" made by the Black Beauty, Ghradeh started to die, gurgling as he fell. Kurt Meninger was also making choking noises, from the kick in the stomach that Joe Kellermug had given him. Meninger made one final sound, a loud gasping, when Captain Griffith stabbed him between the shoulder blades with the Black Beauty.

It was then that Clyde Wolfsob managed to gain full possession of the Soviet PPS sub-gun, which he used with expert speed and precision. He first jammed the barrel into Abdullah al-Mansour's stomach and barely touched the trigger—*BBBLLLUR-RRRPPPPPPPP!* Al-Mansour's lower jaw fell, his eyes closed, and his body went limp. The half dozen 7.62mm projectiles had blown out his stomach and four inches of his spine. He was stone dead within half a blink of an eye.

Wolfsob swung the PPS to the legs of a German struggling with Jerrel Rhodes.

A man who lived life in one long gleeful rage, H. L. Kartz was having one of the prime times of his life. Like Camellion, Kartz had eyes in the back of his head and a built-in sensor that could detect personal danger from all sides. A roundhouse kick to Edwin Hemholtz's lower chest wrecked the man's xiphoid process, the fingerlike tab of cartilage hanging off the lowermost edge of the sternum, or breast bone. This is the insertion of the rectus abdominus muscle on the sternum. Any severe blow that strikes the xiphoid process while traveling upward at an angle toward the heart causes severe bruising to the liver, stomach, and heart, resulting in unconsciousness and even death. In the case of Hemholtz, Kartz's expertly delivered kick caused instant unconsciousness. The German was still falling when Kartz killed him with a right *Chungdan ap chagi* middle front snap kick to the side of the neck. Kartz then turned his attention to the four SSD agents struggling with Wally Chatters and Pini Hilleli. Horst Kastner had both hands around Chatters's right wrist and was trying to force him to release the MatchMaster pistol. Chatters had his left arm around the neck of Gustav Jessner, who was down on one knee. Chatters was doing the best to choke the life out of Jessner with a half-nelson hold while Jessner was doing the best to struggle free, his right arm wrapped around the left leg of Chatters as he tried to pull him off balance.

Hilleli wasn't in a better position. Georg Hartlaub, a broad-shouldered Kraut, was trying to slam Hilleli with his fists and kick him to death at the same time, using his right leg like a battering ram. Konrad Luther—who looked more like a banker than an intelligence officer—was wise enough to keep his distance. He moved in and out like a dancer, waiting for the right moment, a short-bladed knife in his hand.

Before Kartz could intervene, Hilleli managed to pull the TDE Backup pistol he had stashed in one of the breast pockets of his coveralls. With his right hand, he somehow managed to thumb off the safety and turn the weapon on Luther just as the SSD agent thought he had an opening and was trying to rush in to try for a stomach stab. The TDE barked twice, the two .380 projectiles hitting Luther in the chest. The Kraut dropped the knife, staggered back, and his knees began to fold. Hartlaub, assuming correctly that he was only moments away from being shot, backed off and tried to run behind a crate. Hilleli was too fast. Aware that Camellion wanted some of the Germans alive, he used the last three cartridges on Hartlaub's legs, putting one .380 slug in the calf of the man's left leg and the last two .380s in the rear of the right thigh.

Kartz first chose Horst Kastner when he helped Chatters. Kastner seemed the more dangerous since he was close to getting the MatchMaster away from Chatters. A *Seiken* forfist to the back of Kastner's neck forced him to release his hold on Chatters's wrist. Chuckling, Kartz put the slob to sleep with several *Shuto* sword-hand chops to the neck.

"Now you finish the other son of a bitch," Kartz growled to Chatters, who did just that. He first softened up Gustav Jessner by stabbing him in the eyes with a *No Hon Nukite* two-finger spear stab. Chatters then used a series of devastating *Ken tsui* hammer fists on Jessner's neck to send the man into unconsciousness.

SEAL Force 1 was winning, but the Death Merchant didn't have time to realize that the fruits of victory were falling in his orchard. He was too busy staying alive, too busy defending himself against five of the enemy—four coming at him from the front, the fifth man from the rear.

This is worse than living in East Los Angeles!

It was even more terrible for Otto Neimschwitters, who was charging from the rear, to Camellion's left. Sensing the swift approach of the man, Camellion twisted slightly and used a *Ushiro kekomi geri* rear thrust kick, the sole of his right boot connecting solidly with the man's face. It was a grand slam that meant utter destruction. Nasal bones, orbital bones, teeth, philtrum (the front of the upper jaw)—all were crushed. Making animallike noises, Neimschwitters staggered back, doing a wobbly one-two-three step.

God wasn't smiling on Felix Kracaure either. The second mate of the *Prinz Rupert* prided himself on his boxing ability and assumed he would make quick work of the Death Merchant. He received the biggest surprise of the day when the Death Merchant ducked his left cross and right uppercut and very quickly let him have a *Hiji* elbow strike that made colors explode in his brain and the world start spinning around him. The Death Merchant's elbow, striking Kracaure above the bridge of the nose, pulled a yell of agony from him and forced him to fall back as

Wilhelm Meinecke, the chief engineer, tried a knee lift that would have caved in Camellion's abdominal section if the knee had landed. It didn't! Camellion blocked with his right leg, a move that wrecked Meinecke's attack, but permitted Heinrich Leimdorfer to make his move. Leimdorfer rushed in and tried to grab the Alaskan Auto Mag in the Death Merchant's right hand—tried and missed. Camellion had seen the German's hand streaking out, had jerked back his right hand, and now made the East German intelligence agent pay for his mistake. Camellion moved back a few feet and, jumping up, executed a perfect left-legged *Fumikomi* front snap kick and, simultaneously, turned the AMP toward Leimdorfer, who was now wishing he had never left East Germany. The huge stainless steel autopistol boomed at the same split second that Camellion's foot buried itself in Meinecke's groin, the terrific smash flattening Meinecke's testes against the pubic bones and exploding a volcano of agony throughout his body. His nervous system switched to full shock and the shadows became more intense in his mind. He'd be dead in five minutes—300 seconds later than Leimdorfer, who had taken the .44 slug through his chest and, stone dead, was falling to the floor.

The Death Merchant, however, had made a slight mistake. In concentrating on Meinecke and Leimdorfer, Camellion had neglected—for only a micro-moment—Johann Ulbrecht, a fifth SSD gunmen, who grabbed Camellion's right wrist, twisted, and slammed a powerful left jab that rocked the Death Merchant. Johann Ulbrecht was a powerful man, and with several forceful twists he managed to force Camellion's fingers open. The Alaskan AMP fell to the deck. Knowing what a terrible weapon the AMP was, Ulbrecht let his fear and overanxiousness override his common sense. Instead of kicking the weapon to one side, he made the fatal mistake of reaching down, of trying to pick up the Alaskan, a move that not only surprised the Death Merchant but also Felix Kracaure, who had recovered sufficiently from Camellion's *Hiji* elbow strike to rush in and make another fool of himself.

Camellion stopped Kracaure this time with a lightning-fast *Yon Hon Nukite* four-finger spear stab to the solar plexus, delivering the death-dealing slice at the same moment he used his right foot to stomp on the wrist of Johann Ulbrecht, who was reaching for the AMP.

"*AUUUUOWWWWWWWWWW!*" Ulbrecht howled when his

wrist snapped and fell to his side. He didn't have time to do anything else. The Death Merchant kicked him full in the face, the blow not only shattering Ulbrecht's teeth and breaking his lower jaw, but knocking him to his back beside Felix Kracaure, who was on his knees, his arms wrapped around his stomach, agonized sounds coming from his mouth.

He glanced up at the Death Merchant, who was picking up the Auto Mag. The German knew he'd be in eternity within seconds. After all, how can one expect mercy when the enemy is the judge?

"Blessed is the man who shares his neighbor's burden!" muttered Camellion, then stepped back and calmly and methodically exploded the skulls of Ulbrecht and Kracaure with .44 projectiles.

He didn't bother to reload the Alaskan. He shoved it into its hip holster, reached inside his all-weather coveralls, pulled both BP Super MatchMasters, and took a long look at the area around him. Getting a proper perspective was difficult since the illumination from the lightsticks on the deck shone upward, casting everything and everyone in shadows. Even so, Camellion could detect that SEAL Force 1 was winning and that almost every corpse was that of an enemy. He studied the sides and the tops of the shadowed crates. Some had been split off by the hatch cover that had fallen, the cover snapping the metal holding bands securing the cargo.

He let his line of vision drift to a group of crates to port that was still held in place. It was almost the last gaze of his life. If he had been a few seconds slower in spotting the three men kneeling on top of one crate, he would never have heard the exploding 9mm cartridges. The projectiles would have killed him. As it turned out, he saw two of the men aiming submachine guns. One man aiming a Skorpion in his direction, the second man moving his Soviet PPS toward some of the commandos, forty feet away.

"BEHIND YOU!" yelled the Death Merchant as loud as he could, then intuitively made the correct move. A micromoment before Colonel Gunther Flegel fired a long, sweeping burst with his Skorpion, Camellion threw himself to the right. Slugs were thudding into the deck of the hold while he crawled behind a crate and started to move along its side to the next huge container, his plan being to come in from behind the last remnants of the enemy.

197

Suleiman Maghrabi fired a few moments after Flegel triggered off a blast at Camellion, his attention having been drawn to the Death Merchant by the loud booms of the AMP.

The Death Merchant's shouted warning saved the majority of men, who threw themselves to the floor and feverishly started to reach for sidearms or for automatic weapons dropped in the fighting. Donald Ray Yesley, Oscar Hyink, and Wally Chatters were not at all lucky. The subsonic projectiles from Maghrabi's PPS submachine gun ripped into all three men, killing them as fast as a bolt of lightning strikes in summer.

"Kill them! Kill them all!" screamed Colonel Flegel, who had weighed all the factors and concluded that the gamble would be worth it. Flegel, along with Suleiman Maghrabi, Heinrich Reinner, Captain Smoelter, and Konstantin Voelkel, had not taken part in the battle; they had remained hidden behind several crates, hoping in desperation that the Americans would be killed quickly. Common sense told them it wouldn't make any difference. The *Prinz Rupert* was not only drifting in the Atlantic, it was also at the complete mercy of the United States Navy.

Once Flegel had seen that his men were losing, he had snarled in a hoarse whisper, "We'll go up on one of the crates. They won't be expecting such a move. We might be able to kill most of them; it will only take a few seconds with machine pistols."

Only Captain Ludwig Smoelter and Konstantin Voelkel had hung back. They had begun to crawl up the first crate, behind Flegel and the others, then had changed their minds, concluding that suicide was not the way they wanted to die. While there was life, there was hope. On top of the crates was death.

That death found Colonel Flegel, Suleiman Maghrabi, and Heinrich Reinner—in the form of Sergeant Daren Givens and Sylvester "Si" Zanf. Both SEALs had returned from the second deck and had paused by the bulkhead to survey the situation before charging in. They had been in time to see Flegel and Maghrabi open fire. Because the top of the crates were cloaked in black tar-shadows, they couldn't see who was triggering the SMGs. Yet Givens and Zanf were positive it couldn't be any of their own men. For one thing, the heavy firing was neither Ingram MAC-10s or Colt CARs. For another, none of their own side would be stupid enough to expose himself from the top of a wooden crate.

Givens and Zanf raised their own Colt CAR Commando submachine guns and triggered off long, sweeping, side-to-side bursts, the eighty 5.56 X 45mm projectiles butchering Flegel, Reinner, and Maghrabi. The rain of slugs first ripped open the three men, then knocked them off the crates. They crashed to the deck, bleeding from scores of bullet holes, their blood spraying the smoky air. Flegel without a face. Reinner a mass of ripped clothing and bloody flesh, with a only a stump for a head. Suleiman Maghrabi with his intestines pushing out like fat gray worms—and minus a foot of his spine.

The three corpses almost fell on top of Captain Smoelter and Konstantin Voelkel, splattering the two horrified men with blood and gore. Gagging, trying to hold back the bile and vomit, Voelkel and Smoelter dropped their Skorpions and began to stumble to starboard, their minds in a daze, naked horror and dread riding heavy on their shoulders. They had moved only ten feet when they found another surprise in store for them: the Death Merchant stepped out from behind a crate, a MatchMaster in each hand—"Freeze, or I'll turn you both into rotten cabbage."

Konstantin Voelkel fainted. . . .

Aftermath

Searchlights from the *McCall*, the U.S. Navy rescue escort vessel, bathed the port side of the *Prinz Rupert*, with brilliant light reflected in the choppy water. From the officers' mess of the upper deck level, the Death Merchant watched the *McCall* move in closer to the *Frinz Rupert*, the wind blowing snow around him through the shot-out window, and over and around H. L. Kartz, who was standing next to him.

The procedure would be simple: when the *McCall* was close enough, lines would be shot to the East German vessel. Winches would tighten the cables and the *Prinz Rupert* would be secured. The canisters of nerve gas and SEAL Force 1 would then be transferred to the *McCall*.

H. L. Kartz remarked in his rock-hard voice, "It tickles the hell out of me the way Captain Smoelter couldn't tell us fast enough where the tanks of gas were hidden. He sure was a 'brave' one! The Krauts sure had the gas in a good place. That inner bottom was perfect. We would have never found that sealed-off compartment if he hadn't told us about it."

"He didn't want to die," Camellion said. "He'd have been

better off if he had. He can't go home again, and he'll never have full freedom in the States."

Behind Camellion and Kartz, Phil "Foo-Boy" Flint was tightening a tourniquet around the left arm of Roy Wilbur Hill. Hill had been stabbed and, while the cut was not serious, it was painful.

"You're not hurt bad," Flint said reassuringly. "Anyhow, we'll be on board the *McCall* in a short time."

"Don't talk like an idiot," said Hill in indignation. "Any wound is serious to me. Hell, have you ever heard of anyone being hurt 'good'?"

In one corner of the officers mess, Sergeant Givens had just concluded talking with Captain Griffith on a TEL-6Y. Griffith and the rest of the men were on the stern, by the after deckhouse. Givens slipped the walkie-talkie into its case and hurried over to Camellion and Kartz.

"The captain heard from the *McCall*," Givens reported. "After the lines are in place, we'll first transfer the gas and the men. Then navy sappers will come aboard and plant small charges below. Mr. Brent wants this tub sent to the bottom. It will be another fifteen minutes before the lines are shot over."

"What else did Mr. Brent say?" Camellion's voice was soft.

"He said to tell you 'Groucho.' I suppose you know what that means? He said he'd see you at the naval station."

The Death Merchant nodded. Groucho was Courtland Grojean's term for "A job well done."

Sergeant Givens moved off, and Camellion again thought of Grojean's words: *I hope you like El Salvador.*

He gave Kartz a quick, thoughtful glance, a look that was calculating. When it came to social graces, Kartz would have to start in kindergarten and work upward, grade by grade. His faults, however, didn't detract from the Death Merchant's own philosophy of living. Kartz had not been brainwashed by his times, nor conditioned by religious mythology. A realist, Kartz knew one of the truths that few men ever realize: that self-interest is the natural order of nature, that "morality," the "goodness of man," and the rest of the "eternal truths" were relative and subject to interpretation by different generations.

Most of all, Kartz worshipped Death.

Such a man was always invaluable.

Camellion suddenly turned and looked squarely at Kartz. "How would you like to go with me to El Salvador?"

Kartz's gray eyes flickered with intense interest. "I always did consider the rice-and-beans boys on a level with gooks. What's the deal and how much?"

The Death Merchant smiled warmly. "The same price as you got for this job. As for deal—it would be a complete kill-operation. After we got there it would be a slaughter—*a slaughter in El Salvador.*"